It was all Annja could do to hold her ground against the human flood

She glanced back. She could see the priest had managed to stand and let the stampede flow around him. He had his revolver out, pointed safely skyward gripped in both gloved hands.

She vaulted to the top of the low wall to the right of the adobe arch over the gateway. Her feet slipped in the snow. She teetered dangerously, windmilling her arms until she found her balance.

People still streamed through the doorway, breaking around the sealed well with the crucifix and the millstone set in the pedestal. From inside came shrieks that soared above the panicked noise of the crowd.

The crowd thinned out just as she reached the doorway. The screaming from within also stopped.

Cautiously, Annja advanced inside.

Titles in this series:

ROGUE ANGEL

Alex Archer

THE CHOSEN

A GOLD EAGLE BOOK FROM

W✹RLDWIDE®

TORONTO • NEW YORK • LONDON
AMSTERDAM • PARIS • SYDNEY • HAMBURG
STOCKHOLM • ATHENS • TOKYO • MILAN
MADRID • WARSAW • BUDAPEST • AUCKLAND

First edition January 2007

ISBN-13: 978-0-373-62122-4
ISBN-10: 0-373-62122-1

THE CHOSEN

Special thanks and acknowledgment to
Victor Milán for his contribution to this work.

The
LEGEND

...THE ENGLISH COMMANDER TOOK
JOAN'S SWORD AND RAISED IT HIGH.

The broadsword, plain and unadorned,
gleamed in the firelight. He put the tip against
the ground and his foot at the center of the blade.
The broadsword shattered, fragments falling
into the mud. The crowd surged forward,
peasant and soldier, and snatched the shards
from the trampled mud. The commander tossed
the hilt deep into the crowd.
Smoke almost obscured Joan, but she continued
praying till the end, until finally the flames climbed
her body and she sagged against the restraints.

Joan of Arc died that fateful day in France,
but her legend and sword are reborn....

Prologue

"That poor child," Mrs. Murakami said. "We should stop and pick her up!"

The ceiling of gray-and-blue clouds hanging low over the rented minivan was suddenly veined with lightning. The vehicle's interior flashed blue-white.

It might have been the judgment of the *kami*. Alien spirits of an alien place, Mr. Murakami thought.

Obsessed enthusiast that he was for the history and culture of the southwestern United States—so different from his grim industrial suburb outside Tokyo—Murakami should have been in heaven. Instead he was peeved. Not to mention lost.

"What child?" he demanded, as the echoes of a shattering thunderclap died away.

"That child. Hurry! It's about to rain," his wife replied.

This is the desert, he thought. It isn't supposed to rain. Although from his studies he knew that it did. Rarely. But violently. And there was no denying a violent downpour was in the offing. He could smell the rain and the ozone, overlying the sage and dust of the deceptively flat-looking khaki terrain of the Acoma Indian Reservation where he and his family had wandered, small and utterly lost. A few drops splatted against the windshield like fat, transparent bugs.

He looked the way his wife's sturdy arm pointed. "A child!" he exclaimed. "What can she be doing here?"

She stood in the clumpy weeds by the side of the rough dirt track. She wore a sort of blue dress with a scarlet cape around her shoulders, pinned off center with a gold clamshell brooch. Small pink feet in sandals poked out beneath the hem of the robe. She had a plump, round face framed by flowing brown locks spilling from either side of a hat with an astonishing plume and the brim pinned up in front.

Though he couldn't drive faster than twenty miles per hour without jostling the van intolerably on the horrendous collection of ruts and rocks that passed for a road, Murakami hit the brakes so hard the vehicle squeaked and jerked sideways as it stopped. The children, Taro and Hanako, looked up from their furious head-to-head battle on their video game.

"A little girl!" Hanako cried.

"Can we pick her up?" her brother asked. "Can we, Daddy?"

"We have to!" Hanako said. "She'll wash away."

Murakami growled like a bear. His family wasn't fooled. They knew he was a kind man.

But Murakami was also well and truly stressed. They had reservations at the Old Town Hotel in Albuquerque for five that afternoon. He knew that they could be in trouble if they missed their reservation. The whole are was flooded with visitors. But he was a stranger in a strange land indeed. None of his loving studies had come close to preparing him for the unreal size of this western New Mexico desert. The land was so wide he had felt in danger sometimes of falling right off the planet. They had driven through mountains with pine trees, almost like home, between Gallup and Grants. But somewhere south of U.S. 40 they'd found themselves stuck in the middle of a vast bowl of desert rimmed by wind-scalloped mesas.

He stopped the van. His wife hopped out into a barrage of raindrops. She opened the sliding side door of the van and clucked and cooed to the oddly dressed girl.

"What's a child doing alone out here in the middle of nowhere, anyway?" Murakami asked. No one answered him. His children had unbelted their eat belts and were hopping up and down chirping like happy birds.

With Mrs. Murakami's help the child stepped into the van. Startled, Mr. Murakami realized it was a boy.

"Thank you, honored sir, for stopping to pick me up," the child said.

The Murakami children slid the door shut as their mother returned to her seat hastily. Taro and Hanako barraged the curious-looking boy with questions thick and fast as the rain as they helped him buckle himself in the seat between them. He answered only with great, beaming smiles. Gently but firmly he insisted on keeping his staff tucked in a crook of his gowned arm, at a sort of angle to fit the roof.

Murakami started to drive again. He felt a rising urgency. He perceived America as a violent land but had not expected that might extend to its very environment. The growing fury of the lightning and thunder so unsettled him that he had a hard time preserving his stoic demeanor. And the rain suddenly began to rattle off the van's metal skin like ten thousand drumsticks.

Away off to the left he could see the looming sandstone mesa on which an ancient city rested. Its somewhat brutal blockiness was softened by veils of rain that threatened in short order to mask it from view entirely. His objective in driving in to this lunar wilderness was not the great, gaudy Sky City Casino built on the desert, but the real Sky City on its majestic rock slab, the oldest continuously inhabited settlement in North America. People had dwelt up there, over three hundred feet above the surrounding land, since sometime before the twelfth century.

If only he could figure out how to get *to* the confounded hill.

Lightning flashed and thunder crashed around them so constantly it felt as if they had strayed into the middle of one of America's vaunted *shock and awe* bombardments. Through the explosive roars and racket of the rain Murakami could hear his children trying to share their handheld games with their new passenger.

His wife had turned around in her seat to fire solicitous questions at the boy. "Where are you from, child? Who are your parents? Where are your parents?"

Murakami was creeping along. He was genuinely afraid he and his family and their peculiar guest would be swept away at any moment by the horrible, ferocious weather. He tried desperately to remember if they got tornadoes in this part of the U.S.

"Honored sir," the boy said from the backseat.

Murakami drove across a low rise and began to descend. A hundred yards ahead the road bottomed, passing through a gulch with sheer high walls scooped out of the hard earth. Beyond it rose the flank of yet another ridge. He wished his budget had permitted a rental with GPS.

"Please," the little boy said.

"What is it?" Murakami asked. He felt instantly shamed at his brusqueness.

"You must not go down there, *sensei*."

"Ahh!" Murakami drew in a startled, gratified breath. The child had named him "master."

"But what other way can I go?" he asked, wondering how this strange young child was familiar with Japanese customs.

"You must turn around," the boy said. "If you do, you will find a dirt road a mile and a half on the right, back the way you have come. It is hard to see but you will see it. When you take that, it will bring you shortly to a paved road that will take you where you need to go."

Murakami scowled. If the confounded road was there, how had they missed it? The child didn't even know their destination.

He shook his head. "I don't want to turn back. Surely if we keep going this way we shall get there."

The truth was he was afraid to go back. But he would never admit that aloud.

"Master, please. Your danger is very great if you proceed down this road."

"I think you should listen to him," his wife said, her dark eyes, normally calm, wide and worried behind her glasses.

"Yes, Daddy," his son said. "Listen to him, please."

Frowning furiously, Murakami brought the van to a stop halfway down to the gully. "All right," he said, "but if—"

"*Daddy!*" his children shouted in chorus. They flew from their seats to plaster themselves against the passenger-side window.

"Look!" his wife exclaimed, pointing.

Down the narrow gully from the right came something that turned Murakami's blood to ice. Though he had never seen one in person, and didn't live close enough to the coast to be in any real risk, like many Japanese he feared in his bones a tsunami.

That was what he saw rushing down on them. A wall of water, frothing dirty white—tsunami in miniature, six or seven yards wide and two yards tall. He saw with instant, horrible clarity what would have happened had he driven on. That moving water-wall would have caught the minivan amidships, tumbled it downstream like a toy, until it battered open a window and the turbulent water smashed in to drown his precious family and himself.

In silence that seemed almost like a bubble insulated from the raucous storm noise, Murakami and his family watched the flash flood sweep past. It made a roiled river of the road in front of them.

"You are safe now," the boy said from behind him. "But your world also faces terrible danger. Please heed that warning, too."

"Yes, yes," Murakami muttered. He turned. "I thank you—"

Hanako screamed.

The seat was empty.

The child was gone.

1

"Hey, Annja," the wiry red-bearded man in the white straw cowboy hat called out. He stood to his faded-denim-clad hips in a fifteen-by-fifteen-foot hole scraped out of the scrub-dotted chaparral of the Española Valley, about ten miles north of Santa Fe, New Mexico. "Come over here a sec."

The sun looked like a big red balloon about to pop itself on the peaks of the Jemez.

Annja Creed swallowed the last of the water from the cooler settled on the lowered tailgate of what Max Leland, professor of archaeology at the University of New Mexico and dig leader, called his "pick-'em-up" truck. She set the speckled blue metal mug marked with her name on the scuffed black bedliner and walked over, drying her hands on the rump of her brown jeans.

She walked along the lip of the dig, trimmed with tough blue grama grass. Like much of New Mexico the soil was a tough clay that turned into concrete on almost any pretext. Annja was not ashamed to admit—to herself—that she was glad to have missed the drudgery of excavating the site in the brutal summer sun of northern New Mexico. It didn't get all that hot up there, and there wasn't any humidity to speak of. But above seven thousand feet there was also a lot less atmosphere to blunt the force of the sun than down at sea level where she'd grown up. Even though the temperature wasn't that far into the sixties, Annja had been able to feel the ultraviolet rays sizzling on her skin.

Max boosted himself to sit on the edge of the hole. "Check this out," he said, holding up a Ziploc bag.

She squatted next to him, squinting at the scalloped chips of pale stone. They had an almost translucent quality in the dying daylight. The dense overcast, like a ceiling set ablaze by the sunset, gave the light a texture she could almost feel, but did little to aid her vision.

"Flint flakes!" she exclaimed after a moment. "Someone's been knapping."

He nodded, beaming. In archaeo circles—where Annja ran, as it happened—Max Leland enjoyed modest renown as a flint knapper and general expert on the subject of making things from flint. He gestured into the flat-bottomed oblong hole at his feet.

"Found 'em right here, not too far from where the front door used to be. Looks like the inhabitants of this house were rolling their own tools up to the middle of the nineteenth century."

"You racist!"

They both whipped around. An angry young Latina with long black hair stood right behind them shaking a finger at the sunburned tip of Leland's nose.

The professor blinked. "What?"

"You racist bastard! You can't say that about my people."

"Say what, Yvonne?" Annja asked, trying to understand.

"I didn't mean to offend you," Max said in badly accented but fluent Spanish. "I'm just showing Annja what I found."

"But it must have been left here by Indians long before the house was built," the furious young woman said in English. "And don't try to weasel out by speaking Spanish."

The professor's face was turning even redder beneath his tan. "Now, listen. I thought all this got settled years ago—"

"All right, everybody," a husky female voice called. "Just hold on, here."

Everyone turned. Trish Donnelly and Alyson Simpson, the first a graduate assistant and the second an undergrad on the dig, had been loading gear into a second pickup owned by UNM. They had been drawn to the dispute, which was getting louder as the sunset deepened and the air got chillier.

"He's accusing my people of being savages," Yvonne González said. She was a freshman who hailed from Las Vegas, just over the mountains to the east. "He claims they used stone tools like cavemen."

Trish put herself between the combatants. She held up a stubby finger before Max Leland's nose. "Wait," she said. "Here."

She took hold of Yvonne's upper arm.

Yvonne was slim and wiry, with an oval face that seemed to be all flashing anthracite eyes. She tried to resist, but Trish Donnelly, in her blue coveralls faded to gray, with her stiff, upswept brush of black hair and laughing pale-blue eyes, was built like a harbor tug was and about as easy to resist.

"Come on, Yvonne," Trish said in the same easygoing tone she always used.

Annja had known her for years. Trish had invited her to spend the past two weeks on the dig, and wangled permissions from Leland and the San Esequiel Pueblos, who owned the land. In all that time she had never heard the woman raise her voice. Not even in a bar fight.

"We're gonna talk. Annja, why don't you come, too?"

"How about me, Trish?" Alyson asked. She was a willowy Dartmouth blonde from upstate New York.

"You stay here, honey," Trish said. "Keep Professor Max from spontaneously combusting."

"I am *not* spontaneously combusting!" Leland shouted.

"She's a sweet child," Trish said sotto voce to Annja, "but far too innocent for archaeology."

"These Tejanos are all alike," Yvonne muttered darkly. She was still trying to hang back. She reminded Annja of a child balking when a nun was trying to take her somewhere. She was having the same success.

She's like me, Annja thought. She'd always had a problem with authority herself. Growing up under the iron regime of the nuns in an orphanage in New Orleans had hardened rather than softened her resistant nature. Still, in their brief but intense association, she'd never found Leland remotely authoritarian.

Or racist, for that matter.

"Dammit, I'm from West Virginia!" Leland shouted. But he made no move to follow.

Trish marched her little party up to the top of the rise. The clearing went on for ten or fifteen more yards, then rose into some woods of serious pine trees—not the scruffy, hunchbacked piñons that dotted most of the rolling landscape for miles around.

Trish stopped, turned Yvonne to face her, released her arm. "Now, *chica,* what exactly is your major malfunction?"

"He was trying to say the people who lived in this house knapped flint," Yvonne said sullenly, trying to rub her arm surreptitiously.

"And did he have any evidence to back that up?" Trish asked.

"Well, he dug up some flint flakes. But they couldn't have anything to do with the people who lived here. They must have been from long before!"

"Think, Yvonne," Annja said. "They were found at the same level as artifacts we've definitely dated from the 1850s. We have the land records. The Tejada and then the Domínguín families lived here from 1701 until the house burned down in 1863. How could Indian artifacts from some earlier time period have gotten mixed up with stuff from a century and a half *after* the house was built?"

She had broken herself of the habit, however temporarily, of saying "Native American." Burt Trujillo, a stocky middle-aged Santa Clara Pueblo man working with them as a contract archaeologist for the state, teased her and fellow easterner Alyson mercilessly whenever they used the expression. Alyson had actually gotten indignant with him for calling his people Indians, which only made him laugh louder.

Like the rest of the dig team, he wasn't at the site. Annja and her companions were winding down before the early onset of winter shut them down.

"Maybe kids dug them up," Yvonne said. But she muttered the words so low Annja could barely hear them over the ever present whistle of the wind, which didn't lend them particular conviction.

"The point is," Trish said, "where do you think you get off calling Leland a racist? That's a serious accusation. He could lose his job. Shit, maybe go to jail, the way things are these days."

"But it's like he was saying my people were *savages*," Yvonne said, at once intent and pleading to be heard. "Just like…"

Her words trailed away as she noticed Annja and Trish both looking fixedly at her. "What?" she asked plaintively.

"Who's being racist now, Yvonne?" Annja asked softly.

Yvonne drew in a deep breath as if preparing to blast the *gringa* from back East, then she deflated in a hurry. She wasn't stupid, Annja knew. Far from it. But Annja had noticed she did have a tendency to be reactive and defensive. While polite enough, the young Latina had acted wary of Annja since her arrival. She hadn't opened up, but Annja guessed she had some unresolved cultural conflicts going on that made her touchy.

"But," Yvonne began. She let that drop, too. She realized, now the moment's heat had cooled, that she had wandered out of bounds.

"Lighten up, sweetie," Trish said. She caught Yvonne and dragged her into a hug. "It's been a long season. And the clock says it's time to go. We're all a little frazzled. A little weird."

Annja saw Yvonne blinking tears from her eyes. She understood. She hadn't had time to really become part of this crew, yet she, too, felt the camaraderie that arose from long, hard hours spent working to a common purpose. What these women were feeling, she knew from experience, was much more poignant.

Will I ever really know that feeling again? she wondered. She was starting to feel half-misty herself. *Or have I lost that part of my life forever?* Between her semiregular gig with the hit cable-channel show *Chasing History's Monsters* and her…destiny…she wasn't really in position to commit herself to a full season in the field.

She saw Yvonne's eyes suddenly go wide. "Oh, my God," the young woman whispered.

Trish's shoulders tensed. Annja felt her own chestnut hair rise at the nape of her neck below her sleek ponytail. Slowly she turned.

There was a figure standing among the trees. It looked like a tall man in a dark cloak. Annja had the sense he was staring at her. She felt intent so malign it made her knees weak.

She shook her head. I am overwrought, she thought. It was the mellow sunset light, she reckoned.

Trish disengaged herself from the smaller woman and turned to face the intruder. Her bulldog jaw squared. "Can we help you?" she asked in a tone that didn't sound all that solicitous to Annja.

The figure said nothing.

"Listen, buster," Trish said.

Annja waved a hand from her hip in a calming gesture. Soft-spoken and generally easygoing though she was, Trish didn't have the longest fuse.

"I don't know what game you think you're playing—"

Two red glows appeared from the stranger's shadowed black head. "¡Jesu Cristo!" exclaimed Yvonne. She crossed herself.

"Yvonne?" Max Leland called from his truck, where he sat on the tailgate swinging his boots and talking to Alyson. "Trish? Are you guys all right?"

"Holy shit," Trish said. Her hand dived inside her dirt-caked coveralls. It came out holding a flat black pistol.

Darkness unfolded from the mystery figure's sides. At first Annja thought it was a cape. Halloween's almost a month away, and this jackass is about to play Dracula to the point of getting shot, she thought disgustedly.

But it wasn't a cape. Black, tapering wings spread wider than the man was tall. Annja felt her right hand start to curl as if to grab something. *No*, she told herself. *It isn't time.*

Yvonne had dropped her knapsack off her back and was rummaging furiously inside. Leland emitted a startled yelp and, leaping off the tailgate, ran to the front of the truck and yanked open the door so hard it banged against the stops.

A strange sound keened with the stiff steppe wind. It was like a baby crying. Yvonne pulled a Glock 19 out to the full length of her arms in a two-handed grip. She was trembling so violently the gun's blunt muzzle waved wildly.

The figure rose straight into the air. The black wings never stirred. At twenty feet it leveled out and glided over their heads with silent purpose.

Leland had popped out of the truck cab working the lever action of a .44 Magnum Marlin Model 94 carbine. The huge black creature swooped toward him. It passed ten feet over the top of his and Alyson's heads. Leland's face went so pale it was green behind the red beard and rusty freckles. He had not been able to bring himself to raise the gun.

Again Annja heard the noise like a baby crying.

The black figure soared upward to clear a juniper-dotted ridge a hundred yards away and vanished into the lavender dusk.

Large snowflakes began to fall. Alyson threw herself on the ground and covered her head with her hands. "Oh, my God!" she screamed. "They had guns!"

Annja let out the breath she had not realized she was holding in a long, shuddering sigh. Trish came up beside her and rested her right elbow on Annja's shoulder. Her pistol dangled from her hand.

"Wow," she said, as if that summed it all up.

"What was that?" Yvonne asked. *What was it?* Thankfully she was pointing her own handgun toward the clouds, now bluish-black. The sun had vanished from sight, leaving a lemon glow around the Jemez peaks.

"A bird?" Annja said. Her voice sounded like a croak to her. "Eagles have surprisingly wide wingspans."

"Do eagles have *red freakin' eyes?*" Yvonne screamed.

Annja shrugged. "Maybe the sunlight, reflected—"

She gave it up. *She* didn't believe it. Much as she wanted to.

"What's with all the swamp gas?" Trish asked, taking her arm down and putting her pistol back wherever it came from. "That show you're on, I figured you'd be, you know, on the other side and all."

"I'm kind of the reality anchor. You're a scientist, Trish. What else could it be?" Annja asked.

"I've also been hiking the Southwest most of my life. Be real, Annja. That was an eagle like I'm Mary-Kate Olsen," Trish replied.

"What was it, then?"

Trish shook her head. "I'm afraid to find out." She didn't sound as if she was kidding.

Down the hill, Alyson screamed, "Don't touch me!" and rolled frantically away from Leland when he knelt next to her to see what was wrong. He held the Marlin pointed skyward in one hand.

Yvonne had regained control of herself and zipped her Glock back into her pack. Aside from high color in her cinnamon cheeks and slightly flared nostrils she didn't look as if much out of the ordinary had happened. It made Annja wonder. Outsiders told strange stories of happenings where Yvonne came from, way up in the Blood of Christ Mountains.

"What's wrong with her?" Yvonne asked with a sidewise nod of her head at Alyson.

"Easterner," Trish said.

2

Reichenbach Falls, Switzerland

The wind from the glacier gorge whipped mist into the fat man's bearded face like ice-laden fronds. Far beneath him the famed cataract vomited its clouds of spray and roared ceaselessly. The sky above was crowded with clouds, their gray, gravid bellies hanging almost close enough to touch. A storm is coming, the man thought. How very appropriate.

Monsignor Paolo Benigni checked the Rolex watch strapped to his wrist. Next to the black of his overcoat, his skin looked bluish-white.

"Where *is* the man?" he said in irritation. "It's almost time, and I see no sign of him."

The railed scenic viewpoint overlooking the

Reichenbach Falls was deserted except for the fat man and his two younger, much larger companions. October's arrival a few days earlier had brought the annual closing of the funicular that carried tourists from the valley floor to just below the mighty falls themselves. A safe distance back from the sheer cliffs, the hotel in the village was temporarily closed for renovation.

Actually, it had closed at the special request of a man whose influence reached to the core of the Vatican itself. The public was scarcely aware of the name of Monsignor Benigni. But people who counted—the people who really ran the world— knew his name very well indeed.

To his intense annoyance he found himself compelled to meet here with an impudent bastard—a mere priest. A priest without a flock and a damned black Jesuit on top of that. Yet Benigni knew this disciple of the long-dead Basque madman Loyola had an unmistakable influence of his own that was scarcely less shadowy, or pervasive, than the monsignor's own.

Well, Benigni thought, today we shall settle that account. There were many in the Vatican who would thank him for his resolution of this turbulent priest.

"Monsignor," Volker, the German bodyguard, said, peering over the railing above the precipice. He had a lantern jaw fringed with blue-black beard. His pinstriped suit was tailored so immaculately no seam showed the least sign of strain around his vast powerlifter's bulk. Not even at the left armpit, where a Walther P-99 was nestled in a shoulder holster.

"What is it?" Benigni said.

"Perhaps you should come see, Excellence."

Grimacing and puffing in annoyance, the monsignor waddled to the edge. His face sank deep into his own neatly bearded chins as he leaned over slightly, all he could readily manage.

A path wound up the cold granite cliff from the notch where white waters arced down to the River Inn far below. Seemingly out of the falls' very spray came a solitary figure, trotting up the steps with a vigor Benigni would have had trouble matching when he was young and slim, trotting down. The figure wore a long black coat. The head of silver-gray hair was bare.

"That's doing it the hard way," Benigni's other bodyguard said. Semo, the Samoan, was even bigger and broader than Volker, with a mass of crinkly black hair held back from his great tanned face in a braid.

"The fool," Benigni murmured. "Still, if he wishes to exhaust himself in this manner, let him. He will have ample time to rest, soon enough."

As his guards laughed appreciatively, the monsignor pushed away from the white-painted steel rail with a ringed and exquisitely manicured pale hand. The height and sheerness of the drop made him queasy. All this cavorting about in nature was foreign to his constitution. He should be ensconced in a leather chair in some five-star hotel, basking in the warmth of a fire and a snifter of brandy.

As if to emphasize the inconvenience and discomfort to which he subjected himself—for the good of the church, of course—a snowflake struck his cheek and clung. Its cold seemed to bite like some horrid insect. Then he thought about what the immediate future held in store for the vexatious Father Robert Godin, Societas Iesu, who was responsible for dragging him out in this frightful weather. He smiled with lips moist, full and reddish-purple within his goatee.

Godin trotted onto the top of the cliff and slowed to a walk while approaching the waiting trio. He had his hands in the pockets of his black trenchcoat. His breathing seemed normal and his step springy. The monsignor might have suspected the man had a pact with the Devil—but he knew better.

"Monsignor," the new arrival said. He spoke Italian with a hint of a French accent. Benigni felt sure it was an affectation. He knew the Jesuit was as proud of his coarse Antwerp dock-rat beginnings as he was of the unspeakably brutal nature of his early career, before he had entered the bosom of the church.

Benigni smiled. He was not one to lecture another on the sin of pride. To his mind, of all the sins it was, frankly, among the least interesting. Besides, it never did any good to lecture Jesuits.

"Father," he said with false heartiness, extending a hand. Godin shook it. Although he exerted no more than brief, firm pressure it was like shaking hands with a vise.

With the ease of long practice Benigni masked his irritation. As an assistant chamberlain of the Vatican, Benigni was entitled to have his ring kissed. He was also accustomed to it. But the Jesuit has never been born who would bend the knee to less than a red hat, he told himself. And Benigni had purposely avoided becoming a cardinal. Dressing all in scarlet made it harder to operate properly in the shadows, where his most important work was done.

"What exigency drove you to request this urgent conference, Father Godin?" He tried to force an element of lightness. "Or should I say, Father Bob?"

Godin smiled. But briefly. He was sixty-two years of age, the same height as Benigni, but half the weight. He looked like an extremely fit man a decade younger and moved, the monsignor had to admit resentfully to himself, like a fine athlete. His hair was gray, buzzed to white sidewalls and a silvery flattop. His face was oblong and deeply creased, the only sign of age he showed aside from the hue of his hair.

His eyes, behind circular wire-rimmed spectacles, were the palest, most piercing green Benigni could conceive. He made himself not shiver when they looked into his.

"I have come to discuss retirement," the Jesuit said.

"You? The last knight in armor? Or should I say the last inquisitor? Are you ready to hang up the spurs? Or perhaps the scourge." Benigni laughed in vast appreciation of his own wit.

"*Yours*, Monsignor."

The laughter died. "Mind your manners, priest," Benigni said.

"I don't care about your peculations or your secular crimes, Monsignor. I don't care about your involvement in the murder of Roberto Calvi in 1982, nor your dealings with the outlawed Propaganda Due Masonic Lodge. I don't care what deals you worked with the late Archbishop Marcinkus."

Benigni had gone very pale. His breath hissed forth between rubbery lips. "Old man, you over-reach yourself!"

"But when your self-indulgence leads you to invoke demons," Godin continued implacably, "en-

tailing the sacrifice of a human life—then, Monsignor Benigni, you fall within my bailiwick."

"You have no proof!"

The creases of the bloodhound face deepened in
a grin. "All the proof I need, I have in here," Godin
said, tapping first temple, then heart. "And if I am satisfied, the church is satisfied."

"Absurd. You hurl accusations at random. You are
a madman," the monsignor replied.

"Brother Luigi confessed, Monsignor. In Verona.
He is now in custody. Your agents will prove unable
to locate him and silence him. He will live out his
years in silent repentance. His testimony, however,
has been duly recorded and notarized. Should it prove
necessary, I don't doubt several other of your confed-
erates can be prevailed upon to testify. But with the
videotapes in our possession—"

Benigni felt his lower lip quivering. He shut his
mouth tightly, then barked, "My attorneys will laugh
these accusations out of court!"

"Unlikely, were it to go to trial—especially in
some of the nations that have jurisdiction in the case.
But there will be no trial, Monsignor. I am author-
ized to offer you the opportunity to resign your
offices and rank and retire to a monastery outside
Addis Ababa."

"Ethiopia? But they are Copts!"

"No longer—they call their schismatic church Ethiopian Orthodox now. But as you would know were you properly attentive to your duties, Monsignor Benigni, the Ethiopian Catholic Church remains communicant with our Holy Father. They are holy men. They'll ensure you are cared for. And protect you diligently from the temptations of this world."

Benigni stared at Godin with eyes like boiled eggs. Then he looked down at the gray stone beneath the mirror-polished black toes of his Gucci shoes. It was polished almost smooth by generations of tourist feet, slicked by mist from below and snow from above.

"She was just a whore," he said.

"Even a whore has a right to live her life," Godin said, "and not be tortured out of it. Even a whore has an immortal soul. Or do you speak of what you tried to make of our mother, the church?"

Benigni brought his head up. His eyes blazed. "You dare to speak so to me, who bathed your arms in the gore of innocents in the Congo?"

"Anyone whose blood I may have bathed in, Monsignor, was hardly an innocent. But the sins that stain my soul are not under discussion here."

Benigni laughed heartily.

"I anticipated you might attempt some such quixotry, Father Godin," he said. "So I came prepared."

He gestured to the two huge bodyguards who

stood flanking them. "As I said before, Father, you will be retiring this day. Volker and Semo will assist you. In the mist and the snow these steps up the precipice are so treacherous. Alas, you insisted on climbing alone despite the conditions—"

The two bodyguards stepped forward. Godin moved to meet Semo, who approached from his right. Volker reached for him from behind. Godin stopped, spun back and seized the German's thick wrist with his right hand. He dropped his left elbow over the elbow of the trapped arm and pivoted clockwise.

Volker's right elbow broke with a snap.

Godin stepped behind the huge German, twisting the broken arm. Volker, who had initially been too shocked to respond, bellowed in agony as parted bone ends scraped each other.

"Kill him! Kill him now!" the prelate roared.

Semo's bronze face had gone ashen at the brutal abruptness with which his partner's arm was snapped. From beneath his jacket he produced an MP-5K, a stubby pistol barely longer than a handgun, with a foregrip like a miniature table leg. He yanked back on the trigger and held it down.

The pistol bucked and rose left to right. Not even the Samoan's vast strength could control such a weapon firing full-auto. The muzzle flame, pale yellow and orange and dazzlingly bright in the drifting snow, set the front of Volker's black greatcoat smoldering. The burly German's Kevlar vest kept the 9 mm bullets from penetrating. But it only reduced their substantial impact. Ribs cracked and the breath was forced from Volker's lungs straining to draw in air against the blinding pain of his elbow.

Then a bullet hit the German in the throat. Blood spurted in a single thick stream. It gleamed almost black in the faint light.

Holding Volker propped against him, with his own legs braced, Father Godin thrust a CZ-75 under the mortally wounded man's arm and shot Semo twice in his broad chest. The Samoan's vest stopped the slugs.

The Jesuit's third shot struck Semo in the center of the forehead. The huge man emptied the MP-5K into the ground as he sank to his knees. Then he fell to the side like a sack of rocks.

Godin stepped back. Volker simply slumped and pitched forward on his face.

Snow began to fall in earnest. Fat white flakes filled the air, thick as flies on a midsummer evening.

"And now, Monsignor—" the Jesuit said, tucking his Czech handgun back inside his coat.

"You devil!" Benigni put his head down and charged.

He was out of shape, his muscles deconditioned to

the point his flesh felt like pudding to the touch. He could barely walk across a room without panting. But he weighed over three hundred pounds, and a super-charge of adrenaline lent strength to watery muscles. His momentum drove the older, lighter man back to slam his lower back cruelly against the metal rail.

Benigni's arms held Godin's trapped to his sides in a bear hug. His own strength surprised him. Ha! And so I best the vaunted mercenary and counterter-rorism expert, he thought.

Godin snapped his head forward. His forehead smeared the monsignor's broad nose across much of his pie-plate face.

Benigni squealed as agony shot through his brain and eyes like an inquisitor's red-hot pokers. Tears streamed down his cheeks, hot as the blood that poured across and into his mouth and down his chin.

He felt the smaller man's body like a bundle of wire and steel rods, stooping down. Felt hard hands dig into the backs of his thighs.

Then, as Godin grunted once with effort, his jowl to the flab of Benigni's left side, the prelate felt himself dead-lifted. The soles of his Gucci shoes departed slick granite. Holding Benigni's soft, yielding bulk over his right shoulder like a sack of meal, Godin straightened his legs, upending the monsignor.

Benigni screamed in horror as he stared straight

down into the almost black depths of the gorge. Then he was released, launched head downward like a crucified martyr. As the cold air's passage stung his cheeks and eyes he screamed and screamed for God to help.

Godin watched as the monsignor vanished from sight in the mist that boiled from the falls. He put his hands to the small of his back and stretched his body backward as a last thin wisp of scream echoed among alpine peaks. He was capable of dead-lifting far more than the obese prelate's weight, and had used proper form. But his muscles were not so durable as once they were.

Then he doubled over in a coughing fit. What the two huge, hard men and the one huge, soft man had not been able to accomplish, it did; it brought Father Godin almost to his knees.

He hung on to the rail until the fit passed. He dabbed moistness from his mouth with a handkerchief. He put it away without looking at it.

One more job done, he told himself. Doubtless two more will spring up in his place. Yet I can only do what one man can in the service of our Lord.

He checked his own wristwatch, a cheap digital that nonetheless kept time as serviceably as the miniature treasury Benigni had worn strapped to his fat wrist. Then he turned and walked briskly toward the hotel and the highway. He had a flight to catch from Zurich, back to Rome and a discreet rendezvous where he expected to receive the assignment that would cap his long, illustrious career.

And then I will have truly earned my rest, he told himself. *But will I be allowed to take it?*

3

"Ms. Creed," the young Asian woman at the hotel's reception desk said. Her perpetually cheery demeanor had slipped slightly. "I'm afraid I need to let you know that we can't give you an option to renew your room after your reservation runs out the day after tomorrow."

The lobby of the new Ramada Inn on the south side of the small Española Valley town of Pojoaque was decorated in what Annja had come to think of as Southwest Typical. Rounded whitewashed forms hinted at adobe brick beneath—no matter what was really there—rich-colored tile and brass and smoked-mirror trimming were offset by the occasional horsetail-fern accent. It actually produced a pleasant, calming effect even if it had become something of a design cliché.

"Really?" Annja asked. "Why not?"

"We've had a run of new bookings," the young woman said. She had a round, pink face and wore severe black slacks and a white blouse with a bolo tie sporting a silver-and-turquoise sun symbol. "I'm afraid we've committed all of our rooms."

"Is something happening at one of the casinos?" The local Pueblos, clustered thickly in the fertile upper Rio Grande Valley, had already constructed several casinos, giant pyramids of neon and more faux adobe. In fact, the dig site a few miles north and east of the hotel lay on land owned by the San Esequiel Pueblos, who had earmarked the site as part of their own projected casino complex. The tribe would not permit the UNM team to camp on the land; hence the need to find rooms in nearby hotels. The rest of the group were lodged in a Days Inn down the highway.

"Oh, no," the desk clerk said. "They're pilgrims. And paranormal investigators. They're here about the Santo Niño."

"Santo Niño?"

"It means 'Holy Child' in Spanish," the helpful young woman said to Annja, who knew. Annja was fluent in the modern Western Romance languages of Spanish, Portuguese, French and Italian, as well as Latin.

"I see," Annja said.

"It's all over the Internet, you see. There've been sightings here for weeks. People have gotten really excited."

"Who or what is this Holy Child?" Annja asked.

"He's a little boy who appears standing by the roadside. He looks eight or ten. He's wearing some kind of funny clothes—they say totally sixteenth-century Spanish or something. People feel sorry for him and pick him up. He thanks them and warns them something terrible is about to happen. Then he vanishes." She leaned conspiratorially across the counter. "I even read that a Japanese family picked him up a couple days ago. And he talked to them in Japanese!"

"My," Annja said weakly.

WELL, AT LEAST IT's my room for a night or two more, she thought as she sat on the bed a few minutes later, freshly showered and wearing a white fluffy robe and a towel wrapped around her hair as she tapped at her laptop. With the dig winding down, Annja didn't have much holding her in New Mexico. Except—

She felt a strong sense developing that she needed to stay. She wasn't sure why. But she and her companions had seen that terrifying flying thing not two hours earlier. The fear it inspired still seemed to echo in her soul like the tolling of a distant bell.

And now this Santo Niño seemed to be resurrecting the classic vanishing-hitchhiker urban legend. Oddities seemed to be converging on this small area of New Mexico, which was plenty peculiar to start with. And Annja's life was all about strangeness, it seemed.

A few Google search words—"black giant bird anomalous"—took her quickly to a site for a movie from a few years back called *The Mothman Prophecies*. She hadn't seen it. She had little interest in supernatural stuff, being of a skeptical turn of mind. That site led her to a listing for an ostensibly nonfiction book by a man named John A. Keel, and then to a scattering of paranormal and cryptozoology sites. It was all the usual huffing and conspiracy theorizing. She skimmed for a while and then moved on to other subjects. *It probably was just an eagle after all,* she told herself.

A quick check of Snopes.com confirmed what she'd first thought. The tale the girl at the front desk had told her about the Holy Child played out pretty close to the classic vanishing-hitchhiker script. Except in those tales the eponymous prophetic hitchhiker wasn't a child in antique Spanish drag, but Jesus Christ, himself.

Strange, she thought.

She felt a rumbling in her stomach and leaned

over to pick up an apple from a little basket she'd put on the bedside table. The Española Valley was famous for its apple orchards, and a fresh crop had just been taken in. The local apples were all they were made out to be, she had to admit, as she bit into one.

Next she did a bit of flash research into the Santo Niño stories. He was pretty much as the hotel clerk described him, with a gown and a cape and long locks flowing from under a slouch hat with a pinned-up front.

She read a couple of articles. It was definitely a strange apparition for the early twenty-first century—although if he was going to show up any-where, she had to admit northern New Mexico was just the place. It had a character unlike anywhere else she'd been in North America. It was a place where religious pilgrims walked on their knees at Easter to the sanctuary of the church at Chimayó, just a few miles beyond the dig site from where Annja had been working. And where lines of top-flight physicists drove hybrid cars or rode recumbent bicycles, making their own daily pilgrimage to Los Alamos National Labs not so far away to the west.

But Japanese tourists? There were Japanese Christians, indeed Japanese Catholics, Annja knew The Jesuits, austere, learned, ubiquitous and to Annja's mind, a little bit scary—they started out professedly as a conspiracy to take over the world, after all—had sent missions to Japan in the late sixteenth and early seventeenth centuries. Indeed, some authorities blamed the Jesuits and rumors that they were assembling an invasion force in the Spanish colonial stronghold of the Philippines, for Tokugawa Iyeyasu's closure of the country to outsiders. And the Philippines, Annja had just learned, was another locus of Santo Niño sightings.

But, come on. *Japanese tourists?*

She shook her head, letting the towel unravel and whip around her robed shoulders. Her damp hair tickled her neck and cheeks like seaweed strands. Closing the computer, she unwound off the bed and tossed the apple, now thoroughly denuded to the core, into a wastebasket. She realized she'd been up all night. She needed serious food, seriously soon.

Suddenly, her thoughts snapped back to images of the spooky sunset sighting, and the cold that probed through her that had nothing to do with the increasingly icy wind and falling snow. Unlike poor Alyson Simpson, she was anything but alarmed to find her companions on the dig had packed firearms. It wasn't uncommon, but some of the gun handling on display had been casual enough to disturb her. She wasn't sure guns would have been much use against the creature that had silently and effortlessly flown over them.

Twin voices clashed in her head.

Come on, it was only an eagle, said one.

It's good *to have a magic sword on call,* said the other.

"I'm hungry," she said aloud. She discarded the robe over the back of a chair and walked naked and glorious to the closet to pick out some clothes for dinner.

"THERE'S NO SUCH THING as *chupacabras,*" the lean twentysomething eating the Denver omelet said. He wore a scuffed brown bomber jacket over a white shirt with a pocket protector well stuffed with multicolored pens. He had a high, wide forehead and slightly sunken eyes with a tendency to stare. He sat back in his chair with one leg cocked over his knee. "It was a story made up for this Puerto Rican newspaper by a writer guy named Adrian something. *El Vocero.* That's the paper's name."

His bulkier friend with the backward ball cap grunted over his huevos rancheros. He was hunched forward with elbows propped on the table. "What's that got to do with the price of speed in Singapore?" he asked. With his moon face, black beard and black trenchcoat over T-shirt and jeans, Annja *hoped* he was deliberately trying to look like Kevin Smith playing Silent Bob in one of his own movies. Most of all she earnestly hoped he wasn't really Kevin Smith.

The little diner across the highway from the Ramada Inn wasn't a greasy spoon. More a trendy New Age equivalent. A tofu fork, perhaps, Annja thought. More faux adobe—she thought it was faux, anyway—and sand-pink-and-sage decor than the white shoebox with chrome and Formica of the classic American roadside diner. The food was good, portions were plentiful, and they didn't try to foist veganism on the paying customers. Although the customers did pay a tariff appropriate to the famously well-heeled Santa Fe tourist crowd.

Outside, the morning sun shone down on the parking lot and surrounding hills so hard Annja, seated in a booth by the window, half expected it to rattle against the glass. Even though the air was already winter crisp and shot through with the inevitable tang of piñon smoke, the light would sting unprotected skin.

The gloom of the evening before seemed to belong someplace else.

"I mean, we have to maintain a balance as monster hunters," the skinny guy said.

"I prefer the word *cryptozoologists*," the third musketeer said in a surprisingly high voice. Surprisingly because it emerged from a chest the approximate size and shape of an oil drum, wrapped in a black T-shirt with the publicity photo for a band on it. Their getup ran to black leather and pointy metal bits. Annja guessed they didn't do polka.

The man paused, assiduously stuffing a hamburger piled high with mushrooms, red onion and chopped green chili—at this hour of the morning she was impressed—into his mouth. The anthropologist in Annja made him a South Plains Indian of some kind, probably Kiowa. Or maybe a Pueblo or even Apache with Kiowa thrown in. He had incredibly thick and lustrous black hair drawn into a ponytail hanging down his vast back, and a tiny black ball cap perched sideways on his head.

"Whatever," the first man said with a shrug. Annja was surprised to see the three out at such an early hour. They were clearly science fiction fans, or a closely related genus. She'd always thought the earlier before noon they rose, the more strain it imposed on their nerd metabolisms. Apparently they were dedicated to their mission.

"It's important not to let ourselves get sucked in by every urban legend and showy hoax that comes down the pike. I'm just saying."

"But scientists reported seeing it this time," the bearded man said.

"Maybe. How do you know they were real scientists? Do you know the report was real? And anyway, I read rumors this morning that that *Chasing History's Monsters* chick was on the dig site. Doesn't that strike you as just a teensy bit suspicious?"

"The chick with the—" The big Indian held his hands cupped an imposing distance in front of his metal band.

"Naw," the David Byrne kid said. "The skinny, flat-chested one. The archaeologist."

The loud *tink* that startled Annja, she suddenly realized, had come from her melon spoon falling to the dish. She hunched her head between her shoulders and concentrated hard on studying the half-eaten cantaloupe.

I am *not* flat-chested, she thought, looking down at herself surreptitiously.

The three young men, who sat at a table not ten feet away across the maroon-tile floor, paid her no mind. She had her hair pulled back in a severe ponytail and hadn't slept and had huge, round Jackie O sunglasses on to hide the dark shadows under her eyes. On the whole she looked nothing like she did on her occasional television appearances, where a team of people insisted on fussing and painting her heavily with theatrical makeup. She always suspected they felt they were working with a blank canvas when they got their hands on her.

She glanced out the window. Away past the self-conscious Santa Fe–emulating facades of the strip mall across the road, the land sloped to a line of big trees whose gnarled limbs were thronged with tan-and-yellow leaves. Ancient cottonwoods, they marked the course of the Rio Grande—the Big River. It was seldom considered that big by eastern standards, and had probably only struck the Spanish explorers as such after they'd been stumbling around the parched Upper Sonoran Desert for a few weeks. It, not the Rockies and their tributaries that ran alongside it, was the state's true spine.

Annja thought she might walk through the brushy wood alongside it for a while this morning. The dig was done for the year. The Pueblos had gotten wind of last night's adventure and wanted things shut down immediately.

The tribal council was maybe spooked, and definitely pissed. Annja wondered who had talked about the sighting.

"—think about the Mayan calendar," the bearded guy was saying when Annja let herself tune in to the conversation again.

"How do you mean?" asked his leaner companion, who had turned sideways in his chair with his legs crossed.

The bearded guy shrugged. "Well, in connection

with this holy kid's prophecies. He's always forecasting doom, right?"

"But sometimes the percipients have narrow escapes right after he vanishes," the Kiowa-looking guy said. "Maybe he's just warning them."

The bearded guy shook his head determinedly. "There definitely also seem to be undercurrents of long-term doom."

"So what does this have to do with the Mayan calendar?" the third one wanted to know.

"It runs out in December 2012, right?"

The kid in the bomber jacket nodded. Warily, Annja thought.

"So maybe that's what the holy kid is prophesying. The Mayan calendar runs out—time runs out."

The skinny guy had wrinkled his big, wide forehead like a shar-pei and was shaking his head. "I never quite got what's supposed to happen after the Mayan calendar runs out. I mean, what if it's like Y2K? Except instead of all the microchips that were supposed to break down and all, all the world's stone calendars don't work anymore. Hard to see the downside there."

"I read somewhere online that maybe Betelgeuse had gone supernova," the big Indian guy said.

"Hypernova," the bearded guy said.

"Hypernova, then."

"And that concerns us how?" the skinny kid asked.

"Well, it's, like, theorized this happened a couple hundred years ago. Supposedly the star shows signs of being unstable. Its spectra or something."

"But if it happened two centuries ago—"

"But, see, it'd take time for the explosion to get here. Even at light speed. You know how the Mayas made all these precise astronomical observations. So, maybe they noticed Betelgeuse was fixing to blow?"

"Wait," the skinny kid said. "This happened, what? Five hundred years ago? They predicted Betelgeuse would blow up two hundred years ago? Isn't that three hundred years in their future? I'm confused."

"Betelgeuse is 427 light-years away," the bearded guy said, forking up more eggs in *salsa verde*.

"God, you're a nerd."

"We're all nerds. Why else are we here in Snake's Navel, New Mexico? Anyway, wouldn't that mean, if the Maya made their calendar four–five centuries ago, Betelgeuse would've been blowing up more or less the same time?"

"Whatever," the Indian kid said. "The point is, supposedly they knew all these secrets of astronomy and shit. So what if they totally foresaw that the radiation from the hypernova was gonna hit Earth on December 12, 2012, when the Mayan calendar runs out?"

"Seems like kind of a long lead time for the holy kid to be predicting doom in 2012."

"Maybe he wants to give humanity plenty of time to prepare."

"What's humanity going to *do* about the blast wave from a hypernova hitting the Earth in 2012? Invent teleportation and leave? To go where?"

The skinny kid reached out and rapped his knuckles on top of the bearded guy's baseball cap. "Dude, blast waves don't propagate in space. Hello. It's a vacuum? Blast waves need something to travel through. They're like sound."

The bearded guy batted his hand away. "Okay. The expanding shell of lethal hard radiation. Satisfied?"

"You're not taking this seriously," the Kiowa-looking kid said sulkily. "Native peoples had a lot of wisdom about Nature."

"Hey, I was the one who brought up the Mayan calendar. I'm not selling ancient native wisdom short here."

But the skinny guy kid had lost interest in the conversation. Instead he stared at the metal band picture on the Indian's T-shirt as if seeing it for the first time.

"Jesus, dude," he said, "are those ten-penny nails sticking out of that guy's armband?"

4

With a heave of effort Father Robert Godin hoisted his nondescript and battered black duffel bag off the baggage carousel in the brightly lit bowels of the Albuquerque International Airport. Crowded all around him were people wearing colorful pins showing hot air balloons; images of hot-air balloons decked the area. He had had difficulty getting reservations, either for a flight in or a hotel room. The annual Albuquerque International Balloon Fiesta was a major event and tourist draw.

Around him people chattered in a Babel of languages. He picked out French, German, Japanese, as well as English and the locally common Spanish. He half envied them their thoughtless gaiety—and half pitied them.

Yet isn't that your cross to bear, Robert? he told himself. That you should carry in this graying pate of yours fearful knowledge so that these simple children of God need never have to learn it?

Throwing the scuffed black bag over the shoulder of his brown leather jacket, he grinned behind his wire-rimmed glasses and began walking to the car rental agency's check-in counter nearby. God in His wisdom never promised to make life easy for people. Much less Jesuits.

Least of all him. But you screwed up, he reminded himself. You volunteered.

"YOU'RE NOT WELCOME HERE, Father."

There, Archbishop Daniel García thought with guilty satisfaction. I said it.

Although he was as tall as his visitor, and had longer legs, he seemed to be having trouble keeping up with the older man. They strolled in apparent amity around the southern quad of St. Pius X High School, the portion occupied by the Catholic Center, command center for the Archdiocese of Santa Fe, over which García presided. It was a crisp October morning, blustery as usual on the West Mesa bluffs overlooking the Rio Grande. Though it was clear, the winds had driven the hot-air balloons from the sky early. The archbishop's cassock, which he liked to wear during business hours because it made him look official, snapped at his calves like a nasty little animal.

The smile never faltered on the seamed, oblong face. "I gathered as much, Excellency," Father Robert Godin said, "by your body language when I came into your office."

García's face twisted briefly, partly in annoyance, partly in alarm. He had a long, sharp, studious face and a hank of black hair under his skullcap. He was not ashamed that women found him handsome.

Am I that transparent? he wondered. Given what this man had done—and did—that was frightening.

"I don't mean you *personally,* of course," the archbishop said hurriedly. "All God's children are equally welcome. And I do respect your profound commitment to the church. But your mission—it's simply not something that we need."

"With all respect, Excellency, the Vatican believes otherwise."

They can be so retrograde, he thought. But you could not say that sort of thing aloud to a special Vatican emissary. "We don't wish to encourage superstition among our flocks here."

"Such as belief in miracles?" Godin asked.

Precisely, García wanted to say. But of course you couldn't say that, either. Maybe kicked back in some oak-and-leather lounge with aperitifs, cleric to cleric. But not ex cathedra, as it were.

"Let me elucidate, Father," he said, perhaps ever so slightly in hope of befuddling a nonnative English speaker. But he knew better. He had seen the man's dossier, or at least such as was available—even to a man who ranked as high in the church hierarchy as he did. Godin was known to speak at least half a dozen languages, and he spent a great deal of time in North America. And he was a Jesuit. He would have mastered the English language. "Back about thirty years ago a woman in this state believed that the image of Jesus appeared to her in the scorch marks on a tortilla. She presented this as serious evidence of a miraculous apparition. The press, needless to say, had a field day," he finally said.

"It looked more like Mozart to me," Godin said. "Also, the derision seemed aimed as much at New Mexico as the church. Remember, I was a full adult, already in seminary and long in the tooth for that, when the story came out, your Excellency. I'm a bit older than you."

"Yes. Well, it's hardly our desire to expose our parishioners to ridicule. Or our state. After all, we are quite on the cutting edge of technology here, as I'm sure you're aware."

"Yes. Building all those brand-new fusion

warheads, of which there apparently can never be enough."

The archbishop's pale amber eyes blinked rapidly behind his horn-rims. Normally he wore contacts, but for the occasion he had donned the eyeglasses. He felt they gave him gravitas.

Now he felt back on his heels again. *He's the bloody-handed ex-mercenary and spook—and if half the rumors are true, some of the blood on his hands is of much more recent provenance than the end of the Cold War. How did I wind up on the defensive about the bomb?*

They strolled a pathway of crushed pink gravel that ran right along the edge of the bluff above the Rio Grande. Across the river Albuquerque spread like a toy city, looking much neater than it did closer up, tucked away between the tree-lined valley and the foothills of the rather abrupt Sandia Mountains, rising in a blue wall to the east. García was glad the students were all in class at the moment, although usually they stayed north of the center unless they were jogging the path for P.E. The campus had once belonged to the now defunct University of Albuquerque, and was quite extensive.

"Father," he said earnestly, "to be candid, I fear what you may represent."

To his amazement Godin laughed. He had an easy

laugh, easy as the lope with which he walked, loose-limbed as an adolescent. He seemed for a fact to be made out of rubber. And steel.

"I'm no witch-hunter, Your Excellency," the Jesuit said. "In fact some very good friends and professional associates of mine are witches. They can be very useful allies sometimes, in my line of work."

"I'm afraid I don't understand," García said.

"I'm not here to validate the sightings of the Santo Niño. I'm not the devil's advocate on the miracle case. My concern is to establish whether the apparitions might be demonic in origin, and in that case, whether they pose a danger to the church. And to the human race, for that matter."

"Preposterous," García blurted before he could catch himself.

Godin laughed. "As preposterous as being a high-ranking executive in an organization that explicitly teaches the reality of demons and miracles?"

García frowned. "We of the more *modern* generation—if I may speak frankly, Father—prefer to think of such things as allegories. Metaphors for the human condition. We much prefer to leave the biblical literalism to our, shall we say, more zealous Protestant brethren."

Godin nodded. "Fair enough. You've been spared certain experiences that would remove a lot of doubt in no uncertain terms. I have not. But after all, Your Excellency, I do not ask for your belief, nor even your cooperation. Merely your permission to operate within your archdiocese."

"But some of your experiences give me pause, Father—again, speaking candidly. Not as an exorcist, or whatever you may be—"

"Not that, either—thank God."

"—but rather your past, shall we say, political experiences. You have been a fairly active exponent of, even a warrior for, the forces of reaction. I can only be concerned as to what sort of methodology you might find appropriate to employ in pursuit of your mission."

Godin stopped and took off his glasses and polished them with a spotless white handkerchief. "You will believe this or not as you choose, Excellency," he said, "but I am, and always have been for all practical purposes, apolitical. When I fought against the followers of Pierre Mulele, I saw myself fighting against sadistic murderers, rapists, torturers. The fact that the Soviet Union chose to use them as counters in their great game made little difference to me. Fighting evil—evil I could see, and hear and smell—that was my role."

García shook his head. No point in getting drawn into a protracted wrangle, he told himself sternly. "I fear the very mission you've been sent upon indicates a strain of reaction within the church herself," he said, trying for more sorrow than anger. "Like much of the world, the church seems to have taken an alarming turn to the right of late."

He knew he skirted the edge. He was of course speaking to an inferior, hierarchically speaking. But the man was a direct representative of the Vatican. And a Jesuit. Some—most—of the Jesuits he knew were all-right guys, down with liberation theology and the true mission of the church in the modern world, which was to spread social justice and environmental enlightenment.

But the church still harbored deep, dank recesses of reaction, some even within the Society of Jesus.

Godin had started walking again, north toward the cluster of not particularly attractive flat buildings with flaring, slanted tops that made up most of the campus. "I'm not interested in heresy, either, Your Excellency. Either professionally or personally. My own faith's likely little more orthodox than your own."

"You—a Jesuit?"

The priest laughed again as the archbishop, cheeks burning, had to trot to catch up.

"You should read more history of the church. We Jesuits have often been accused of unorthodox views— though nowhere near as often as we're guilty of it."

"What do you want of me, then?" García asked at length.

"As I said, your permission to operate freely."

"Under the circumstances, the archdiocese can take no official cognizance of your activities."

"Meaning what, if I may be so bold as to ask, Excellency?"

"Meaning that what you do here is your own concern. I do not give permission. It is not in my purview to deny, much as I might wish otherwise. You enjoy the same rights and privileges—and responsibilities—as any other communicant, and any other ordained priest. But the archdiocese will extend no cooperation."

"That's fine, Excellency," Godin said easily. "I'm used to operating on my own."

García felt his thin cheeks grow hot. "And if you violate the laws of the land, the archdiocese will have no choice but to repudiate you. Should you break the law, and should I find out about it, it will be my pleasure to report you to the authorities."

To García's amazement the priest turned to him with an engaging, boyish grin. "Sure, sure," Godin said, patting his shoulder. "You'd be shirking your responsibilities to do otherwise. And don't worry. Over the years and the miles I've gotten pretty adept at not getting caught."

Such was the twinkle in the man's eyes that García found himself able to believe the words were spoken in jest. Almost. It was impossible, he found, to dislike Godin as a person, much as it may have been his duty as a progressive Christian to do so. He hoped God would forgive him.

"I will take up no more of your time, Excellency. I thank you, and trust that this is the last time I bother you."

"For both our sakes," García said gravely, "I hope so."

Without being entirely sure why he did so, he extended his hand. Godin bent to kiss the ring. Then he turned and strode off toward the parking lot at a land-devouring gait.

Archbishop Daniel García stood staring after him with the wind snapping his cassock like a sail. He is a dinosaur, he thought in wonder. And quite possibly dangerous.

So why do *I* feel shame?

5

"I have to admit," Dr. Lauren Perovich said, "that it's an exciting place and time to be a professional student of folklore. I'm actually getting to see it in action—see folklore made." She smiled and shook her head. "Then again, New Mexico's seldom a dull place. Not for anyone with a taste for the strange."

You can say that again, Annja thought.

"After all, this is the land of the McDonald's coffee verdict and the holy tortilla, Ms. Creed."

"'Annja' is fine, Doctor."

"Annja, then. And call me Lauren."

Despite the gray streaking the professor of American folklore's long, straight, ash-blond hair, she looked little older to Annja than Annja herself did in the mirror most mornings. Perhaps it was the late-afternoon light filtering between the half-shut blinds of Dr. Perovich's little office tucked away in a corner of the University of New Mexico campus in central Albuquerque.

Or maybe I'm just getting old, Annja thought.

The folklorist was slim and youthful in her grayish turtleneck pullover and jeans. Her blue eyes danced behind round glasses. Annja thought her students lucky, hoped they appreciated the fact. The professor had graciously agreed to meet with Annja after her normal office hours, when afternoon classes were done for the day.

"If you don't mind my asking," Perovich said, "what's your professional interest in these Holy Child sightings, Annja?"

"Well, as an archaeologist I deal in people—societies—cultures that are dead and buried. It sounds awful when put that way, I suppose. But it's true. So I find it useful to, I guess, reconnect to the dynamic world of a living human culture, the interactions of living beings. So I keep touch with how people really work—to avoid embarrassing situations like thinking some artifact whose purpose I can't identify must have ritual significance, when it's, like, a pot scrubber or back scratcher or something else everyday."

The conversation she'd overheard in the diner that morning had actually suggested action to her.

She laughed and brushed away a strand of chestnut-brown hair that had drifted in to tickle her forehead. "Or maybe I'm just abusing professional courtesy to gratify simple curiosity."

Dr. Perovich sat rocking slightly in her swivel chair and nodding judiciously. Then she grinned impishly.

"I admit I'm just a bit disappointed," she said. "I had visions of seeing myself on *Chasing History's Monsters,* I suppose."

"The Holy Child doesn't exactly fit my definition of a monster. Or at least not my producer's. Now, if he had murdered eight or nine people…"

"But the show also deals with more general paranormal events," Perovich said.

"You seem awfully knowledgeable about it."

"I admit I'm a fan. Since I'm not a 'hard' scientist—" her fingers made quote signs in the air "—I don't have to pretend to some kind of reflex skepticism. Frankly, a lot of what passes for skepticism I can't tell from rather ingenuous faith in conventional explanations."

"Um," Annja said, feeling more than a bit uncomfortable. She liked to style herself a skeptic, too. "Well. I'll certainly keep you in mind for the future. You'd be a good talking-head expert. You're articulate and interesting. It doesn't hurt that you're photogenic."

"Not, I'm afraid, like that hostess—what's her name?"

"Kristie Chatham."

"That's the one. Just so long as it doesn't matter if your experts aren't quite so profoundly endowed."

"Not to me," Annja replied.

She was grateful for the banter. There *were* monsters on the prowl, her instincts told her. Doug Morrell, her producer on the show, would, in the fullness of time, be all over the black anomaly of the night before—the more so since one of his own people was among the witnesses. *An eagle,* she told herself firmly.

That's all it was.

Perovich crossed her legs, laced her fingers over a knee and sat back. "So how can I help you?"

"You're keeping up with the recent rash of Santo Niño sightings, I take it?"

"Oh, yeah." Her eyes gleamed.

"What's your professional take on them?"

Perovich swung around in her chair. "Fascinating. Really, really. We're seeing a synthesis of truly ancient folk legends with modern urban myth. Although I suspect the vanishing hitchhiker first appeared to Egyptian chariot drivers, portraying himself as the god Horus. Falcon head and all."

"Can you tell me a bit more about the myth?" Annja asked.

"Yep. A staple of the Automotive Age. Really seemed to hit its stride back in the seventies— although I'm never sure whether that's just because people began to be aware of urban legends as such, and keep track of them, about that time. That's always a risk, with sociological or psychological disciplines, even medicine. How much of an increased volume of reports of something is due to actual increased occurrence, and how much to people simply being more aware of it, and even having someone to report it to? Also, I ran up against the legend myself in those days, as a blushing girl—not to date myself too much.

"The basics are a young man appears by the side of the road with his thumb out. Although he's long-haired and bearded and maybe a bit scruffy in appearance, a kindly motorist stops and picks him up. The young man is very polite and friendly. Then his manner turns grave. He warns of some impending disaster, usually global in scale. Then something distracts the motorist. He looks away. When he looks back the passenger is gone."

"And he figures it was Jesus?" Annja asked.

"Sometimes. Who else would be long-haired, benign and prophetic? Well, of course, a raft of personages, even from the New Testament, although who ever sees an apparition of John the Baptist?

Sometimes the enigmatic passenger explicitly identifies himself as Christ, but that's rare."

She shrugged. "Actually, my personal encounter with the legend involved a friend telling me about a hitchhiker his uncle picked up who claimed to be a scientist. This scientist—a young, kind of scruffy, polite man—claimed he had learned that the Earth was going to run out of oxygen by 1980. After that he dropped out of school and decided to wander and see America, spread the warning, for what good it would do. Of course, both my friend and his uncle swore it was true. It wasn't strictly a vanishing-hitchhiker yarn in the classic sense, although, if memory serves, the uncle claimed he did lose track of the guy kind of mysteriously at the next truck stop. But not long after I heard that story, I ran into an aunt who said a friend of hers said a friend of *hers* had had an encounter with Jesus. When I heard that tale I instantly hooked it up in my mind with the dropout-scientist yarn. And I was hooked. That's the actual urban legend that gave me my vocation—that and the choking Doberman."

"Choking Doberman?" Annja laughed. "I seem to be turning into an urban-legend echo machine."

Perovich waved a slim hand. "Master finds dog choking—finds house broken into—learns when he calls the cops that a burglar was just picked up in an emergency room missing some fingers…no need for more details. If you've ever seen a slasher flick your imagination will fill them in more than well enough. Oh, yeah—and the lover's lane, with the escaped maniac killer with the hook. Anyway."

"So you actually set out to study urban legends?"

"They were what drew me to folklore in the first place. When I went to college—be a dear and let me slide as to exactly when—there wasn't anything like a discipline of urban-legend study, although the term had come into use and a couple of books had been published on the subject. I'm afraid I don't have the stuff of pioneers in me. I didn't feel capable of forcing urban legendology into legitimacy all by my lonesome. The up-and-coming study of folklore was the closest thing available—though tending to be overrun with annoying granola eaters. Not that I, um, haven't been known to munch on the occasional granola bar, you understand."

"All the way around," Annja said, laughing. "How do you see what's happening now?"

"As you may know, the Holy Child—the Santo Niño—first appears in Spain, during the resistance to the Moorish occupation, feeding Christian prisoners in a village called Atocha. The apparition was supposed to be the infant Jesus."

She shrugged. "You can see why the oppressed

Christian minority would want to believe that, certainly. From there the legend makes its way to New Mexico along the same twisty, colonialist trail that most of the colonists and trade goods did. Through the Spanish holdings in the Philippines, then through Mexico and finally up into northern New Mexico, which was the nether end of nowhere in those days."

"I see," Annja said.

"Now, it strikes me there's a natural match here," Perovich said. She was clearly enjoying herself. She liked spinning yarns—which Annja could guess might be a useful asset in a folklore prof. "The Holy Child associated from the get-go with *succor*. And of course any spiritual manifestation worth its spiritual salt possesses the gift of *prophecy*.

"While sightings are reported all across the Southwest from about the eighteenth century, when the myth made it up here from Plateros in Mexico, the main local belief centers upon an image of the Holy Child kept in the Sanctuary de Chimayó, in the Sangre de Cristo Mountains north of Santa Fe."

"We're doing a dig not far from there, on San Esequiel Pueblo land," Annja said. "Or were. It's kind of wound down for the season now."

"Winter comes early and hard to northern New Mexico. You know what 'Sangre de Cristo' means?"

"'Blood of Christ,'" Anna stated.

"Exactly!" The professor smacked the arm of her chair. "See why I love it here?" Perovich asked, eyes shining in the gloom. She hadn't turned on any interior light. The soft polychrome glow of her computer monitor lit the side of her face and struck the occasional rainbow accent off her long hair. Annja did not feel compelled to ask for more lights. If her subject was comfortable, so was she. "You don't get that sort of thing back in Ohio."

Perovich rocked back in her chair. "Then again, you don't get *mountains* in Ohio, either. Not like around here. So, anyway, the image in the sanctuary is supposed to bust loose occasionally and wander the countryside doing good deeds. There's this really wonderful tradition of bringing children's shoes to the shrine, to replace the ones he wears out on his errands of mercy. And of course, he's spotted from time to time—and as mysteriously disappears."

Annja nodded. "I see where this is going."

"Wandering-saint yarns of pretty similar content are common to many cultures and religious traditions around the world. Like sightings of a benign and powerful feminine spirit. Before the Spanish got to the Valley of Mexico, they called her Tonantzin, a fertility goddess. Later they called her the Virgin of Guadalupe."

"Yes. You see her image everywhere around here," Annja said.

"Another reason to love the place. A lot of what I study isn't folklore to the people around here. It's *real*. Anyway, I'm researching my own paper on that very subject. How the Santo Niño may have engendered the vanishing hitchhiker. Would you like me to send you a draft?"

"I would, please. You've got my e-mail address."

"In any event, it's easy to see how the current concept of the vanishing hitchhiker might blend—or blend back—into the Holy Child myth. That's what I see happening now. It's like all those clichés we New Mexicans are so fond of. I laughingly call myself a New Mexican after living here ten years, when the real New Mexicans have roots here going back to the sixteenth century."

"Or the ice age," Annja said.

The professor laughed. "True, true. Please don't report me for having a Eurocentric moment, there. Could be fatal in my position."

"Your secret's safe with me."

"Anyway, we always like to tell ourselves about New Mexico being a land of contrasts—from ancient petroglyphs to the atom bomb. But like most clichés it's true in some important ways. And I think we see it in effect here."

The professor leaned close to Annja. Her eyes were big in the twilight. "I'm going to propound a theory that I'm sure would make your cultural-anthropologist friends hold their fingers up in crosses and hiss at me. I hope this doesn't ruin my shot at a gig on your show."

Annja laughed. "I'm not so good at political correctness myself."

"All right. You've been warned. The southwestern U.S. is basically uninhabitable. It's desert and mountain. Arid and uninviting. Even the river valley— well, you've seen our river, so-called?"

Annja nodded.

"There weren't such drains on its flow upstream back in the day, of course. But no one was ever going to mistake it for the Orinoco. So the people who settled here were the ones they wouldn't let settle anywhere else—anywhere, well, nice to live. The natives you got were human-sacrificing hardcases like the Anasazi, or Pueblos, who kept getting chased out of wherever they settled by mean people, or Athabascan raiders. Even the Aztecs—not a kind and gentle bunch—took one look and kept on moving. Right through the Jornada del Muerte.

"The Spanish settlers were largely converted Jews and Moors for whom Spain had become too hot. Literally—ba-bum!" She did a top-hat sting on the arm of her chair. "The Christians were mostly bandits—heavily weighted to Basques and Catalans, whom any good Castilian of the day would tell you were the same thing. The Anglos, well, you know what kind of sociopaths and escaped doorknobs our pioneering forebears were. Again, they pushed compulsively west because the decent, civilized east wouldn't hold 'em."

Annja nodded. "Okay. I may have to turn in my anthro card, but you haven't said anything I'd disagree with."

Perovich reared up, looked at her and pushed her glasses up her straight nose. "Well. You're a rare one."

"That's what the nuns said." To the blank look she expanded, "At the orphanage."

The professor nodded. "So what we get here is the confluence—no—the three-way, full-on, pedal-to-the-metal *collision* of the most extreme elements of three pretty disparate cultures. The aftershocks reverberate into the present day—spend some time on the streets listening to people, just open your eyes and look around. You can see them—you can feel 'em."

"I already picked up on that," Annja said seriously.

Perovich sat back, unfolding her hands to her sides. "So there you have it! I was an Ohio suburban chick with a taste for the strange. Goth hadn't been invented yet, or hadn't reached Columbus. So what's a girl to do? First I got into the study of folklore, because it was the accepted discipline closest to my interest. Then I came here for grad work. And I've been here ever since."

Annja nodded. She wasn't sure if she'd discovered anything she could use. She was definitely getting a better feel for the place, though, as well as its innate weirdness. It helped her put in perspective some of the things she'd observed during the two weeks she'd spent with the dig. As well as the occasional sense of eeriness she'd experienced even before the incident the previous night.

"What do you think about the reality underlying the stories?" she asked. "Is there any?"

Perovich laughed. "That's a tricky question. But since I've already opened up to you, what the hey? First, I think it's fatuous to say that all legends or myths or other stories 'must have' or 'always have' some basis in reality. People lie. They make things up, to amuse themselves, to amuse others, to make themselves look important. You can twist the definition of 'based in reality' to fit anything, up to and including most horror movies—there are teenagers and they have nightmares. I've had some doozies myself, let me tell you. So, on that basis, you could say those movies are based on something factual.

"At the same time, not all urban legends are false.

Sometimes they include elements of real events. Sometimes yarns that get repeated—by word of mouth, at one time, by photocopy, then fax, then e-mail—are quite true. Like the story about the lawyer who fell to his death after hurling himself against a picture window in a high-rise to show it was shatterproof, or the guy who flew by tying helium balloons to a lawn chair, and descended by shooting the balloons with a pellet pistol. The details may be off sometimes, but those things are well documented. They really happened."

"So what you're saying is—" Annja began.

"I come down firmly on the side of waffling. We also spin yarns because we have a hardwired desire to believe in the strange—something beyond the horizon, beyond what we know. I have the same desires. At the same time, I try to keep a level head. What I do hasn't got many metrics, not a lot of re-producible results. But I try to take a rational approach.

"But still. Just rationally, looking at evidence I consider pretty trustworthy, it seems to me that things do happen in this world that defy conventional expla-nation. These people are experiencing *something*. They are talking to someone. Is it a hoaxer? When you get a Japanese family reporting that they were warned away from impending calamity by a child dressed in classic Santo Niño costume—well, something odd is happening by definition. Wouldn't you say?"

Annja shrugged. "I do wonder if we have enough information to form an opinion."

Perovich nodded. "True enough!"

She slapped a jean-clad thigh. "Well. Just be glad we're not having an outbreak of sightings of one of our *really* scary apparitions."

Annja felt invisible mice with cold feet run down the nape of her neck and right down her spine. "Such as what?" she asked, not sure she wanted to hear the professor's answer.

"La Llorona. The Weeping Lady. Brr." Perovich shook herself theatrically. "Those stories always give me the willies."

"The Weeping Lady," Annja repeated in a small voice. "What does she do?"

"Wanders rural areas weeping for her lost children. She murdered them herself. In some versions of the legend she was burned at the stake for it. She's also supposed to lure lone travelers—usually young men, for obvious reasons—to their doom. She keeps turning up even today, although modern encounters are sadly short on actual doom. I have collected some pretty unnerving reports that seem quite credible. I've interviewed several percipients myself, off the record. Most people who run into something really strange seem very reticent to talk about it."

That would be me, Annja thought. Unfortunately, it would not be whoever spilled the beans about our sighting last night. It was an eagle, anyway, she told herself again..

"One odd thing I've noticed," Perovich said. "Sightings of the weeping lady are usually associated with the sound of a woman screaming—big surprise, huh? But sounds like that have also been cropping up in the monster-sighting reports that have started to cross my desk of late. You know—shadowy cats, anomalous dogs, bigfoot kind of things, but black and foul smelling. Peculiar, isn't it?"

Once again Annja thought she could hear the chilling noise that had accompanied the black form as it glided off out of sight—piercing screams like a woman in distress.

"Very strange," she said.

OUTSIDE, TWILIGHT WAS well advanced. Over and through the old trees across University Boulevard she could see the dying embers of another gaudy black-velvet-painting sunset silhouetting an old church steeple. The narrow parking lot between the Maxwell Anthropology Center buildings and the street was empty but for her rented Honda and a battered minivan parked twenty or thirty yards away. She gave the van a glance and put it from her mind. It looked like the sort of third-hand vehicle a college student might own.

"'Scuse me, lady." A voice broke the silence from her left.

She snapped her head up and around. She had parked with the car facing away from the street. A raggedly dressed man—early thirties, she guessed—was walking none too steadily toward her across the strip of grass separating the inner and outer sections of the parking lot. He was gaunt. His face was half-covered by patchy dark beard.

"Sorry to bother you, ma'am," he said, speaking a little too crisply, as the mildly intoxicated tend to do when they want to decisively show they aren't drunk. "My car ran out of gas about a quarter mile back up University here." He gestured vaguely to the north. "I need to go pick up my old lady at work. She's pregnant and gets tired real easy, and I need to ask if you could please help me out with a couple of bucks for gas."

Annja frowned. She hated these situations. She'd heard such sob stories before—not infrequently repeated word for word on consecutive days, by the same "distressed" motorist. He obviously does need money, she thought. But do I really help him if I give it to him? Or only encourage him to persist in self-destructive behaviors?

"Really, lady," he said. He sounded weary and desperate. "I'm not bullshitting you. I really need it."

She almost reached in her pocket for some money. Almost. But he had entered the customary cultural limits of her personal space and kept coming. Warnings shrilling in her mind, she turned to face him squarely.

Her arms were suddenly seized from behind by powerful hands.

6

The Vatican

Grunting, the man slowly pushed the weight-laden iron bar upward from his chest. The body lying supine on the bench was well into middle age, and had expanded and softened considerably around the middle. But he prided himself that he had lost but little of the bull-like strength that had characterized him in his youth. This despite the sedentary and indeed intellectual profession where he had spent his entire adult life since leaving the seminary.

Straining, eyes tightly shut, he fought to straighten his arms against the massive weight. Finally, with a last exertion of his will—an organ exercised perhaps more regularly and rigorously than his body——he forced his arms to lock.

Instantly they began to tremble. He felt strength flee. In a heartbeat they would buckle and drop the weight to crush his chest. In half panic he opened his eyes, although he knew his spotter stood waiting, attentive to just such situations.

Yet the spotter did not seize the bar. The man on the bench began to perspire profusely as the bar started oscillating in the air above him. He squeezed his eyes shut again, as if by not seeing his doom he could forestall it.

He felt the bar move, then, tardily, steady as it was grasped. But still the awful weight pressed down on his arms, turning them into jelly.

"*Deus meu!*" he gasped. "My life is in your hands."

"Yes," a deep voice said.

He opened his eyes.

The hands guiding the heavy bar as if it were featherlight were not the pale, relatively soft hands of Franz, the Swiss attendant at the modern gymnasium below the Vatican. They were as hard and sunbrowned as a common laborer's, and covered with expensive rings of ruby and sapphire, gold and silver.

"You," he gasped as Garin Braden, clad in his customary Fleet Street suit, lowered the bar into the waiting rack. After his initial start the cardinal felt little surprise at seeing Braden, although access was most carefully restricted. Garin Braden seemed to appear anywhere he willed within the confines of the Vatican.

"Thank you," the cardinal said when he caught his breath.

"It is nothing, Eminence," the newcomer said in the prelate's native Portuguese.

He knelt, took the still-shaking white hand proffered and kissed the ring of office. Braden was a big man, with dark hair, a neat black beard and mustache and piercing black eyes. He rose smoothly to his feet.

Cardinal Adalberto de Souza sat up. He gratefully accepted the towel and bottle of water the wealthy industrialist handed him. He mopped his high, sweat-sheened brow and drank.

Then he looked around. They were alone in the small but brightly lit, clean and wonderfully appointed weight room, one of many dotted throughout the sprawling Vatican City complex. The modern church had begun to pressure its shepherds to tend to the condition of their bodies, rather than regarding such as vanity and indeed the sin of pride, as in years past. Cardinal de Souza was still one of relatively few among princes of the church to avail himself of the weight rooms, although many of the younger priests were quite passionate about fitness.

He shook his head. He had seen many changes come to the church. Not all were for the better.

He looked up at his guest. "Good morning, Mr. Braden. It is an unexpected pleasure to see you."

"The pleasure is mine, Eminence," the shaven-headed man said in his exquisitely modulated baritone.

He reached a manicured hand inside the coat of his dark suit and brought forth a manila envelope. This he handed to the prelate.

"The negatives," he said.

VANITAS VANITATUM, omnia vanitas, Garin Braden thought. He had seen it all before.

Braden and Sons was one of Europe's most established and respected industrial concerns. The company was second only to arms maker Fabbrica d'Armi Pietro Beretta in age. It had long outlasted such one-time peers as the Fugger and Medici banking empires. One thing had mystified the cognoscenti for centuries. It seemed each Braden son looked unnervingly like the last, and all the others before him.

Garin Braden knew a secret. He knew many. He had grown rich trafficking in secrets long before it became a cliché that knowledge itself constituted wealth.

One of the deepest secrets he knew was that there *were* no Braden sons. He and his one peer—his deadly rival, former mentor and sometime best friend Roux—had no heirs. Garin Braden remained eternal in many guises.

"With my compliments, Your Eminence," he said.

The cardinal snatched the envelope as greedily as a small boy with a Christmas present. "They're all here?" he asked.

Braden smiled. "Have I given Your Eminence cause to doubt my diligence?"

"No, no. Forgive me, my son. I know you to be most scrupulous."

It might have been hard not to laugh at that, had Garin not had so many years of practice.

Garin had betrayed Jeanne Darc—whom moderns had until recently miscalled d'Arc—to the English. He had been motivated by simple jealousy, born of insecurity. He'd felt his master was devoting too much time and attention to his female protégée, and too little to him. It was intolerable that a brilliant, apt pupil and apprentice should be pushed aside for a teenage schizophrenic with a sanguinary cast of mind.

He had repented it long since, of course. It had been petty. Worse, it had been out of control.

Garin Braden was all about control.

He had forgiven himself. It was mere youthful folly. And he had accepted—even embraced—the consequences.

"And the blackmailer?" de Souza asked.

"He will trouble you no further, Eminence."

The flesh merchant had proved unwilling to see reason. Consequently he had suffered a fatal accident two days before, when his vehicle had overturned on a treacherous back road, breaking his fat, greasy neck. Or at least, so read the official finding.

It would do no good to Cardinal de Souza for his enemies to come into possession of evidence of distasteful acts. Powerful men—and Cardinal de Souza was powerful indeed—had many enemies.

Garin knew all about that, too.

The cardinal clutched the envelope protectively against his undershirt, which was sweat soaked and glued to his matted, graying chest hairs. "I thank you, my son," he said. "You have performed a great service. Not just to me, but to the church."

"My pleasure to serve," Garin said.

He thought it a great pity his old master, Roux, was so sunken in self-righteousness and hence self-pity. Roux hadn't changed much over the years. He was still in the grasp of the same vices as five centuries ago— wine, women, gambling, a tendency toward sloth.

Garin, meanwhile, had explored without compunction the furthest extremes of human behavior, vice and virtue. He had jaded himself with excess— and spent decades in self-denial so total it had excited both envy and suspicion among the Christian Trappists, Sufi dervishes and Tibetan Buddhists in whose monasteries, and more, he had studied and meditated. Garin had seen, and done, it all.

"And the sword, Eminence?" Garin asked.

The balding head nodded gravely. "You served us well in that, too, my son. It was a grave matter you called to our attention."

Garin thought about his youthful betrayal of Roux's protégée. For half a millennium Roux had attempted to make amends. Whereas Roux liked to steep himself in drink and self-pity and rail against the modern world, Braden embraced it with both arms.

But suddenly there was a terrible threat. The loss and breaking of Joan's holy sword had frozen them in time. The rediscovery and reforging of the blade threatened the status quo.

Indeed, Braden had initially feared he would simply age all at once, like the head vampire at the end of a horror film—drying to dust and blowing away. That had not happened. But he woke each morning alert to every pang, and each time he looked in the mirror, scrutinized beard, eyebrows, head for the telltale appearance of a gray hair. The existence of the sword was a threat to his existence. If Roux could not understand that—or worse, was fool enough to welcome the prospect of oblivion as a rest

from his endless bouts of guilt and self-recrimination—
then so much the worse for him. Garin would do
what needed to be done.

He would do whatever was right for Garin
Braden.

Just as he had always done.

Cardinal de Souza looked up with a bushy gray
eyebrow raised. "If your information is correct?"

"I am likewise scrupulous about my information,"
Garin said smoothly. "And Your Eminence knows
my resources are vast. Would I have troubled your
Eminence with a mere fairy story?"

"No. No, of course not. Forgive me." De Souza
shook his head and mopped his brow again. His
breathing had mostly returned to normal. "It's just
that what you told us was so…difficult to credit."

"In this modern world of ours, with its vaunted
science and reason," Garin said, "I can see how that
would be so."

"Nonetheless it is as well to have certain…spiritual
realities recalled to us. Even to princes of the church."

"So you have done me the honor of taking my
warning seriously, Eminence."

"Just so. I myself spoke to God's Hound before he
left on this mission of his. He goes, you see, to in-
vestigate whether something demonic lies behind
these apparitions in New Mexico." He shook his

head. "His superior, Secretary Cangelosi, insists he actually finds such infernal influences. And dispatches them in a most efficient way."

"God's Hound?" Garin asked.

"It's what we call this Walloon Jesuit. He looks like a hound. He is tenacious as a rabid dog. And can be as ruthless. *Domini Cane*."

Garin laughed. "He might take umbrage. The term was once used to refer to the bitter rivals of his order, the Dominicans."

"Really? I had no idea. Well, I personally took Father Godin aside and charged him to recover this relic. To think—the sword of St. Joan restored! You are certainly correct. It must be returned at once to the bosom of the church!"

Garin bowed to hide his smile. He found Roux's new project, Annja Creed, to be a thoroughly delightful young woman. She was beautiful, vibrant, resourceful, indomitable. But if she stood between him and his continuing ageless immortality—well, was it not the way of mortals to wither and fall from the vine?

He knew about Father Godin. The former Belgian paratrooper, Congo mercenary, French Foreign Legionnaire had a list of doctorates as long as his arm. He was one of the world's most esteemed counterterrorism experts. Indeed, certain of Garin's companies had at various times hired him to consult on security, although Garin had never met the man. But his great passion and his life's work were to serve as the special secret operative of the church, answering only to the Pope's confidential secretary.

Despite advancing age he was deadly as a krait. And for all his genius-level intellect he had the single-minded tenacity of what Cardinal de Souza blithely named him, and what he resembled—God's Hound.

If any mere mortal could separate Annja Creed from her cursed blade, it was Godin. Garin was counting on that.

"We live in an age of miracles as well as dangers, Eminence."

"Just so, my son, just so."

The cardinal rose and made the sign of benediction over the industrialist, who piously crossed himself in turn.

"May God bless you, Garin Braden."

"He has, Your Eminence," Garin said with a wholly genuine smile. "Many times."

7

Two men pinioned Annja's arms from behind. She had never sensed them coming. She looked back over her shoulder. The man on her right had a head like a Muppet, all blond shag and gap-toothed grin. He wore an oversize Army jacket and smelled sour.

The scruffy man who had originally approached her had shifted to place himself between Annja and the street to screen what was happening from cars passing in the twilight. He smiled at her.

"Don't scream or struggle, honey," he said. "Or we'll have to hurt you."

The man who held her left arm rammed a fist into her kidney. She gasped as pain shocked her system. Her knees buckled.

The men hustled her toward the minivan. They

moved around to flank her, making themselves look more like helpers and less like abductors while keeping pressure on her shoulder and elbow joints.

They've done this before, Annja thought. Adrenaline coursed through her veins. The aftershocks of pain made her blink. She forced herself to breathe deeply and focus.

The first man moved around her to open the van's back doors. The rear row of seats had been discarded, leaving an extralarge cargo space. Her two handlers, grunting from the exertion, hoisted her into the van.

"Damn," the man on her left said with a Latino accent. "Bitch is heavy."

"Muscular," the gap-toothed guy said. "Watch her. She might get ideas."

"No way," the first man said, climbing in after them and shutting the doors.

The sunset gloom was replaced by darkness that seemed complete. Annja felt panic fluttering around inside her belly and rib cage like a bird trying to break free. She drew in a deeper abdominal breath.

"She knows she'd better be a good girl. And if you are a good girl, we'll make you feel real good."

Rapists? she wondered. It was the most obvious explanation for this attack. But from the very outset she doubted it was the motive.

The first man was pleasant-looking, if you overlooked the patchy three-day beard and an overlay of grime that she strongly suspected had been applied by hand rather than hard living. He had his hand inside his jacket. When it came out Annja saw a glitter as her eyes adjusted to the last rays of daylight filtering in the front windows of the van.

The grubby hand held a hypodermic syringe. There could be no mistake.

Annja sagged. "There, sweetie," the man said. "This'll sting at first. Then you'll feel fine."

The fear she felt on seeing the needle turned her stomach. It was time to stop pretending to be a victim.

She ripped both arms forward. The two men holding her were caught off guard in spite of their previous discussion. She clapped her hands together on the sides of the bearded man's head as if clashing the cymbals.

He bellowed in surprise and dropped the syringe, reeling back. Annja slammed both her elbows straight back. She felt her left one glance off the Latino's forehead. The shaggy man caught it right in the mouth. She felt teeth break and gouge her elbow through her windbreaker.

She was pretty sure the gap in his teeth had been blacked out. He'd have a gap for real now. He fell back from her, howling.

"Jesus Christ!" the Latino guy shouted. Holding her biceps with his left hand, he let go to do something urgent with his right.

Suspecting what it was, she pulled her knee to her chest. The man who'd held the syringe crouched before her. His eyes were glazed but starting to refocus with purpose—and rage.

Annja kicked him in the sternum with all her strength. The force blasted him backward. He had not fully engaged the door latch. The van doors blew open and he flew out to land hard on the pavement.

Annja was already twisting clockwise. The Latino was bringing a handgun to bear. It was a serious handgun—a Heckler & Koch USP of some kind, big and black. It was expensive hardware for a penniless, panhandling derelict.

Annja recognized the standard equipment for a professional killer.

She caught his right wrist in her left hand, pushed the barrel upward. It went off with a bang that seemed to bulge the thin-gauge metal van walls outward and Annja's eardrums inward. With her eyes stinging from the muzzle-blast Annja squeezed. Hard.

The Latino's dark eyes went wide. His mouth worked. No sound came out.

His wrist bones broke with a crunching sound, like rocks breaking beneath the tires of a heavy truck.

He screamed. With a twist, to make sure raw, splintered ends and loose parts ground against nerves and shocked him into incapacity, Annja flung him bodily against the shaggy man, who now had a bloody beard to go with an authentically vacant black gape of mouth.

She leaped from the van. The man who had first accosted her had struggled to his feet. He had his hands down in his pants. As she sprinted the few steps toward him, Annja did not reckon he was playing with himself.

The hand popped out of his waistband clutching some kind of black autopistol. It was blocky: maybe a Glock, she thought. She crescent-kicked with her right foot, up, across. The inner side of her boot slapped the handgun spinning from his hand. She used the kick's momentum to plant her right foot, pirouette on that leg and deliver a spinning reverse kick to his jaw with the heel of her left foot.

Bone broke with a loud snap. The man's head whipped to the side, trailing blood and saliva. Whether it was his neck that gave or his jaw she didn't much care as she spun through her kick, then took off running for her rented Honda.

She had crested the adrenaline rush and now rode it like a surfer on a wave. Without any fumbling she got her keys from her pocket and into the door. Forcing herself to move deliberately, she unlocked the door, removed the keys, opened the door, slid inside.

Annja was no stranger to danger. She was experienced enough to know that in immediate lethal peril the main predictor of survival is not strength or fitness or even skill at fighting. It's whether or not you keep your head.

Keeping her head had kept Annja alive before.

She looked back. The man who had first braced her lay sprawled face-first on the ground. He didn't seem to be moving.

The Honda kicked to life at the first twist of the key. She had parked at the north end of the ribbon lot. The van was parked to the south, cutting her off from the only exit. Directly behind her was a landscaped strip, dry and sparse as autumn had settled, and then another row of parking places paralleling the street beyond. She could easily back into that row and head to the exit that way. But if the van had anybody in shape to drive, it could just as easily block her exit like a cork in a jar.

She put the Honda in Reverse and backed out, turning to face south. At the same moment the van backed out into the middle of the drive to face her. She rolled her window down quickly and hit the gas.

Engine whining, the Honda shot forward. She couldn't see who drove the van. Whoever it was probably wasn't acting or reacting at top speed. The bigger vehicle made no further motion to block her.

She stuck her left hand out the window, fingers curling as if to grasp, and reached with her mind to a different place. As she veered right to whip past the van through the space it had just vacated, a fantastic broadsword appeared in her left hand. She slashed it forward and down, felt impact. The van's front left tire exploded. Drawing the sword rapidly back, she thrust out again as she passed the rear tire. The weapon bit deep, yanking her arm brutally as the rubber closed around the double-edged blade.

The sword came free. She was past the van. She made the sword return to that pocket universe, or whatever it was, where it dwelt until she summoned it. With both hands on the steering wheel she spun around the end of the divider toward the exit.

The van tried to follow. Its driver had trouble controlling it with two flats on his left side. The van was lurching up the drive when Annja burst out onto University, turned right and raced into the darkness.

She watched her rearview mirror for suspicious headlights as she squealed through another right turn on Lomas, the next major street north. But she saw no sign of pursuit.

"MIND IF I JOIN YOU?"

Annja looked up from her plate of blue corn enchiladas. A man stood by her table, smelling strongly of the piñon smoke outside. He looked to be about her height and trim, so far as she could tell given that he wore a loose brown leather jacket. He had hair buzzed to a pale plush, round wire-rim glasses whose reflection masked his eyes and a well-creased oblong face wrapped around a boyish grin.

It was standing policy of the Shed restaurant, tucked into a little courtyard off the Plaza in Santa Fe, that during crowded times new diners could be seated in unoccupied chairs at otherwise occupied tables. The smiling young female hostess had explained it to Annja when she'd arrived around eleven o'clock, finding her breakfast burned up by a leisurely morning spent visiting museums and window shopping.

The lunch rush had hit about the time she'd placed her order. The place was packed to the *vigas,* the heavy dark wood beams exposed from the ceiling. She saw no other place nearby the man might sit.

Something about him immediately intrigued her. She wasn't long on company these days. Or any day.

"Certainly," she said, smiling.

"Thank you," the man said. "You are most kind." He had an accent that fascinated Annja. It sounded partly French, but with a certain guttural undertone she could only think of as Germanic.

I could do worse for a mandatory lunch partner, she thought. Though once he settled himself and began unzipping his jacket she saw that his hair wasn't blond but silvery-gray; he was older than he looked at first glance. Still, he was obviously in excellent shape and politely well-spoken. And I'm as big a sucker for a man with an accent as the next girl, she thought.

"I'm Annja," she said.

"Robert Godin," he said.

Smiling, he reached across the table. As he did his jacket fell open. Beneath it he wore a black shirt with a white clerical collar. Annja tried not to stare. It had been years since she had seen a dog collar worn outside a church.

"Father Robert Godin, Society of Jesus. I'm a Jesuit."

Feeling a marked drop in internal temperature, Annja took his hand and shook it. His grip was cool, dry, and hinted at a strength that could crack walnuts without mechanical aid.

"I'm pleased to meet you, Father," she said.

He laughed, turned sideways in his chair as he reclaimed his hand. "I assure you, Annja, we Jesuits don't bite."

"I—I'm sorry. I know you don't. I didn't realize I was that transparent," she said, embarrassed by her childish reaction.

"I have perhaps an advantage in experience and training over most people. Your secret is safe with me, my dear. If my presence or profession make you uncomfortable, I shall be happy to wait for a seat at another table."

"No, no. I really am sorry. It's just that I was raised in an orphanage. In New Orleans. A Catholic orphanage. I—I'm afraid I still have a little bit of a problem with authority."

He laughed. Not loudly but richly. "I do, too. For much the same reason." He held up the heavy crystal water glass a server had deposited unobtrusively at the table. "I propose a truce. You will rein in your natural fear of priests—I will refrain from putting a poison tack on your chair."

It was her turn to laugh.

He leaned forward slightly. Behind his lenses she could now see the color of his eyes. They were extremely pale green. They danced.

"I take it you recognize the reference," he said.

"Sure. It's from a supposed argument in the late sixteenth century by a noted Jesuit scholar—I don't remember who—who claimed that while it wasn't permissible to poison someone's food, because a man must eat to live, it was permitted to place a poisoned tack on his chair, because man doesn't *have* to sit."

"Close enough. We've gotten more inhibited since then. Or at least more circumspect."

He ordered pork medallions marinated in red chili and they settled into a pleasant conversation. Annja told him about her work on the dig. He asked her about Southwest archaeology. She found herself falling readily into conversation with him. He asked questions like a well-informed amateur who was genuinely interested in knowing more.

He told her he was a Walloon—a French-speaking, Catholic Belgian, accounting for his curious part-Germanic accent. He regaled her with stories about growing up wild on the docks in Antwerp. Though the stories were pretty sordid and sad, if looked at carefully, he somehow made them seem lighthearted and nostalgic.

Annja realized how good it was to have somebody to talk to. She led a pretty solitary life. She was around other people a fair amount; any New Yorker was. But she so seldom got to *talk* to them.

She finished her meal and found she'd ordered coffee just to sit and talk a little longer. Even if he was twice her age and a Jesuit, her companion was entirely charming, as well as knowledgeable and witty. He had a gift of putting her at ease.

Or a skill, she cautioned herself as the coffee was delivered.

The crowd was beginning to thin out. A pair of expensively dressed and very fit women in middle age passed close by their table. They stood beside a pillar bedecked with artificial flowers, one aisle away from a window that looked out onto a courtyard alive with late-season blooms.

"You really should report it," the woman with hennaed hair cut in a bob said. "There are reports coming in from all over the area."

The other woman, taller, with frosted blond hair, shook her whole body in a shiver of negation. "It scares me even to think about it," she said. "Besides, who's really going to believe me?"

"Well, there have been a lot of sightings of strange animals. It's even in the paper."

"I just remember seeing that shape crouching on the slope right over my garden wall. All I could see was a shadow the size of a Shetland pony. It looked at me with those eyes—those red-glowing eyes! I'll be having nightmares forever. And that strange sound it made, like a baby crying. Or was it a woman screaming—?"

They passed beyond earshot to the cash register up front. Annja felt a strange sort of shuddering emptiness within.

She was aware of Godin—Robert, he'd insisted she call him—watching her intently. Those pale jade eyes missed very, very little, she was sure. As she was sure there was a very great deal he wasn't telling her about his life.

"'And power was given unto them over the fourth part of the earth, to kill with sword, and with hunger, and with death, and with the beasts of the earth,'" the priest quoted softly.

Annja glanced sharply at him. "Revelation 6:8," she said. "The fourth seal, if I recall correctly."

"You do."

"Do you believe these are the end times?" Annja asked.

He gave slight smile. "I shall leave such speculations to your primitive Protestant millenarians," he said. "Nevertheless, it does seem we may be entering upon very perilous times."

"Why do you say that? The economy? The situation in the Middle East?"

He tipped his head to one side and hunched a shoulder upward. "Those, too. And these sightings of mysterious black creatures, prowling not just up in your legend-haunted mountains, but even appearing along the ridges of the affluent suburb of Lamy, seem to me ominous. And surely you have heard the prophetic pronouncements of this mysterious child who keeps appearing?"

"You take those seriously? I mean—I know you're a priest. I just think of Jesuits as having a more…scientific bent."

"Because you know much of our history. Many of

my order have been scientists of note. The least of us is supposed to be, at minimum, a scholar. I have yet to evaluate these apparitions of an ostensibly Holy Child, much less validate his alleged prophecies."

He shrugged again, this time with both shoulders. "Still, my preliminary investigations suggest that those who report meeting this Santo Niño are sincere for the most part. It certainly raises questions."

"You think these appearances might be miraculous?"

"I sense skepticism in your voice, dear lady. In this you resemble our good archbishop here in New Mexico, who, it seems, prays most fervently that no authentic miracles should appear on his watch. They might disrupt his simple faith in dialectical materialism."

"I guess I am something of a skeptic by inclination," Annja admitted.

"As attitudes go, there are worse. So long as one does not permit doubt itself to become an article of faith."

"Do you believe in miracles?" she asked.

The smile he showed her seemed bittersweet. "I believe in strange things, surely," he said.

Such as swords that can appear and disappear at will? she thought incongruously.

"But I fear I have seen far more," he went on soberly, "and more concrete evidence for the existence of evil in this world than of good."

"A crisis of faith? In a Jesuit?"

He laughed. "We are human—all too human, to borrow from that most misunderstood of Western philosophers, Nietzsche. You must know, since you know so much of our history, that we Jesuits are notorious for such crises. As well as for our outbreaks of outright materialism. If not cynicism.

"Worldly education—the pursuit of *knowledge*— wars with faith. Even as the early church fathers perceived and feared."

"But you've pursued what you call worldly knowledge pretty vigorously, haven't you?"

He nodded. "I continue to, my dear. Pursuit of knowledge is pursuit of truth, is it not? And did not our Lord Himself name Himself the truth? But understand, please. A weakening of faith in *faith*—in things taken for granted, without questioning—does not necessarily imply weakening of belief in God."

She sat back, crossed one long leg over another and regarded him.

"You could always give up on the whole God issue."

His eyes narrowed and his brow furrowed briefly.

It was a low blow, she admitted to herself. Why do I suddenly feel an urge to bait this old man, who's shown me nothing but kindness and respect?

"Alas, my dear," he said softly, "that option is foreclosed to me. I know there's a God. I simply must suffer likewise knowing I shall never understand Him."

She found nothing to say to that, and sought refuge staring at the dregs in the bottom of her heavy blue pottery mug.

Father Godin leaned forward with his elbows on the table and his fingers laced above his coffee mug. "One wonders, in all this—might there be some connection between the apparitions of this Holy Child and these other—how shall we say—less holy sightings?"

Feeling unnerved, Annja glanced at her watch. "Oh. I'm sorry. I have to be going. I'm afraid I've got to rush away. But it's been lovely."

He stood up as she did. She offered her hand. He took it, bowed over it, kissed it briefly.

It's a corny, male-chauvinist gesture, she reproved herself sternly. Yet she found herself utterly charmed.

"I just have a plane to catch," she said. "Down in Albuquerque. And with the balloon fiesta, and all the security hassles…"

"I quite understand," he said, holding her hand for a lingering moment. His other hand came up and pressed something into hers.

"My card," he said as she looked at it. It identified him as Father Robert Godin, SI. The card also showed his cell phone number and e-mail address.

"SI?" she asked. "Oh. Societas Iesu."

"So you know Latin?" he asked.

She saw no reason to dissemble, although something had suddenly put her on her guard. "Yes."

"An affectation on my part. So, then, where must you be off to in such a rush?"

"Mexico City," she said.

8

"We can be somewhat defensive here in Mexico," Dr. Lorenzo Márquez, of the Department of Meso-American Studies of the National Autonomous University, told Annja as they strode along a corridor with modern Mexican folk-style paintings spaced along the polished wood wall to their right. On their left was a series of tinted windows looking out on a spacious courtyard garden of ferns and broad-leaved tropical bushes, surrounding a huge round helmeted Olmec head carved of stone. "The whole concept of diffusionism strikes many of my colleagues as nothing more than Northern Hemisphere patronization."

Her escort through the capital's expansive Museo de Antropología was young and tall, his lean, long-legged body swinging along beneath a white lab coat hung from wide shoulders. His dark face was round, from bone structure rather than fat, of which he seemed to carry little. Beneath an unruly hank of thick hair, black as a raven's wing, he had a prominent jut of nose and piercing black eyes sunk in deep sockets. They seemed connected by a dark band, giving him a slight resemblance to a raccoon. Actually, Annja thought, he would have looked sinister had his manner not been so relentlessly cheerful.

"So you don't take seriously theories that space aliens taught early native peoples in the Americas to build step-pyramid temples?" Annja asked lightly.

His brow creased slightly.

Oh, dear, she thought. That sounded patronizing, didn't it?

"I'm sorry," she said quickly. "I was only being facetious."

He smiled and bobbed his head. "Of course, of course. And of course I do not. Nor do I believe anyone—whether intrepid Polynesian navigators or ancient Egyptians—taught my ancestors to do so, either. A step pyramid, any pyramid, is the simplest structure possible. You place a smaller square of blocks on top of a slightly larger one. Even if one uses undressed stones, just piles natural rocks on one another, they will achieve an angle of repose to produce a rough pyramid of sorts."

"And the temples?"

"For all our cultural and physiological differences, we're the same organism—and forgive me, please, Señorita Creed, for telling you what you no doubt abundantly know. I suspect a fascination with the heavens is hardwired into our species. The sky, after all, is the one realm of natural Earth that is inaccessible to us. So a belief that gods must dwell there springs naturally to our minds. The urge to be closer to them, so they can better hear our pleas and complaints, drives us to high places. How many cultures boast stories of priests and shamans climbing high mountains in search of revelations? And getting them.

"So the urge to build high places—artificial mountains—for communing with the gods is universal, as well. When you combine that with the equally universal desire of rulers to express their power and intimidate rivals—and their own subjects, usually—by building vast monuments—" he shrugged "The worldwide prevalence of pyramid-shaped temples becomes not at all mysterious, and requires no diffusion whatever."

"So you reject the notion of pre-Columbian contact between American natives and Old World outsiders?" Annja asked.

His laugh surprised her. They had come into a large hall, in the midst of which rose a replica Mayan temple, with bas-reliefs seeming to writhe up its heavy square columns of poured concrete. He led her inside. Groups of visitors, mostly tourists by their dress and accents, clumped around pools of illumination under the watchful obsidian gaze of security guards. These squat, dark men, despite their European khaki uniforms, reminded Annja of Nahua statues themselves.

"Not in the slightest. Indeed, recent discoveries in North and South America make it abundantly clear that there was much traffic between the so-called Old World and the so-called New. Archaeologists in South America have possessed evidence for years of continuing contact with the Pacific peoples dating hundreds of years before the Europeans. Sadly, the tendency of North American archaeologists for years was to dismiss such evidence blithely. After all, who were we but mere natives?"

"It's true," Annja said. "Too true. I'm sorry."

"But you didn't do it, did you?"

"No. I was always something of a rebel against the established order in the orphanage school." She had made a point to establish her upbringing in a Catholic orphanage early in her correspondence with young Dr. Márquez. She had long ago learned that even fairly secular Latin Americans related more readily to Catholics. Not that she was communicant, or even considered herself Catholic, but she felt small inclination to raise that point.

And then I became a student of science, she thought. Did that transform me into a reflex defender of a different established order? A lot of her colleagues still ridiculed any notion of pre-Columbian contact across either ocean as chariots-of-the-gods rubbish.

He nodded. "Well, then. Not guilty. It pleases me to live in a time, Ms. Creed, in which such questions are beginning to be frankly examined by science, rather than reflexively ridiculed and explained away."

"Me, too," she said.

They came to a major clump of tourists sporting shorts revealing legs like uncooked sausages. From their mutterings Annja thought they were German, although she understood little of the language despite her gifts for learning tongues. She also knew that despite her own Anglo-American prejudices concerning body-mass index, these stout middle-aged and elderly men and women could more than likely hike her straight into the ground. Fit as she had always been, on her few side trips to Germany and Austria she had grown accustomed to finding herself halfway up a trail to some mountaintop castle or another, laboring along with her tongue all but hanging out, only to be passed at effortless speed by parties of jovial Germans of all shapes, sizes and ages.

Dr. Márquez steered Annja to the side so she could see what had the tourists so fascinated. "Now, here we have a fine specimen of the famous Mayan calendar," he said, beaming as if he'd invented it.

Propped atop a black stone pedestal in a blaze of yellowish light was a thick wheel of yellowish rock. Its center showed an angry-looking face missing a nose. Rings of intricately carved glyphs radiated outward from it.

"There are actually three distinct Mayan calendars," Márquez said. "There is a 365-day calendar, the Haab', which describes a standard solar year. There is the Long Count calendar, which is the one that involves all the controversy. This, though, is the calendar the Maya themselves most used—the Tzolk'in, the Sacred Round. It depicts a 260-day cycle."

"Which recurs throughout Mesoamerican cultures," Annja said.

Márquez nodded. "Just so. This is what people usually mean when they talk about the Mayan calendar."

"But the Long Count—"

"Is the one that involves the so-called prophecy," Márquez stated.

He ushered her onward to a less crowded niche containing a tombstone-shaped slab. "This stela was unearthed in the Yucatán four years ago. It makes use of Long Count dating."

It showed two vertical rows of glyphs indecipherable to Annja. Fascinated as she was by the whole broad scope of archaeology and anthropology—all of humanity and its multiplex history—she specialized in Middle Age and Renaissance Europe. The Chimayó dig team had welcomed her involvement in large part because the early New Mexican colonists, cut off from almost all contact with Europe for most of their history, retained many aspects of culture long archaic in the rest of the Spanish-speaking world. As a matter of fact the language still spoken in the high mountains of the north resembled sixteenth-century Spanish, just as the speech of certain mountain populations in the southeastern U.S. retained much of Elizabethan English.

"The Long Count was based upon cycles of just under four hundred years," Márquez said, "each called a *b'ak'tun.* The current *b'ak'tun,* the thirteenth, began on September 6, 3114 B.C., in our Julian calendar. It ends on December 21, 2012, although there's a certain amount of wiggle room, amounting to a week or two."

"Thus the end of the world," Annja said.

He grinned. "You might think so."

"What do you think?"

"What I *think* is that the makers of the calendars on which some people base end-of-the-world prophecies didn't see any particular reason to project more than half a millennium into their future. In fact I like to think their funding ran out."

Annja laughed.

"You must be familiar with the phenomenon."

"Oh, yes."

"Stargazing and astronomical calculations were a monopoly of the Mayan state. As in most of the world's more complex cultures, particularly the Chinese, calculating dates and astronomical events wasn't just an important activity, but a major source and mainstay of power. The public literally couldn't get rid of the state—though individual components, such as emperors, could be and were replaced—because then they'd have to do without vital knowledge. Both key ritual knowledge, such as the timing of eclipses, as well as when, in a given year, crops needed to be planted. So, long before the vaunted computer revolution of our own lifetimes, knowledge was, in fact, power."

"Really," Annja said. "I didn't know."

"And since we speak of knowing, I know for a fact that the Maya did not regard 2012 as the end of the world, or near to it. Or in any event, not all Maya did."

"Why not?"

"First, in Palenque in the state of Chiapas, we find record of projections to October 13, 4772. For those Maya, history did not run out a handful of years from now. Also, a monument at Coba in Quintana Roo projects the end of creation at many powers-of-thirteen of the cycle of *b'ak'tun*. According to it we've barely begun the cycle."

"So the world," Annja said, "will not cease to exist on December 21, 2012? Or thereabouts."

"According to the Maya, I'd say there's no more likelihood than that it will end on any other given day, including this one." His smile frosted over. "There are times when I suspect that 2012 is a most optimistic date for how long we have left."

Annja sighed. "I hear you, Doctor. Thank you very much."

SHE HAD A BUS TICKET to Fresnillos in the central Mexican state of Zacatecas, north of the Federal District, for the following morning. Her modest but comfortable little three-star hotel was in Coyoacán, near the university. Instead of heading back there after parting company with the helpful young Dr. Márquez she decided to spend the afternoon cruising the bright, chattering street markets of the immense city square known formally as the Plaza de la Constitución and universally as the Zócalo.

She took a quick pass through the museum showing artifacts from the Aztec Templo Mayor unearthed during the construction of the underground station. Quickly, because she had done a lot of museums recently, and suspected more lay in her near future. She loved archaeology. She loved glazed doughnuts, too. Continuing to savor life's loves, she had learned, was done best by metering their doses.

She emerged blinking into the heat and spear-sharp sunlight—and eye-watering pollution—of the plaza. Leaving the climate-conditioned subterranean realm of the station was like getting hit in the face with a wet blanket. A none-too-clean one, at that.

Like Los Angeles and Denver, and, on a smaller scale Albuquerque, Mexico City was built in a big bowl in the desert, with mountains for walls, ideal for trapping both heat and pollution. It was also naturally humid despite high altitude and relatively low annual rainfall, being built in a lake, into which it was gradually sinking. Moreover, the world's third-largest square, after Tiananmen and Red, was well fenced by big buildings, from the cathedral to the Palacio Nacional. They served the same function for its microenvironment as the surrounding mountains did for the Valley of Mexico. The Zócalo, in short, was a heat sink wrapped in a heat trap.

Annja wandered past some rather tawdry and dispirited Aztec dancers and in among the brightly colored kiosks, and the crowds of tourists, notably less colorful. In fact the latter were mostly pale but well-larded North Americans, Northern and Eastern Europeans. The season had grown cool in New England and Europe. The sunbirds had begun early migration to warmth.

One place that caught her eye was a wooden booth offering pre-Columbian artifacts, mostly figurines of weird Aztec and Mayan gods. She made a beeline to it, a frown starting to furrow her brow.

Still a few feet away, it became apparent that these were all reproductions, not necessarily of museum grade, and not plundered archaeological treasures. Though when she picked up an effigy of Tezcatlipoca to find a yellow Made In China sticker on its base she thought that was a bit over the top.

Feeling somewhat chagrined, she moved on. She looked distractedly at white dresses with bright trim, hung next to sticks of cinnamon in clay vases and, improbably, brass Buddhas. I don't know why I bother, she thought. It's not as if I have any room for more stuff. Between artifacts—all legally held—and stacks of books, magazines and manuscripts, her Brooklyn loft apartment was well packed.

I've never been a shopping goddess, anyway. She took pains about her appearance, not a universal constant among archaeologists. But that was mostly confined to making sure her clothes were clean and color coordinated. Sturdy and serviceable were big items with her. As was cost. The closest she came to being a fashionista was her expertise at thrift stores. But that wasn't shabby chic; that was spending almost her whole life poor.

As for labels, it seldom occurred to her to look. People like her female associates from the *Chasing History's Monsters* staff sometimes caught her and forced her to spend a little money on nice clothes and accessorizing.

But her acquaintances had learned to their exasperation that unless they arrived at her loft and stood guard over her as she dressed, Annja was still just as likely to show up for one of the rare girls' nights out they could coax her to in khaki cargo pants, a secondhand man's shirt and comfortable boots. Exactly what she wore at the moment, except for substituting a lightweight saffron cotton blouse.

She was content, though, to let herself drift. Listening to the tourists natter in German and French and nasal English as they bargained with the cheerful shopkeepers, she knew that however strange, or even crass or tacky the goods on offer, she was participating in a ritual at least as old as civilization. More than likely Nahua vendors with plugs in their lower lips had dickered on this very spot, half a millennium ago, with copper-haired Tlaxcaltecans and cynical, pipe-smoking Mayan missionary-traders.

She found herself under an awning at a booth offering plates and pots and mugs of heavy, lovingly hand-painted pottery. She picked several up and examined them. No two were alike, and there was nary a Made In China sticker to be found.

A cat with a swirled brown-and-gray back and a white belly and nose lay in repose in a bin on top of a stack of serving platters, apparently enjoying the cool. As its pale green eyes caught hers it rolled over on its back with a loud, hinting purr.

She scratched its proffered belly. It writhed and purred louder in appreciation.

Maybe this is why I came here, she thought. It was as good an answer as any.

9

Annja put her hands to the heavily tinted glass of the taxicab window. "Wait," she said in English. "Where are we going?"

"*No intiendo*," the driver said, a stout, sweating, droopily mustached man who had both understood and for that matter spoken English perfectly well when he had picked her up outside the hotel.

She repeated her question in Spanish, which was the first foreign language she'd learned in the orphanage in New Orleans—a city where the Spanish influence was almost as strong as French, though much less publicized. It attracted both the affluent and the penniless from all across the old Spanish Main and much of Latin America. Not to mention from right across the Gulf of Mexico.

The cabbie only shook his balding head and waved a handful of rings that had turned the fingers blue-green around them.

She was on her way, or so she thought, to the airport. Yet somehow the taxi had turned decisively off any kind of main drag. Initially the driver had muttered something—again in heavily accented but quite clear English—about avoiding traffic jams. And traffic jams there were aplenty, with upward of twelve million people poured together in the big, high bowl of the Valley of Mexico. At first Annja accepted he was dodging apparent gridlock because she could see he did so. The street ahead had been solid with cars immobile as some modernistic ribbon statue of sun-gleaming metal.

But they had wandered way too far from the beaten path. Annja's instincts were screaming.

The street was narrow, unlike the wide, tree-lined boulevards that veined the vast metropolis. That wasn't entirely unexpected of a back route. But the buildings all looked old, without either the affected quaintness or authentic grandeur of, say, the buildings around the Zócalo. They ran to cracked white or pink stucco and bulging, tilting walls that looked to consist of no more than random piles of ill-chosen rocks. Where much of Mexico City resonated with the energy one encountered in midtown Manhattan or Buenos Aires or Río, this place had a stealthy, half-deserted vibe.

Nor did it seem the lack of activity on the claustrophobic street resulted from early-onset siesta. Annja had the acute sense of being watched, from every dark hole of a doorway or gap between badly fitting stones. By eyes that were anything but friendly.

Too late she remembered reading about taxis being a popular medium for armed robbery and kidnapping in the violence-plagued Federal District. But this taxi had an official emblem, she thought wildly. It was identical to the others lined up in front of the hotel.

"Turn around," she shouted.

Instead the taxi turned into an alley that been invisible to her a moment before and stopped. Instantly she yanked the door handle.

It came off in her hand.

The driver jumped out so ferociously his door scraped pink stucco dust off the wall of the building to the cab's left. He ran away down the alley.

Annja slapped her palms twice experimentally against the window. She couldn't remember if side windows were made from sugar glass the way windshields were, to minimize the risk of their turning into sprays of shrapnel sharper than any razor when broken. She wasn't too sanguine a

Mexican taxicab would have such amenities anyway. Especially an outlaw cab—even an outlaw with official sanction.

Instead she lay back at her full length, which put the back of her head and shoulders against the far door. She placed the corrugated rubber soles of her hiking boots against the door and pushed with all her strength.

The flimsy door banged off a cracked concrete patch of wall and fell into the hard-packed alley dirt with a clatter and crash of glass breaking. With the strap of her overnight bag already looped across her shoulder, Annja flew out of the cab almost as fast.

She saw both ends of the alley were blocked.

There were six of them, spread out across the alley. The trio facing her, approaching the rear of the stalled cab, had two machetes and a rusty-looking revolver. The three coming from the front carried two semiautomatic pistols and a length of white-painted metal pipe.

Knowing her only hope was to act quickly, she darted straight at the bunch with the two big knives. The guy with the revolver promptly cranked off his entire cylinder.

Even before he cut loose, Annja had dropped flat on the ground, just catching herself, palms and toes. The bullets passed harmlessly over her. Two starred the taxi's rear windshield and made the red-and-green-and-white fringe inside bounce. One knocked a maggot-colored divot in the pink wall on the driver's side. Two went who knew where.

The last smacked, audibly, into the forehead of the tall man coming up right behind Annja, a big 45 autopistol in his hand. The shot killed him so quickly his finger didn't even twitch enough to set off the sensitive single-action trigger.

When she heard the sixth shot crack Annja jumped. She snapped herself upright as if springloaded, then vaulted over the top of the car.

The guy on the far wing from the deceased *pistolero,* coming up on the cab's front passenger side, blazed away at her with some kind of 9 mm pistol. He held the piece on its side, rendering it utterly impossible to aim.

The impact of seeing his intended victim hurtling through space, apparently right at him, startled him. He sprayed the ground, the car, the walls, the sky even more comprehensively than the first guy had, and with a good deal more bullets.

Shooting the way he was, he would only hit Annja by sheer luck, even at close range and closing fast. Annja felt the left side of her blouse, which had come out of her cargo pants during the proceedings, tugged as if by invisible fingers. Another shot brushed her right forearm.

She cleared the entire taxi, hitting the far side on her feet. She went instantly into a forward roll as her target finished emptying his high-cap magazine through the approximate space she would have occupied had she stayed up. As she came over she drove both heels into his chest in a sort of combination ax-and-thrust kick. Impact shivered down her legs. She heard ribs crunch. Her target was thrown into a wild backward somersault. His head hit the pavement at a deadly angle and the pistol dropped from his lifeless hand.

Annja brought her feet down and snapped herself standing again. Then she threw herself into another roll. As she did the pipe came whistling down in a two-handed overhead stroke meant to turn her skull to mush. Instead it glanced off her left buttock.

Pained but not injured she came up yet again onto her feet. She turned left. The pipe man was cocking his steel club over his head for another crack. She skipped sideways and pistoned a side kick into the pit of his stomach. She didn't have time to roll her hip over and get the full weight of her body behind it; it was just a leg kick. And his stomach was well padded. But Annja had powerful legs. He doubled as if he'd sucked a slug to the belly and sat down hard.

Loud noises from just up the alley indicated the man with the revolver had managed to fumble at least a couple of cartridges into his weapon. Annja darted past the pipe wielder, who was struggling to breathe. She crouched by the front bumper as glass, blasted from the windshield by a back-to-front shot, rained down on her head and shoulders.

"I got the bitch," a voice shouted in Spanish from her near left.

"Kill her!" someone shouted.

Things were getting tight for Annja. She had a machete coming up fast on her left. There was almost certainly another coming down the other side of the car to catch her. And all too soon the pipe man was going to suck enough air back into his lungs to kickstart his central nervous system and get back to the party.

It was time.

She willed the sword into her hand. And sprang like a panther.

The man who'd claimed he had her howled and swung his big, wide blade at her from beside the front tire. Striking across her body, Annja caught it with the sword, guided it past her and down. As momentum carried her attacker by she rotated her wrist and swung her weapon backhand. Right up the line of his extended arm.

The sword caught him right between clavicle and Adam's apple. It cut through skin and cartilage with only the slightest hesitation. When the edge hit his neckbone she felt a jar. His head drooped. She pulled back the blade.

The man's body hit the ground hard and slid, limbs sprawling, neck pumping great gushes of blood into the dust.

Annja was already looking the other way, brandishing the sword in a glittering horizontal arc over the cab's dented hood.

The machete man coming around from her right yelped. He jumped back. The sword's tip swished harmlessly before his scrawny chest.

A shot cracked. The taxicab roof sounded like a Caribbean steel drum as the soft-nosed .38 slug skipped off it like a stone off a millpond. At the same time a shadow loomed in Annja's peripheral vision and her nose filled with the stench of stale sweat.

She threw herself into a forward roll as more ineffectual shots echoed down the alley. The steel pipe buckled the taxi's hood with a bang. She rolled to her feet in time to parry a downward machete stroke with a ring and a shower of sparks.

A blur of motion in her eye's corner brought her a quarter turn right in time to parry another ax-style stroke of the pipe with the flat of her long blade. For a moment she stared past the crossed weapons at the fat, astonished, sweat-streamed face of her opponent.

She pushed off to deflect a wild machete slash over her head. She was a whirlwind, parrying rapid hacks and slashes from both increasingly desperate men.

She was breathing hard, almost gagging on the diesel fumes and stench of blood and dust and viscera. The air was thin—but at 7,240 feet it was almost the same altitude as the San Esequiel dig, where she'd spent ample time to be acclimated.

But nothing drains like combat. It was why prizefighters did roadwork so obsessively. Intense exertion took it out of you. But the mental stress was what really sucked you dry.

The revolver began to go off like spastic firecrackers again. All three combatants ducked as a bullet moaned low over their heads, then jumped as another kicked up dirt right beside Annja.

The machete guy turned to curse out his buddy with the gun.

Annja was not feeling chivalrous. She side-kicked the pipe man in his capacious belly once more and turned right, unleashing a wheel-like stroke, looping high and down to the right.

Her sword took the machete wielder transversely across the back. It opened him right up. His head snapped back, his knees gave way and he fell into the alley grit.

Screaming with surprising shrillness for one so

huge, the fat man rushed her with pipe held high. She pirouetted, lunged, thrust.

The tip of the sword took him in the sternum, punched through ribs, heart and ribs again to stand a foot out from his back.

He fell over backward.

The tight embrace of bone and flab pulled the sword right out of Annja's hands.

She looked back over her shoulder. Her final attacker stood thirty feet away. He had the revolver open and a new scatter of silvery empties at his feet. He was frantically trying to fumble a fresh cartridge into the cylinder.

Their eyes met. She experienced a strange sense of darkness, felt an inexplicable internal impact.

The cartridge at last slid into the chamber.

Annja spun and flowed forward as he shut the cylinder with a snap. As he raised the pistol with both hands, feet braced, she reached the fallen body of the second machete man. His weapon lay in the dust by his side.

She grabbed its hilt. The revolver came on line. The click as it was cocked seemed like the loudest sound in the world.

Annja was still twenty feet from the muzzle. She would never reach him before he dropped the hammer. And this time, it seemed, he aimed true.

She cocked her arm back, threw. The unwieldy two-foot machete turned over twice in the thick, humid air and punched its wide tip vertically through the gunman's forehead.

For a moment he stood there staring at her. His eyes had gone very wide.

A single trickle of blood ran down between them.

He collapsed. The old revolver did not fire.

Annja dropped to her knees. Her lungs burned as she gasped in huge breaths. Her eyes stung with tears, whether from pollution or emotion she could not tell.

Police sirens rose and fell like a chorus of electronic locusts from all around her. There was little chance of a tall, leggy *gringa* on foot escaping unnoticed from some wretched warren of a Mexican slum. *Especially since only God knows how much blood I've got on me,* she thought frantically.

She hauled herself up enough to stagger over to sit sideways in the rear driver's-side seat of the cab, with her legs out the now-missing door. It was time to play soft and sheltered American tourist lady much too totally freaked out by an eruption of sudden violence and her own near brush with death to give a coherent account of the proceedings.

It would not be much of a stretch.

10

As the Airbus A319 circled to altitude Annja finally felt her muscles unclench. It's really over, she told herself.

The police, as she anticipated, had spun their own story of what happened. It did *not* include an active role for a delicate middle-class American tourist in the back-alley bloodletting, extreme even by the standards of Mexico City street violence, that had left half a dozen hardmen dead. They assumed she could have been nothing but a helpless victim in whatever it was that transpired. Therefore she was no suspect.

As a tomboy who'd occasionally managed to cut loose from the orphanage and wander the seamy, steamy byways of predeluge New Orleans, Annja had picked up a bit more than a modicum of street wisdom. Among other things she had perfected a technique she'd used on the sisters themselves. The best alibi was to give the authorities a tale to tell themselves that didn't include you. She'd seen it succeed time and again.

This time the prevailing hypothesis was that one or more gang members had gone amok, resulting in internecine slaughter. The fact that one would-be kidnapper had a bullet hole from his buddy's revolver in his head, while the man with the revolver had another comrade's machete embedded in *his,* lent great credibility to that scenario.

Of course, drugs were also involved. Annja would not be surprised if toxicology tests on the decedents supported that, too. She'd be surprised if it *didn't.*

The fact that someone recognized her as a television personality had helped. Considerably. She already knew that the various Knowledge Channel networks were popular in Latin America. Thank goodness for satellite, she thought.

She took a deep breath, forced residual tension to flow out of her with the air. She was bound for Albuquerque. The police had kept her overnight so she could answer further questions, under guard in her hotel room. By morning their theory had evolved enough tha they had lost interest in her. They suggested she leave the country as quickly as possible. She was up for *that,* even though it meant forgoing

her intended trip to the silver town Plateros, near
Fresnillos. She reckoned she had learned what she
needed to in Mexico.

A male attendant, slim with receding hairline and
hands crossed behind his back, passed by and nodded,
smiling. She reciprocated. She sat by the window over
the right wing of the modest two-engine Airbus. Right
behind the starboard emergency exit, it was one of the
best seats on the plane, with extra room to stretch her
long legs. It was such a good seat she wondered if the
police had bumped someone to get it for her.

The captain spoke up over the PA system. "If you
look out the starboard windows, folks, you'll see one
of Mexico's most spectacular sights—Mount Popocatepetl. MEX traffic control has routed us to pass
near it as we climb to altitude. It's only seventy kil-
ometers, or about forty-four miles, from downtown
Mexico City. Rising 5,452 meters, or almost 18,000
feet, Popo is, like its legendary companion Ixtaccihuatl, that flat-topped mountain visible a bit to the left
and past it, an active volcano. Fortunately, at present
neither is acting up much."

Annja turned and pressed her nose to the glass. The
sight was breathtaking. Popocatepetl was so dramatic
it looked more like a matte painting than anything
real. A perfect cone, bare silvery gray rock thrusting
into the sky from a base of green whose top indicated

the treeline. The Smoking Mountain lived up to its name: a thin gray strand trailed away to the right from its summit. A thrill of delighted apprehension passed through her. Here was a genuine monster. Not like black phantoms flitting through New Mexico dusk…

She sighed again and got out her iPod. She stuffed the earbuds in her ears. She hated them. The right one would never stay put, but they gave good sound and most of all were highly portable. She dialed up a New Age playlist. New Age music drove her crazy in short order if she actually *listened* to it. But it soothed her wonderfully as a background, especially when it blotted out the incidental environmental sounds of airplane travel.

Laying her head back against the headrest, she slipped quickly into sleep.

DRIVING HER RENTED Honda back to the motel room she'd relocated to on Albuquerque's west side, Annja realized with a start she was skating around the big thing, the elephant in the room—an image that momentarily gave her the giggles.

But that was sheer venting. There was nothing humorous about two attempts to murder her in the space of three days.

She had wondered, sitting in the sterile fluorescent

police offices shivering in the air-conditioning and after-action adrenaline crash, why she'd never even tried to talk her way out of the ambush in the alley.

She knew she'd sensed a purpose even darker than kidnapping the instant the cab had turned into an inexplicable alley and stopped.

Perhaps it was because of the attack in the parking lot. Although that may also have been nothing more than a kidnap attempt. But she felt certain, irrationally perhaps, a darker force was behind it than that.

Perhaps it was the presence in those grubby hands of a very clean hypodermic—and equally clean firearms. Obviously, little about that incident had been as it seemed.

You're going into conspiracy-theory mode, the debunking part of her mind sneered. But the thought rang hollow. For two attempts on her life to be made in two different countries, a thousand miles apart, by sheer *coincidence* was a theory as far-fetched as anything she could imagine. In a purely abstract, hypothetical sense, it could happen. But had it?

Stopped at a red light waiting to turn north up the entrance to I-25, she rolled down the window. She hoped the night wind blowing in her face would sharpen her thoughts.

Why would anybody want to kill me? Who?

One answer came to mind. Garin Braden. She knew

he unabashedly enjoyed the immortality that Roux claimed to regard as a curse. He feared that the reunification of Joan's sword might jeopardize his apparently infinite life as a young, robust, healthy man. He had taken drastic steps to eliminate the sword before.

Garin had professed a liking for her. Frankly Annja found him charming and even likable, as well. But she knew he was willing to do absolutely anything necessary to get his way. He'd tried to claim her sword before.

He certainly had the reach. He was tremendously wealthy and influential, both acknowledgedly and, like an iceberg, she was sure, enormously more so beneath anyone's range of vision. But why now? Why here?

Freeway speed blasted cool air into her face. It helped keep her awake but forced no insights. She shook her head. Maybe Garin wasn't involved. Or maybe his involvement was very indirect. That's certainly his style, she reflected.

Whatever the truth was, she had to assume the attempts against her had some connection to her investigation. And that in itself meant she was on the right track.

SITTING CROSS-LEGGED on the bed in her Motel 6 room Annja almost deleted the e-mail. The subject—Urgent Meeting Requested—tripped her mental spam filter. As did the sender's name, Dr. Raywood Cogswell. A lot of scammers styled themselves "Doctor."

Her virus-protection hadn't detected anything unusual so she clicked on the header to read the message.

Cogswell claimed to be a retired biologist turned cryptozoologist. He wished to meet with her to discuss anomalous sightings—including the one she was rumored to have shared. She grimaced but kept reading.

He was familiar, naturally, with her work on *Chasing History's Monsters*. He believed he might have information that could be of use to her.

She sighed and unwound the towel from her hair. It was mostly dry. That was one thing you could say for the high desert, she thought. Things dried quickly. She shook still-cool locks tickling down her T-shirted shoulders and tossed the towel at a chair.

Shut out of her hotel room in Pojoaque, she had shifted operations here. It was just as well. Even on the off chance the Pueblo could be talked out of pulling the plug on their dig, a heavy early snowfall had blanketed the area during her Mexico City jaunt. The dig season was over anyway. And the interesting action, for the moment, seemed to be developing in

Albuquerque. Unfortunately, more centrally located rooms were unavailable with the balloon fiesta in progress.

Annja leaned over to the bedside table and picked up a hair brush. As she began to brush out her tresses she thought about where she was and what she was doing.

Someone or something had drawn her to this place. Maybe it was the sword itself. She couldn't be sure. She didn't like to think about what the sword's existence implied.

Her mentor, Roux, was half-cynical, half-devout, half-mad and a few halves beyond that. He had found her when she found the last remnant of the sword— the last piece for which he himself had been searching ever since Joan herself had been taken and executed, her sword destroyed. If he understood what forces were in play, he refused to tell her.

The sword belonged to her now. Whatever, exactly, that entailed. Neither the sword nor her new life came with an owner's manual.

She had always felt an impulse to protect the weak and defy the bully. If there really was a difference. If anything she felt more strongly now. She felt an over-riding, almost obsessive desire to preserve inno-cence—where she could find it, and of course, where it could be preserved.

Maybe that was her mission. It would do until something better came along.

Meanwhile something strange was going on in central New Mexico. Several somethings.

Maybe. That was what had hooked her, she thought. The strange creature sightings and the sudden spate of well-attested encounters with the Holy Child. More coincidence?

No way to know yet, she reflected, grimacing as she broke through some split ends. Nor was she sure if innocence was involved, or if so, who the innocent was. The Holy Child himself? Whatever he was, it was difficult to envision what could threaten a being who apparently could disappear at will.

Ah, well, she thought. If no one going to give me any hints, I guess I'll have to go on relying on my intuition. It had always served her well—even before she encountered Roux, the sword and this madness.

Her instincts told her that whatever was going on here, she was meant to take part in it.

She sighed and put her notebook computer back on her crossed bare legs. A little practiced Google searching turned up some background on her mystery correspondent, Dr. Cogswell with the curious first name. He had a respectable if not extraordinary curriculum vitae. He had worked for Monsanto, apparently researching ways to make agricultural insecticides safe for creatures that weren't insects. From there he had gone to a professorship at an agricultural college in Nebraska, from where he had recently retired to the warmer climes of Albuquerque. Along the way he had contributed numerous articles on cryptozoology—the study of creatures whose existence was not acknowledged by science—to various publications. More recently he had been an active participant in Usenet newsgroups and on the Web.

He struck her as one of those scientists who, despite genuine intelligence and knowledge, tended to go a bit bizarre as soon as they set foot outside their own specialties. Nonetheless, he was as close to a lead as anything she had. Unless she wanted to hang around and try to interview the next tourist to encounter the Santo Niño before he, she or they fled home—as almost all the previous claimants had.

She reread Cogswell's message then hit Reply. He had suggested they meet for lunch.

So be it.

THE MORNING AIR HELD an edge as Annja pushed the glass door of the motel lobby. Not enough to cut— just enough to make itself known. It was the sort of cool you tasted as much as felt—along with the inevitable exhaust fumes from the vehicles streaming past a parking lot dotted with cars whose windshields were white blazes of reflected sun. And a hint of that ubiquitous piñon smoke. Annja already knew she would associate that scent with New Mexico for the rest of her life. Adjusting the strap of her shoulder bag, she strode forth into the full light of the sun in search of breakfast.

From directly above her head a hissing, roaring sound cut loose.

She ducked. She almost summoned the sword.

She looked up to see a gigantic bloated shape, blotting the painfully blue high-desert sky mere feet overhead.

And then a chubby arm waved at her from a wicker-looking basket hanging from beneath the vast, globular shape, and a smiling little face appeared framed by blond pigtails.

"Hi, lady!" the little girl called from the gondola of the hot-air balloon. The man standing beside her, wearing a bright yellow jacket, did something that caused another jet of blue-edged yellow flame to shoot up into the open mouth of the envelope. Rising slowly, the balloon, painted in jagged horizontal stripes of blue and red, swept across busy Coors Road and off over a shopping mall.

Beyond it the sky was full of balloons. The weather was different down in the Lower Sonoran life zone than up North, where a glance showed her dark banks of cloud piled high above the Jemez and Sangre de Cristo mountains flanking the central river valley. That was a boon to participants in the vaunted Albuquerque International Balloon Fiesta, it seemed.

What struck Annja was that the sky really was full of balloons. Some took bizarre form. She saw cartoon character heads, a taco, a fire hydrant and at least one totally implausible cow. Mostly they were standard fat-teardrop shapes like the one that had overflown her, painted in a dizzying range of colors and patterns.

She had paid little attention to the balloon fiesta. It didn't really impinge on the dig, eighty miles or so north. It struck her as just another gimmick to draw in tourists, and as such, of small interest to her. She was concerned with ancient things, things that lasted. Not tacky ephemera.

But nothing she had ever seen in her life had quite prepared her for the sight of several hundred hot-air balloons in the air at once.

Her shoulders rose and fell in an exaggerated sigh. "Okay," she said aloud. "I'm impressed."

She had turned to face toward the uneven wall of the Sandia Mountains, a blue backdrop to the lower balloons. She was facing right back toward the motel lobby entrance.

Her eye happened to fall on the newspapers displayed in dispensers in front of some juniper bushes beside the door. There she saw, beaming at her, the beatific countenance of Santo Niño himself.

She rushed to the rack. The likeness was plastered all over the front of a local alternative-looking paper calling itself by the unlikely moniker *Alibi*. It was free. Bonus, she thought.

She plucked one right out. The painting was almost breathtaking in its sheer kitsch. The Holy Child was portrayed as a huge-eyed waif in cloak and robe and weird hat.

Splashed across the image were the words Holy Kid Sightings At Chiaroscuro Fest! Below it the legend continued:

"Holy publicity stunt! Albuquerque art prodigy Byron Mondragón attracts nationwide attention to local gallery opening, just as his current favorite subject puts in personal appearances all over the state.

"Whoa," Annja said. A rumble from her stomach reminded her of her prime mission of the moment.

Folding the paper, she tucked it under her arm and strode off to her rental car. She was assured of interesting breakfast reading material, at any rate.

11

"Hi! Welcome to Chiaroscuro!" the gorilla said as Annja swung in through the open ironwork gate.

She nodded and smiled to the black rubber mask. After all, the sign out front did say Chiaroscuro Guerrilla Art Compound.

She had smelled the place even before she saw the entrance.

She parked on a sidestreet that lay just north of the gallery. The surrounding houses ran to painted cinder block and squeaky-tight little lots, scrupulously clean and tended for the most part, but giving a definite air of staving off the encroachment of far less appealing environs. It was not so much poverty—certainly not by the standards of Mexico, to say nothing of South America—as a prevalent hardness. On the drive

down Broadway she'd seen a few too many small
packs of lean young men with slouching backs and
out-thrust jaws to feel any too complacent.

But the smell that greeted her on the warm late-
afternoon air as she walked the half block south was
totally inviting. It was a warm smell as of something
cooking, a wonderfully pungent smell that teased
with faint hints of familiarity. It did seem to sting,
slightly, at the edges of her eyes.

The entrance was not terribly obvious. It was a
narrow gate of black wrought iron wedged between
down-at-heel storefronts with stucco peeling off in
tectonic plates and soaped-over windows. She would
have missed it but for a group of kids with colored
spiky hair and piercings you could see at thirty yards
who drifted in ahead of her.

The welcoming smell grew stronger as she walked
on past the tall guy in the gorilla suit. She found herself
in a short passageway with big, irregular slate flag-
stones. The sun, falling toward the cinder cones on the
West Mesa behind her, cast her shadow long before
her. A door stood open into interior afternoon gloom
in a brown building to her right. To her left was a big
picture window revealing a crowd of people drifting
among art exhibits visible on the other side. The music
of a live ska band came from somewhere ahead.

The compound opened to her right onto a courtyard with benches and grotesque twisted-metal sculptures and an ash tree with small, bladelike leaves just beginning to turn in the middle of it. People drifted or clumped among them in the mingled soft shadow and curiously rich buttery light of late afternoon, drinking from plastic cups, chatting and laughing and smoking. Not tobacco exclusively, her nostrils told her. They were mostly but not exclusively young. She spotted Goths, retro punks, hipsters, hippies and a wide selection of unclassifiables.

At the courtyard's far end she saw what looked like a builder's yard, a big, open building with a sheet-metal roof, partial walls and wooden shelves piled with lumber and metal bar stock. On the right side of the courtyard stood a single-story structure with several doors that might lead into apartments.

As she entered the courtyard heat washed over her from the right. She looked to see a man standing by the wall, turning the crank on a sort of metal meshwork drum half-filled with green chili pods, rotating them above a set of blue propane-burner flames. That was the source of the marvelous smell.

If the sounds coming out the open door were any indication, the main action was in the building next to the gallery on her left, a two-story structure that had apparently started life as a warehouse. Though the gallery's front door stood open, she wandered past to enter the warehouse.

Inside was a blare of noise. Loud, cheerful conversation competed with riotous ska brass and the piercing whine of a cutoff saw biting metal. A sort of greeter's booth stood right beside the door to her right, covered with pamphlets about the exhibitors and Chiaroscuro itself. In a room behind it Annja saw a curious apparatus like an outsized hood for a kitchen stove above a large square table at which men and women in goggles sat doing dangerous-looking things to metal.

"Hi, I'm Randy," shouted the guy standing by the table. "Welcome to Chiaroscuro Guerrilla Arts Collective."

"I'm Annja," she replied, likewise shouting to make herself heard. "I thought it was the Guerrilla Art Compound."

"That's the place. The collective is us. Can I help you make yourself at home?"

He looked like a Kiowa—tall, burly, well bellied, with olive skin and a ponytail of heavy, glossy black hair.

She gestured past him at the big copper hood arrangement. "What's that thing?"

"Negative-air-pressure hood," he said. "Draws up nasty fumes and all kinds of other stuff we don't want getting loose. We do a lot of metalwork here. I draw and paint, myself." He handed her a business card, printed with a pen-and-ink drawing of some kind of Goth goblin girl with pointed ears and a definite attitude.

She laughed. She liked him. She liked the place, and the energy of the people. "This is very good. Do you have some work on display here?"

He nodded at the door behind her that led into the display room she had first seen from outside. "In there. But look all over the place. We have a lot of talent here."

He gestured deeper into the building. Past the partition at the other side of the metal shop lay a much bigger room. The music came from there, as did most of the other party noise. Though the band was hidden from view, Annja saw paintings and drawings hung on the walls.

"Thanks," she said. "I will. Where would I find Byron Mondragón's work?"

"Through that door right behind you, then through another door on the right. It's great stuff. He's a great guy, a good friend of mine. Although I hate him."

His big smile belied the latter. Annja could not refrain from asking, "Why?"

"He's too damned young to be so good!"

"Is he here? I'd like to meet him."

"So would everybody else. But because you're you, I'll see what I can do," he said with a wink.

ALTHOUGH ANNJA FELT DRAWN into the back room and Mondragón's Holy Child paintings as if by a magnet, she resisted. Exercising her willpower was all to the good, she told herself. And if that's just token rebellion against my destiny, she thought defiantly, then good for me. I didn't ask for the sword. I just wanted to do archaeology.

Telling herself to simmer down, she took in the art on display. She looked at paintings, drawings, small sculptures of wire or stone. She was surprised by how good most of it was. Randy's artwork mostly followed the lines of his business card, pen-and-ink cheesecake. But it was cheesecake with an edge. The scantily clad females, some with pointed ears and little wings whom she presumed were punk fairies, displayed not just sexiness but a definite insouciance. As if they'd as soon kick your ass as look at you— and could. It wasn't exactly to Annja's taste. But it definitely made her smile.

She moved on. She had visited many of the great art museums in Europe and New York City. While she didn't doubt the cognoscenti would want to subject her to her famous predecessor's fate for daring to believe so, she thought to see much of the same inspiration here in this desert backwater. If that wasn't an oxymoron. She'd never claim to be an expert of fine art. But she was endlessly fascinated with the human drive to express vision with skill—whether in the caves of Lascaux, the studios of Renaissance Florence or here.

I don't know if it's art, she thought, amused at herself, but I like what it stands for.

She found herself staring intently at a huge photograph on the back wall. It was very strange. It looked for all the world like a winter snowscape, with snow dusted or clumped on bare tree limbs, drifted on the ground around dry grass bunches. Except it wasn't white. It was orange—and glowing.

It was, in fact, fire. Embers, actually, although if she looked closely she could see little blue ghost wisps of flame dancing above the brighter concentrations. It gave her goose bumps.

"I know the feeling," a voice said from behind her right shoulder. "It kind of creeps me out, too. Makes me think of a winter wonderland in Hell."

She jumped, turned. A young man stood there. He was just taller than her, wispy, with almost blue-pale skin that made the blackness of his eyes and wavy, slightly wild hair especially intense. He was dressed in black pants and white shirt, as if he'd just shucked suit coat and tie.

But for an obvious but indefinable Latino cast to his features, he might have stepped from a Beardsley drawing. Annja thought he was beautiful.

"I'm sorry," he said, smiling. "I didn't mean to startle you. I'm Byron Mondragón. My friend Randy said you were looking for me."

"Yes," she said, returning his smile with interest. "I'm so pleased to meet you. I'm Annja Creed."

"It's my pleasure, Ms. Creed," he said. "Have you seen my work?"

"I haven't yet had the pleasure."

He gestured toward the next room. "Would you like to?"

It was what she had come for, of course. She preceded him through the door. The ska band had finished their set and were filing past the door to the main room in their Goodwill sports coats and little hats, carrying their instrument cases.

The *Alibi* piece had characterized Mondragón as something of a child prodigy. He was certainly kicking up a sensation. Annja was dubious herself. The pieces pictured in the article struck her as tacky, just a step up from black-velvet paintings. She felt trepidation. She'd liked the young sensation on sight, with his pleasant, ever so slightly diffident manner. He was a far cry from the social-lion artists she was familiar with from the East Coast.

There were a half dozen of his paintings displayed, propped in a darkened corner of the room with a tracked spotlight overhead focused on each. Her first look at them in person was a disappointment. They're amateurish, she thought, and wondered if he might be no more than a beneficiary of the global attention drawn to the Santo Niño flap. Did he just win the lottery on this?

She glanced at him sidelong. He hung back. Though he maintained calm well enough, she could tell he was on tenterhooks. She opened her mouth to lie…

Then she found her eye sliding back to the middle painting. It was the largest, at least three feet high in its blond-wood frame. It was a conventional enough representation, the usual Holy Child portrait, with his archaic outfit, his staff, his little basket. She found herself noticing the intricacy of the woody vines the artist had used to frame his central figure, the detail, unobtrusive yet meticulous. They drew her attention gradually inward to the child himself.

The eyes, huge and dark, no longer looked so clown-waif tacky. They seemed to stare deep inside her, responding to her, recognizing her for who she really was, approving. *Forgiving*.

Odd, she thought. The skin, pale cheeks blushed faintly pink, seemed alive. It was as if she were looking at a real being through a window. Despite the lifelike quality the painting was not photorealistic. It went beyond that. It transcended the *appearance* of reality while seeming to reveal…truth.

"It's fantastic," her mouth said before she even knew she meant it.

"Thanks," he said.

She looked at the other paintings. Each had a similar impact, but no two quite the same. She found them utterly compelling. She realized she was looking not just at remarkable skill for an artist so young, but authentic genius. He somehow used an idiom of bad taste and cutesiness to reach down and grab the viewer's soul. The semblance of vulgarity actually induced the viewer to let down her guard.

She realized she was holding her breath. After she set it free, she turned to the young man and said, "It's amazing how you've managed to capture such an overwhelming sense of innocence."

"Thank you," he said with a self-deprecating laugh. "I had a good model."

She raised a brow at that. A woman of about Annja's age, height and build suddenly appeared at Byron's elbow. She was pretty, without makeup, with big pale gray eyes, and hair dyed into a rainbow cockatiel crest. Had Annja been insecure about her own appearance she might have hated her on sight.

"Hi," she said to Annja. "Please forgive me, and thanks so much for coming out and supporting us, but I have to steal our guest of honor. Byron, the Travel Channel video crew is here."

Byron gave Annja a helpless shrug. "I enjoyed meeting you, Ms. Creed. I'd better go."

"Can I have your card?" Annja asked. Suddenly her mind was crowding with questions. She feared losing the chance to ask them.

"Sure." He gave her one embossed with a thumb-size reproduction of the main Santo Niño image.

Out in the main space a middle-aged man with a knobby face and disheveled russet hair had commenced playing an acoustic guitar. He sang a song that seemed, implausibly, to have to do with hunting tigers. A large, mostly young crowd was clapping and singing along on the choruses.

"Billie here does some great stuff," Byron said, nodding to the rainbow-haired woman. "There's some of her paintings hung in the main room. You should check them out."

Billie patted his cheek. "He's sweet, as well as pretty," she said. She firmly grasped his elbow. "Now quit stalling and come with me." With a last, apologetic smile over her shoulder to Annja she hustled him off into the large space.

Regretfully, Annja watched him go. Some of the

crowd in the next room began elbowing each other and pointing. Byron Mondragón was clearly the man of the hour.

Annja's amber-green eyes, scanning right across the crowd, slammed to a halt and tracked back. She focused on a suddenly familiar form.

Father Robert Godin was wearing his scuffed bombardier's jacket open over his black silk shirt and dog collar. The Jesuit was smiling and talking to someone. He didn't seem to notice her. He had the friendly, easy face of an old hound dog. But his eyes were the eyes of a cat.

"Son of a bitch," Annja said. Half under her breath. And half not. She didn't really care if he heard her. She smelled a rat.

She turned, pushed back into the front gallery, then out into the main room. A quick glance into the main room showed no sign of Godin. She didn't waste much time searching. She felt a sudden strong desire to be gone from there.

I knew I should never trust a Jesuit, she thought. Why is he following me?

Outside it had come down almost pure night, with only a bloody line along the horizon above the river, some purple streaks in the sky and magenta underbrushings on a few clumps of cloud overhead. She made her way upstream of a fresh crowd streaming into the compound and headed out the narrow half-concealed gate right onto Broadway.

She strode down the half block as fast as her long legs could carry her without appearing to hurry. She wondered now at her reaction. After all, Godin had expressed an interest in the Holy Child. Indeed, he had given her the impression he had a professional interest, as it were. He might have come to Chiaroscuro for the same purpose she had. Quite innocently.

Innocent, she thought. She snorted. A Jesuit. Right.

She turned right on the side street and walked quickly toward her parked Honda. Fishing in her jeans pocket for the key, she heard a car's tires squeal as it turned off Broadway. Its engine snarl crescendoed as it accelerated behind her.

Without knowing why, she launched herself in a long dive, just clearing the ornamental but still perilous spear tips topping a wrought-iron fence sprouting from a hip-high wall of whitewashed brick.

As she fell to the neat but dry lawn behind it the white front of the cinder-block house strobed yellow as an automatic weapon yammered at her back.

12

Glass exploded from behind security bars on the house's big front window. The slats of the venetian blinds behind made musical twangs as bullets plucked them like strings.

The car roared by. Cautiously Annja raised her head. Her heart hammered in her chest, and her pulse was drumming in her ears. She hardly believed in drive-by shootings in the real world. She couldn't imagine gangbangers targeting her.

Unless the shooting was connected with the recent attacks on her in Mexico City and the none-too-distant campus of UNM. But that's conspiracy theory! she insisted.

And this was lethal and immediate *reality*. The vehicle was an American muscle car of some kind,

low-slung and painted dark. She saw its brake lights
go on just short of the next corner. Then it accelerated backward toward her.

For a moment she lay frozen, unsure what to do.
The car screeched to a stop right in front of the house.
The doors swung open. Young men in long plaid
shirts piled out. They carried guns. Serious guns.
Short, blocky MAC-10s with stub barrels, shotguns
with barrels sawed back to the end of the pump
action.

"Where'd she go?" the driver asked in Spanish.

"I think she went over the wall," the one getting
out the passenger door replied.

A whistle came from the direction of Broadway.
Annja looked that way to see a small knot of young
men rounding the corner from the north. In the shine
of the streetlight she saw they were similarly attired
to the five who had emerged from the car. And similarly armed.

Gotta go, Annja thought as the thugs from the car
approached the front fence with cocky assurance.

She leaped up and sprinted east, down the block
away from the traffic on Broadway. The lights and the
witnesses drew her like a siren song. But the second
contingent of bangers had her thoroughly blockaded.

A dry rosebush clutched a low chain-link fence on
the far side of the house's empty driveway. Annja was

hurdling wall and bush before her hunters even reacted by shouting startled curses and raking the house front with random gunfire.

On the far side of the fence she immediately tripped over a hunched ceramic bunny. She went sprawling with a yelp of alarm. Then she jumped up and was off again. Her right ankle hurt ferociously but nothing seemed broken. The leg held, in any event.

Bullets cracked past her. She heard more glass breaking. A motion-sensor light came on from the porch to her right and was instantly shattered, most likely by a stray shot.

She vaulted another low fence. The block sloped slowly upward before her. With her long legs and natural speed she was quickly distancing her pursuers.

There was no question of charging this much fire-power, sword or no. Her only hope was to make herself as poor a target as possible while pulling away from the cursing, puffing gangbangers. She continued running at top speed, dodging garden gnomes and plaster Virgin of Guadalupe shrines and jumping fences and hedges.

It finally occurred to somebody that she couldn't outrun a car any more than she could bullets. A second vehicle snarled around the corner and whipped past her, a pimped little Mitsubishi Lancer Evolution with a huge spoiler and pointy tribal-tattoo decals on the sides. It skidded to a stop a couple of houses ahead of her. Three more thugs leaped out.

The driver leveled another sawed-back pump gun at her from the hip. At that range the pellet spread gave him a chance to hit her even with lousy aim. She immediately launched herself in a long, low dive, past a front porch and between a garage door and the front of an old Ford Taurus.

Annja scraped elbows and knees on concrete. She was grateful for long pants and a jacket. Her left knee banged painfully on the pavement but didn't buckle when she came up to a crouch with a juniper hedge right in front of her, separating the drive from the next yard.

She called forth the sword. A banger appeared at the end of the driveway. He fired a MAC-10 at her. Bullets skipped off concrete and punched through the metal garage door as she ducked down in front of the Taurus. By chance she was in the safest location possible in the immediate circumstances. The little pointy 9 mm slugs would never make it through the big car's engine block.

Her attacker still tried. He held the piece up above his head two-handed, firing downward at a shallow slant. Bullets went into the car body through the roof, sent the windshield cascading away in glittering particles, thumped through the hood to clang into the engine. None came close to the crouching Annja.

The gunfire broke off as the magazine emptied. With no notion where his two buddies were, but certain the rest of the pack was catching up quick, Annja moved fast. She darted around the driver's side of the sedan and charged straight back just as the banger hopped out on the same side into a straddle-legged stance, screaming and firing his reloaded machine pistol from the hip.

She dived beneath his bullets. She smelled burned propellant and lubricant. Oddly she heard nothing. She rolled up with the yellow muzzle flare dazzling her eyes and fast-flung primer fragments stinging her cheeks. She swung the sword down.

The blade caught the chattering machine pistol and split it open. The gunman's screams went up an octave as the chamber opened up just as a cartridge went off, causing a bubble of blue-and-yellow fire to scorch his hands and scraggly beard. The powerful blade carried on downward, scarcely impeded by cutting the gun in two, slicing his left hand transversely across the palm.

She found herself sitting right in front of the man as his seared right forefinger continued to pump the trigger of his ruined weapon uselessly. With no better option in view, she jabbed the sword up, fast and short. The tip took him under the chin, cleaved his tongue, pierced the roof of his mouth and went straight into his brain.

His howls abruptly stopped. As he collapsed life-lessly, pithed like a lab frog, she tore the sword free with a desperate full-swing wrench of both hands. She was already looking right to where she heard thudding footsteps, glad not to have to see what that did to his face...

One of his comrades loomed up over the hedge. He was almost on top of her. This one had a full-on AK-47. He raised it to his shoulder.

She knocked the broken-nosed barrel up with the flat of her sword. The gun went off, a full-auto snarl, flame stabbing four feet into the night sky. The weapon's considerable recoil at such an unwieldy angle drove the gunner back, off balance.

Annja was over the hedge and on him like a leopard. She slashed at his winged-out right elbow. His arm parted to her blade. A final shot torqued the heavy rifle from the hand that still held the foregrip. He sat down shrieking horribly until Annja silenced him with a slash across the face.

A white-painted metal yard lamp exploded right in front of her. She screamed in surprise and terror, then dropped straight down as a second charge of buckshot moaned over her head to take out most of what the first blast had left of the front window of the house.

The assault rifle lay on the lawn right beside her. She sent the sword away and grabbed the rifle.

Blasting away from his hip, the shotgunner ran forward from the middle of the street. Annja yanked the Kalashnikov into firing position, pointed it at him and squeezed off a 4-round burst.

At least one shot struck home. The man reeled, stopped and went to one knee just on the other side of the short block wall at the front of the little yard. He raised the shotgun. Annja got the hooded front sight in front of her eyes. The first part of him it bore on was his head, with a ball cap turned sideways. She squeezed off a single shot. He fell.

She put the steel buttplate to her shoulder as she aimed back the way she had come. A pursuer came into view in a flying leap across the far fence of the yard she'd just escaped, a shotgun in his right hand. She fired a short burst across the hood of the shot-up Taurus. It caught him in the center of his chest. His legs flew up before him, and he landed heavily on his back.

The first car that had tried the drive-by peeled out after her. She fired an aimed burst into the driver's side of the windshield. To her gratification the car veered left and slammed into the front of a parked pickup.

Then she realized the Kalashnikov's charging handle was locked back. She'd fired the banana magazine dry.

A wild burst from somebody running up the street cracked against the stone front of the house beside her like hail. She threw down the empty AK-47 and ran for all she was worth.

TWO BLOCKS EAST of Broadway a green park opened up to the right, climbing a hill covered with turf grass that, well watered by the city, was still mostly green. Paths graveled in crushed pumice from the Jemez Mountains wound through it. Halfway up the hill sturdy playground equipment, a slide and swing set rose out of a little depression. At the hill's crest stood some kind of a statue. Gloom and the shine of the streetlight by the play set hid details from Annja's eyes.

Her pursuers had quit shooting to concentrate on running. There were at least half a dozen of them left. They were obviously out of shape for the chase but kept after her regardless of tongues hanging out—and regardless of the casualties she had already laid on them.

Why are they after me? she wondered. Matters had gone far past the point she could pretend this was some random act of violence against a chance victim. They wanted Annja Creed. And they wanted her badly enough to die.

As she came upon the park a pair of headlights appeared over the top of the long slope that continued a block past the park. They came fast. She knew that her tormentors had just received reinforcements.

She raced up the gravel path into the park's interior. The folds in the ground, the landscaping, the swing set bolted together from heavy railroad ties would provide some concealment and more importantly cover from bullets.

Gunfire ripped from the just-arrived car as it squealed to a stop. Bullets tore divots from the sod around her.

She reached the little hollow where the playground equipment stood. For all her fitness she was breathing hard, so winded by exertion and the stress of mortal danger that she had to put a hand on a splintery wood upright to brace herself as she gasped for air. She made herself take control of her breathing. She drew air through her nostrils deep into her lungs, using abdominal breathing from Asian martial arts and meditation practices, which would oxygenate her system far quicker than panting like a dog in a hot car.

She glanced up the hill. The statue seemed to portray a somewhat larger-than-life-size youth in what she took for not very accurate Aztec warrior garb. He knelt cradling a maiden in a long gown who was apparently expiring across his knee. The statue gleamed as if made of something shiny, possibly painted fiberglass.

From the other side of the hill she heard more voices—harsh, masculine, calling out in slangy and not very grammatical local Spanish. These were homegrown bad boys, not immigrants. They sounded like a pack of hunting dogs giving voice as they pursued a fox. Their evil intent was clear even though their words were not.

Where are they coming from? she wondered in desperation. She summoned the sword again. She wasn't sure what good it would do her against ten or a dozen foes armed with shotguns and automatic weapons, no matter how gangster-terrible their marksmanship was. But dying with it in my hand will let me feel as if I'm doing something, she told herself.

Feeling the weapon's heft and hardness in her right hand, she knew that what she was truly arming herself against was the sense of *helplessness*. She knew giving in to despair would rob her of the resourcefulness that was the only thing that could give her whatever sliver-thin chance of survival she had.

They were all around her now, laughing and bantering, approaching slowly. The predators were playing with their food. She grasped the sword in both hands and stood with legs slightly flexed, ready to dive in any direction—or lunge in counterattack, should a chance blessedly present itself in spite of the odds.

Their heads started to come into view over the lip of the little depression. Their attitude was almost relaxed. They were still twisted near the snapping point, she knew—but entirely confident now of the kill. They were ready for fun.

"Remember your buddies back there," she called to them in Spanish. "You can join them if you want."

They laughed at that. "Give it up, girly," called their apparent leader, a small, wiry, swaggering man with tattoo-covered shoulders and arms bared by an undershirt despite the chill and hair shaved within a millimeter of his scalp. He carried a Beretta autopistol in his hand. "We won't hurt you."

"Much," added a tall, lanky man with snag teeth and a head of wild black hair who walked beside the leader. He carried another AK-47. Like his buddies he held it at a careless angle, barrel down.

One of the men cursed in Spanish. "She's got a sword!"

"Who's afraid of her little knife?" the bandy-legged little leader said. "Miguelito, why don't you shoot her in the leg for me?"

The tall guy started to bring up his rifle. Annja coiled herself for a final futile spring. The gunman was twenty feet from her. She could cut him with her sword, but she would also take a burst of jacketed Russian 7.62 mm bullets, pulping muscle, smashing bone.

The left side of Miguelito's head suddenly erupted red.

13

Annja was already in motion, cocking the sword back to her right side, racing with all her speed at the leader. From her left she saw a man raise a shotgun. Then the leader lurched forward as if punched hard between the shoulder blades. His shirtfront blossomed blood. His head snapped back with blood starting from his mouth.

Eyes wild as a trapped animal's, the blood-soaked gang leader tried to shoot. He had no chance. Screaming in a release of terror and fury, Annja swung her blade savagely right to left.

Shots flashed and cracked all around her. She spun to her right, found herself confronting a gang member hammering futilely on the charging lever on top of an evidently jammed MAC-10 with the heel of his fist. He looked up and screamed as her blade flashed.

Ten feet beyond him another man pointed a shotgun at Annja's face. Before he could fire, a bellowing burst from an assault rifle took him and sent him spinning to the gravel.

The remaining gang members were fleeing, with the spraddling, loose-jointed panic of those who know death's gaping jaws are slavering an inch from the seats of their baggy pants. Attacks from at least two directions had finally shattered their morale.

Annja looked around to the south, from where the interloping shots had come. She had a feeling who her rescuer must be, improbable as it was.

"They will run until they literally drop now," Father Godin said as he tossed away a Kalashnikov and drew a bulky, short-barreled revolver with a black-gloved hand. "It will be weeks before they sleep through a night without waking screaming from the nightmares. If ever.

"No thanks are necessary," he added.

"Thank you," Annja panted. Her knees felt like overboiled pasta, and her stomach churned with exhaustion and after-action nausea. She staggered a few paces to brace herself against the swing set. "I can't believe they were that determined," she said.

"Evidently they were strongly motivated," Godin said. "One suspects both a large carrot and an equally large and heavy stick. You have made someone very powerful most unhappy, Annja Creed."

She lifted her head and looked at him through strands of loose chestnut hair. "Like the Pope?" she asked.

He laughed. "His Holiness doesn't find it necessary to operate through the agency of street gangs."

She watched him closely as he approached. He had opened the cylinder of his brushed-nickel gun, dropped six empties connected by a black spring-steel full-moon clip to his palm. He transferred them to a pocket, and came up with a fresh clip.

Despite the fact that he had come to her aid she felt uncomfortable at his proximity. Or even his presence.

"How is it," she said, still sucking in deep breaths, "that you happened by at such an opportune moment?"

"I was following you, of course," he said.

"Why?" she asked angrily.

He aligned the six cartridges gripped in the moon clip, slid them into the cylinder and snapped the revolver shut. Then he stretched out his arm, cocking it as he aimed it straight at Annja's head.

"Because I fear you have something that does not belong to you."

Deliberately she straightened. She forced her focus past weapon to meet his eyes with angry intent. "The sword?"

"Indeed."

Anger flashed inside her. "Why should you have the sword? Look what happened to the last sword bearer!" she shouted.

"Mistakes were made," Godin said. His voice was level, his eyes calm. They held hers. She realized he was trying to lull her. "Surely, they will be made again. Still, the church can be the only proper caretaker of such a holy artifact."

She held her hands out open to her sides. "Where is it?"

He shrugged. Somehow he managed to do so without the muzzle of his handgun wavering in the slightest. "An excellent question. Suppose you answer, and save us both a great deal of unpleasantness?"

She laughed. It had a frost-brittle sound in her ears. "If you kill me, how do you plan to find the sword? Using a Ouija board?"

"You frame a most astute objection," he said, and shot her in the leg.

Or tried to. As he dropped his arm, time seemed to slow for her. She'd anticipated his move and noticed the black-gloved finger as it tightened on the curving trigger with its longitudinal grooves.

She was moving, diving sideways to put a six-inch post of splintery gray-green pressure-treated wood between herself and her opponent. The handgun flashed. The bullet kicked up bits of porous white gravel behind the heel of her boot.

She put down a shoulder, rolled, came up crouching behind another upright. Godin stood placidly, regarding her with an odd smile on his face.

"Very good," he said, and snapped a shot for her face.

Again she read the intention in the ripple of the fine calfskin of the glove echoing the movement of muscle and bone in the finger beneath. Before he had completed triggering the shot, she had ducked back. The bullet sailed past her head and struck the grassy slope behind her with an audible thud even as the aftereffects of the painfully loud report rang in her ears.

As the ringing subsided she heard the crunch of his crepe-soled shoes on the pumice. He was walking clockwise, trying to flank her.

She sprinted right, straight out in front of him. She kept her eyes at soft focus so as to perceive the widest possible vision field. She saw his arm once again tense to fire.

She stiffened her left leg as she swung it out for the next step, dug her heel deep through the gravel to the soil below. She pivoted around her heel, away from him, as another shot cracked out—horribly loud, the noise like knitting needles driven into her eardrums. Wheeling through 270 degrees, she ran straight at him, trailing her right arm.

The sword appeared in her hand.

He was trying to shift aim to shoot her in the face. She ran fast. The sword sang through the air in a rising backhand cut.

Somehow the Jesuit managed to twitch his heavy revolver far enough that the mystic blade did not shear it in half. Instead it knocked the dull silver weapon from his grasp. It spun end over end, glittering in the light of the single streetlamp that illuminated the little depression beneath the hill with its curious gleaming statue.

It took her a moment to halt her disarming cut, which had passed over Godin's head as he recoiled. In that immobile instant he grasped her sword wrist with his own right hand and, using legs and hips, turned his body hard clockwise. His strength and mass were sufficient to complete the locking out of her already straightened elbow. He put his left palm on that elbow and applied pressure as his right hand yanked the trapped arm across his body and twisted the captive wrist cruelly counterclockwise. Annja was forced to bend double at the waist as pain shot up her arm.

"Ah, splendid," he said, puffing slightly. "I knew the sword would put in an appearance if I put your life properly in danger. Now, release it, please. I really don't want to hurt you."

"Is that why you shot at me?" she asked.

"I believed you would dodge. As indeed you did. I observed during your running fight with those young hooligans that you possess quite extraordinary physical abilities. But I'm afraid I have you at a decisive disadvantage."

"I guess so," she said. She relaxed her muscles in defeat. Her fingers opened. The sword fell from them.

It vanished halfway to the ground.

Not even the too clever Jesuit had anticipated *that*. In his astonishment he relaxed his own grip a fraction.

Annja threw her body forward and down, no longer resisting the pressure on her arm but literally rolling with it. She kicked her right leg out straight behind her, brought it up. Her long hair dragged across the pumice. Then she completed her walkover, freeing her arm from the terrible torsion.

Before she finished her rotation, Godin released her and danced back. He respected her strength and agility even if he didn't quite grasp the extent of them.

She planted her left leg as it descended, fired a right side-kick at him. He stepped back with his left foot, pivoting backward out of the way. She continued her spin, putting her right leg down and whipping her left foot in a blinding spinning roundhouse kick for his face. He leaned aside. Her corrugated sole just grazed his ear.

"Ow," he said mildly.

She threw a furious punch at his face. He got the back of his hand up against her inner arm, deflecting the piledriver blow just enough that it missed his face as he ducked into her. She threw a left. He fouled it with his elbow. She launched a furious flurry of punches, faster than he could possibly move.

Yet he fouled or deflected and slipped them all. His muscles could not match up to her youthful power. But he never opposed his strength to hers. He applied deflecting force at ninety degrees to her angle of attack, or simply closed inside the blows so they lacked force when they did make contact.

After an interval of wild but fruitless activity she stepped back, breathing hard. Her cheeks felt hot as a forge. Incongruously she wondered what her body temperature was, given her unnatural exertion.

"How can you dodge me?" she shouted. "I'm faster than you could possibly be."

"The same way you dodged my bullets," he said. "By reading your intent from your eyes, your breathing, the play of your muscles. Most of all, your balance. I salute you, by the way. It has taken me years of practice and brutal experience to become so proficient."

With a cry of frustration she charged him.

She had some vague intention of grappling him and taking him to the ground.

It was a poor choice. Rather than trying to dance away, Godin stepped up to meet her and jabbed her in the face with his right hand. The blow did not break her nose but it stung and filled her eyes with a rush of hot tears. It did break her momentum. He followed with a left cross to her ribs that sent a white-hot stab of pain through her chest and clenched her lungs like a fist.

She gasped and staggered past him at a diverging angle. Momentum carried her out of range of any intended third shot to his combination.

But not out of range of her long legs. She halted herself, did a little stutter step and pistoned a side-thrust kick into his ribs just beneath his right arm. The impact jolted her teeth together and sent fresh spikes of pain through her torso.

It lifted him into the air and knocked him over. He rolled over twice and lay on his face.

Annja almost collapsed. She just caught herself, bent over, bracing hands on knees, gasping and moaning as she tried to suck in breaths. She knew it was the worst thing she could do. The posture created both physical and mental stress that actually restricted her ability to draw in air. But she was momentarily overcome by a drowner's desperation.

After three heaving breaths she quit feeling as if she were about to die and began to force herself to breathe from her diaphragm, compressing her abdominal organs to create room to allow her lungs to fill all the way to the bottom. As she winched herself fully upright, she saw the Jesuit stir, then begin with obvious pain to pick himself up. As he did he was hit by a coughing spasm so violent that it sounded as if things were tearing within him.

He's an old man! she thought with a pang of self-reproach. She had to remind herself sternly that old or not he had given her as tough a hand-to-hand fight as she had experienced since coming into her destiny. He was a skilled, tough bastard.

Yet he didn't seem so tough as he spit something dark into the gravel from all fours then raised the back of one gloved hand to his mouth to wipe it. She wondered if she had broken his ribs.

"*Ave Maria,*" he gasped. Another spell of coughing shook his body.

With a mighty effort he came up to his knees. He jackknifed forward, coughing brutally, stopping himself with hands on thighs. He forced his body vertical, raised a knee, got his foot planted. "*Sancta Maria,*" he said, and thrust himself upright.

"'Mother of God,'" he rasped in English. His face contorted, his body began to buckle. He clutched at his side with a black-gloved hand, which seemed to arrest the spasm.

"'Pray for us sinners—'" he stood fully erect once more "'—now and in the hour of our death. Amen.'"

Without meaning to Annja echoed his final words. As he crossed himself, she did the same.

"You are a daughter of the holy mother the church," Godin said, with more than a touch of the raven's croak, "no matter how hard you pretend not to be."

"But I've seen how the church treats her daughters!" she retorted defiantly, the more because her cheeks were wet, for some unaccountable reason.

"And may God have mercy on my soul, child, for I do what I must—" He reached behind himself.

She charged him. The sword sprang into her hand. She brought it looping up into a side cut at his neck.

He snapped a black autopistol out right into her face. She heard the safety snick off as the muzzle aligned with her right eye. She froze.

For a few heartbeats they stood that way, her blade pressed into the skin of his neck, the barrel of his pistol almost touching her eye.

"You should come back by daylight and examine that statue up the hill," he said conversationally. A trickle of blood was drying down the right side of his chin, maroon in the bluish light. "It's a naive representation of popular Mexican myths. The warrior is the personification of Popocatepetl, the languishing maid his lover Ixtaccihuatl. I mention this because I believe you have recently seen the originals first-hand, yes?"

She had to smile. But she never relaxed the sword's pressure against his neck.

"Is it just me or are you even more full of bullshit than any man I've ever met, Father?" she asked.

His grin made him look almost boyish. "Given my order, and my life experience, I would most assuredly hope so," he said. "And now we seem to find ourselves at a New Mexican standoff."

"Now, you can blow my head off with that piece of yours," she told him. "It's *possible* I'll just relax, and my arm won't twitch enough to sever your carotid artery before I fall. So you need to ask yourself just one question, Padre. 'Do I feel lucky?'"

He laughed incredulously. "You quote Clint Eastwood?"

"It was all I could think of," she said.

Sirens began to wail. They weren't far and they were getting closer in a hurry. From multiple directions, by the way the sounds surrounded the pair.

Godin tipped his gun toward the star-filled sky. His thumb let the hammer down and snapped the safety back on.

"If you want to cut my head off," he said, holstering the weapon behind the small of his back, "now's your chance. But I'd suggest you do whatever you choose to do quickly and leave with alacrity. The police will not care for any of the answers you will be able to give them."

For a moment she still stood, feeling the pressure of her steel against the skin of his neck through her hand and arm. Then she deliberately moved the blade sideways before making the sword disappear.

"I don't have it in me to kill a man who doesn't pose a direct threat," she said. "I hope I never do. But I also hope I'm not making a mistake not going ahead and taking your head off and letting my soul take the consequences."

"Refraining from burdening your soul with such a weight is never a bad choice, child," he said. "And now by your leave, I bid you adieu. You have given me much to contemplate."

She watched him walk away. Just before he passed out of the direct shine of the light illuminating the play area he stooped to scoop up his big, gleaming revolver and stuff it back inside his jacket. Then he continued on his way, moving along with no apparent hurry. Once beyond the circle of light he seemed to dissolve into the night.

She turned to run in a different direction.

14

"Sit, sit," the big man in the herringbone coat with the black fake-fur collar said, gesturing her back down with a gloved hand. He beamed at her through his full salt-and-pepper beard. Cars choked the narrow street behind him. A horde of tourists, many wearing brightly-colored lapel pins in the shape of balloons, milled along the sidewalks to either side.

Halfway out of her metal chair on the small patio in front of the Purple Sage Coffee House, Annja halted. "You're Dr. Cogswell?" she asked.

"Affirmative, affirmative," he puffed. He was a tall man, heavyset, with round pink cheeks and lively brown eyes beneath extravagant black-and-white eyebrows. Like his beard his thinning hair was gray with a showy black streak down the middle. He held himself almost militarily erect and moved with brisk authority. "And you are the famous Annja Creed?"

"Not that famous," she said, resuming her seat. "I'm pleased to meet you, Doctor."

The coffee house was tucked back from San Felipe Street, just north of Old Town Plaza in Albuquerque. San Felipe Cathedral stood across the lane. It was a bright autumn noon. The sun was warm enough Annja had taken off her jacket.

"Puff," Cogswell said, taking his own seat across the round metal table from her. "The pleasure's all mine. I'm flattered you took time out of your busy schedule to meet with an old coot like me."

For a moment he sat regarding her. He had a keen gaze. His scrutiny could well have been taken as obtrusive and inappropriate, though she detected nothing sexual in it. She wondered if he understood that and was using the fact that his age and professorial mien made him relatively innocuous, or whether, like a great many scientists of her acquaintance, he knew too little of human interactions even to be aware of it.

Make no assumptions, she told herself sternly, behind a carefully bland smile.

He nodded his round head once, briskly, as if she had passed examination. He leaned forward slightly. "We live, it would appear, in interesting times."

He nodded to Annja's left, where a thirtyish

brown-haired man dressed in slacks, a pullover and red-and-white athletic shoes sat reading an early-afternoon paper. The headline read, or rather screamed, Nine Die In Gang War.

Her smile crumpled a little. "Yes," she said. "I guess we do." She had never really thought she'd be grateful for the War on Drugs, but she had to admit it kept providing excellent cover for her. She wondered how long that could last.

Cogswell cocked his head to one side. "Ah, but I suppose you know that better than any of us," he said.

Her blood turned cold. She felt as if he had read the thoughts right out of her head. Her cheeks burned. *What does he know?*

The next moment he reassured her by saying, "You are acquiring quite a reputation in paranormal circles."

"Ah," she said. "Well. I hope they aren't too hard on me." Some people were, she knew. She had once made the mistake of wandering onto the public forum the Knowledge Channel maintained online for *Chasing History's Monsters.*

He smiled. "I suppose you've been quite occupied researching the remarkable events transpiring here in the land of enchantment. In fact, I gather you've been a firsthand witness of one of the more alarming phenomena."

"I'm afraid that's been a little blown out of pro-portion, Doctor," she said. "I don't think I saw anything but an eagle. The light wasn't very good."

"You maintain scientific detachment. Very good. But an eagle that flies without flapping its wings? An eagle that makes a sound like a baby crying? Or was it a woman screaming?"

She was getting those insects-crawling-down-the-spine sensations again. She searched her memory frantically. How much had the anonymous post from the San Esequiel dig revealed?

"A baby crying?" she asked.

"So what you heard sounded more like screaming to you," he said. "Reports vary. Still, the one seems rather similar to the other, don't you think?"

He smiled at her merrily. His coat had come open. Beneath it he wore a bright red vest and an emerald-green tie. It went beyond aging-professorial fashion blindness almost to the point of deliberate bad taste. Though the combination, she had to admit, lent him a certain cheery premature-Christmas air. And who am I to play fashion fascist anyway? My friends all accuse me of dressing like an archaeologist.

"Wait," she said. "An eagle has a pretty impressive wingspan. They glide pretty well. And while I'm no authority, I believe they have some pretty shrill, piercing cries."

"Could a bird as imposing as an eagle take off without flapping its wings?"

She shook her head. "I don't think so. But if you're familiar with my work on the show you know I'm sort of the house skeptic. I try to resist jumping to any exotic conclusions."

He nodded. "Commendable, commendable. But please, tell me truthfully, do you really think that all that's going on here is childish pranks and misapprehension of natural creatures?"

"Let's leave aside what I think, if we can, Dr. Cogswell. You have a most impressive résumé, I must say."

"Ah, the wonders of Google. You probably don't even remember the days when checking a person's bona fides required at least a trip to a well-stocked library, if not lengthy and tedious correspondence."

"My love for the past does not blind me to the advantages of climate conditioning and antibiotics and the other blessings of modern life. But you said you had some information for me. I'm very eager to hear it."

"Yes. Are you familiar with the works of Charles Fort?"

"I've heard the name."

"In his writings he maintained a careful distance between the anomalies he reported and his own belief system. Nonetheless, whether jocularly or not, he indulged occasionally in speculation."

"Didn't he write at one point that 'we are owned,' presumably by some nonhuman intelligences?" Annja asked.

"Yes. Which may have more merit than we like to believe, but does not bear directly, insofar as I am aware, on our situation here. Rather, I find fascinating his suggestion, later expanded in the sixties and seventies by American monster hunter John A. Keel, that a great many sightings of anomalous beings can be attributed not to undiscovered life-forms from our own Earth, but rather are strays from somewhere else."

"By somewhere else do you mean other planets, Doctor?" She felt her interest begin to slip. UFO conspiracy nonsense was all that needed to be added to the mix to turn it all into a hopeless web of confusion.

"Not necessarily. Rather, I suggest the possibility that some manner of small, localized dimensional shift allows beings to enter our world from, as I said, somewhere else—which for now must remain unspecified owing to a lack of data. Whether these slips are accidental or deliberate, or some mixture of both, is likewise speculative."

"With all respect, Doctor, it all seems pretty speculative to me. Are temporary holes between dimensions really a more plausible explanation than people seeing wild animals or escaped pets—or just shadows magnified by their imaginations?" Annja asked.

"Sightings worldwide, and over a very lengthy period of time—spanning centuries at least—show remarkable consistency. Such as the ability of these anomalous creatures to appear, sometimes do great harm and then simply disappear, even when hunted by professional trackers with dogs."

"Like the Beast of Gévaudan?" she asked blithely.

He chuckled. "Give me credit for doing my research, too, Ms. Creed. I watched that particular episode of your show. You did a most creditable job of getting across your reasoned hypothesis that the beast was some kind of unfortunate mutation of a natural animal, possibly a large wolf-dog hybrid."

She decided that she liked this older gentleman.

"The beast was reportedly killed," he said, "which seems to remove it from our particular anomalies. Not so with others. We have just recently seen another spate of mystery large-cat sightings in England, where no cats of any size have dwelled in the wild since before the last Ice Age. By comparison, in his book *Strange Creatures from Time and Space,* Keel reports that according to the records, in August of 1577, a beast like a giant black dog killed several worshipers at a church in Suffolk, England. The creature vanished without a trace. Incidentally, the British Ministry of Defense has repeatedly, if discreetly, dispatched experienced SAS sniper teams with the most modern night-vision equipment to chase down the phantom cats that have killed sheep, chickens and household pets. Without result, needless to say."

For some reason his words chilled her. She shook herself, annoyed at being susceptible.

"Certain other phenomena are repeatedly reported in such sightings," Cogswell went on. "One of the most persistent is the frightening sound associated with the creatures, usually described as sounding either like a baby crying or a woman screaming. A sulfurous smell is another. Black color, red eyes, flying without visible flapping of wings—the latter were common features of the Mothman sightings in West Virginia in the sixties, which Keel himself made famous, although they have likewise been reported in myriad cases before and since."

She stared at him. She willed herself strongly not to remember that last evening at the dig site. There was no future in that.

"What about the Santo Niño sightings, Doctor?" she asked, hoping her tone didn't ring as brassy false in his ears as in hers. "Do they bear some relation to these extradimensional phenomena you suspect?"

He smiled his big smile and bobbed his head. "Precisely! How else to account for the fact that our phantom hitchhiker has repeatedly shown a distressing tendency to vanish from people's automobiles? In the Murakami case near Acoma—which is the farthest west and south the Holy Child has been reported in this current spate—the family reported the child vanished from within arm's reach of the two children, sitting in the backseat of a minivan. What else could account for that, but an ability to travel dimensions usually debarred to us?"

He sounded so enthusiastic she almost felt herself going for it. "Well, since we have names and even video of real people who have reported the Santo Niño, it's hard to pass him off as an urban legend," she said. "Still…wouldn't you really think it's more likely that some kind of clever street magician, somebody like David Blaine, has come up with an especially ingenious disappearing stunt?"

"That would seem a high level of conjuring skill for an eight-year-old child."

She shrugged. "Well, then, a very small David Blaine. A little-person David Blaine. Who actually does, you know, tricks."

"Who's grasping at straws now, Ms. Creed?"

"That would be me," she confessed. "But—you've hit me with a lot, here, Doctor. I need some time to assimilate it."

She made what she hoped wasn't too much of a show of checking her wristwatch. "I have to ask you to forgive me. I've got another appointment coming up here—"

"Of course. Of course." He nodded sagely.

They rose together. "Should you uncover anything you find it difficult to account for," he said, "you have my contact information."

"Thank you, Doctor. I will remember that. And thank you for the time. What you've told me is highly intriguing." That was the truth.

"Just one thing," he said, arresting her as she began to turn to walk back to the parking lot to reclaim her rental. "These warnings the Holy Child issues—"

"Don't most of them involve immediate peril to the people who report seeing him? Like a flash flood, in that Murakami case?" she said.

"Yes. But percipients also report, rather unanimously, an impression that he was also trying to convey some greater danger, some common danger we all face. Here's the thought that makes *my* blood run cold. Could that greater menace possibly have anything to do with our own current spate of sightings of strange and very scary animals?"

I sincerely hope not, she thought. Aloud she said, "One thing's for sure, Doctor. It doesn't concern the Mayan calendar."

He laughed at that. "Indeed. A very good day to you, Ms. Annja Creed. And remember to look behind you."

ANNJA WAS STANDING in her motel room in her underwear trying to figure out what to pack in her overnight bag for her imminent jaunt overseas. The small stack of clothes on the bed beside her open case was not giving her any hints.

Damn that smug old bastard, with his look-behind-you bullshit, she thought peevishly. He got me so rattled I'm actually dithering about doing something I've done a thousand times. It was true. It seemed she had spent far more time moving from place to place than fixed at any given address. Even the Brooklyn loft where she'd lived for the past few years served as little more than a *pied-à-terre*. She should have been able to pack for a short trip in her sleep. As a matter of fact, she was pretty sure she had.

On the television, which she had on as a sort of background, a man with a young face and a richly coiffed head of silver hair was interviewing a lean, tanned man who seemed to smile perpetually.

"—really think there's nothing to these reports coming out of New Mexico, Don?" the silver-haired man asked.

"Just call me Mr. Skeptic, Miller," his subject

said, grinning. The crawl beneath him read Donald "Mr. Skeptic" Triphorn, Editor, *Skeptic Eye* Magazine. "And the answer to your question is, of course not."

"How could so many people be mistaken, Mr. Skeptic?"

"I'm glad you asked me that, Miller." He turned the unrelenting grin to the camera. "I'd say it's a classic example of an overwhelming will to believe. We're inundated incessantly with fantasy—stories that take us out of our humdrum daily existence, reassure us that there really is magic in the world, regardless of what the mean old scientists say. From Harry Potter to Roswell conspiracy theories, it's very popular. The fact is, Miller, a lot of us *want* to be fooled by easily explainable events. Or publicity stunts. Or simply to buy into urban legends."

"But don't urban legends usually have no traceable attribution, Mr. Skeptic? Don't these stories usually get told as happening to a friend of my cousin, third- or fourth- or sixteenth-hand? Whereas these stories have names and faces associated with them," Miller asked.

Mr. Skeptic's grin had turned a bit glassy. Hearing part of her own discussion of a couple of hours earlier with Dr. Cogswell replayed, Annja had stopped staring fruitlessly at her piled clothes. She gave full attention to the television screen.

"In one recent case our alleged Holy Child appeared to a young couple whose SUV had broken down at night in an early blizzard near Red River. If you'll recall, he actually gave them a silver thermal blanket to keep them warm until help arrived."

Miller—Miller Pemberton, an on-screen flash identified him—nodded his silver head. "We have some shots of that." The screen showed a pair of hands displaying a thermal blanket.

"Not only is that a perfectly normal thermal blanket you see there, Miller," Mr. Skeptic said as his grin reappeared, along with the rest of him, "but thanks to the magic of modern inventory-tracking technology, authorities have been able to identify it as an item shoplifted from a Wal-Mart near Interstate 40 in Albuquerque."

"Hard to reconcile petty theft with an entity popularly rumored to be the infant Jesus," Pemberton said.

A great, warm wave of reassurance washed over Annja.

Cogswell was clearly full of nonsense; that much was obvious. He was an intelligent, very learned man, well meaning. But misguided, like so many devotees of the strange.

"I understand you actually believe there is a threatening aspect to these sightings, though, Mr. Skeptic."

The grin went away and was replaced by a look

of concern so studied it almost made Annja burst out laughing:

"Yes, there is a considerable threat here, Miller," Mr. Skeptic said. "Tall tales such as these cause people to question proper authority, disbelieving what scientists or even our government tells us. I don't think I have to tell you how dangerous such antigovernment sentiments can be. If people trust their own untrained observations instead of what they are told by qualified professionals, the possibilities for unjustified panic or worse are infinite. Don't you agree, Miller?"

"Of course, Mr. Skeptic. Of course I do." Another camera focused on his head as he turned to look into the lens. "And now a few words about a very special program coming up called 'We're All Going to Die'…"

"Christ," Annja said. She reminded herself that in the late sixteenth century, popular broadsheets distributed all across Continental Europe described the Spanish Armada as an overwhelming success for King Philip and Spain for weeks and weeks after the battle. *The more things change,* she thought.

Shaking her head, Annja turned off the television. My plane leaves in three hours, she told herself. I have to make some executive decisions here.

I don't have time to wonder who's crazy—me or the rest of the world.

15

"Pretty, isn't it?" the little man asked.

From the small platform built out over the second-floor scenic overlook Annja observed the great spray of palms and other tropical vegetation springing from the middle of the huge atrium. "Yes," she said, "but definitely not what I expected."

"You expected some kind of mystic or historical shrine," he said, hopping from foot to foot. "Instead I give you a shopping mall."

Her host, who rejoiced in the name Dr. Eleuterio Bobadilla, was a professor from the even more impressively named Departamento de Historia Antigua, Historia Medieval y Paleografía y Diplomática of the

Madrid Autonomous University. Both his name and that of his department were substantially longer than him. The top of his shiny brown head, egg bald but for a little black fringe at the back, barely came to Annja's shoulder. He had lean features, a neat little mustache and skinny arms and legs sticking out, improbably, from a grotesquely large white jersey that came down almost to the bottom of his black silk running shorts. Annja recognized it as a Real Madrid home jersey. A pair of red-and-white running shoes completed his ensemble. She gathered he'd actually jogged from the university to meet her. It was impossible to guess how old he was, but he somehow reminded Annja of a young Mohandas Gandhi.

"I admit I was wondering why you weren't showing me the basilica devoted to the Virgin of Atocha."

"Well, you know, you told me you had seen ample images of the virgin and child," Bobadilla said, his running-in-place cooldown finally coming to an end. His appearance in exercise clothing had taken her somewhat aback. In her experience, most Europeans were terribly formal in dress, especially in front of Americans. "The basilica is not so much about the Santo Niño. Our Lady of Atocha is far more significant to us. She is rival to the Virgin of Almudena for the devotions of pious Madrileños. A few years ago our king, Juan Carlos, recognized the Lady of Atocha as protectress of the royal family."

Annja leaned on the rail. Below, a few tourists stood snapping digital cameras at the gardens while locals strolled by. Overhead the space rose to a high half-cylinder ceiling, ribbed with metal girders and pierced with a great skylight to allow the sunlight to pour down on the tropical jungle in miniature. Structurally, the mall looked like nothing so much as a turn-of-the-twentieth-century train station. As it once had been.

"But wasn't the church built on the site of the original Santo Niño manifestation?" she asked.

"No. To tell you the truth, no one knows precisely where that took place. The church was originally consecrated by Alfonso VI, who credited an image of the virgin for his reconquest of Madrid from the Moors in 1083. That was two centuries before the events commemorated in the Santo Niño legend supposedly took place. Why Alfonso picked the site is anybody's guess. For much of its history the church lay derelict. Indeed, the current cathedral is younger than this, the old Atocha station."

He gestured around to encompass the echoing space. "The station was rebuilt after a fire in 1892. Meanwhile the image of the virgin wasn't even housed at the church until 1926, shortly after a rather desultory reconstruction began."

"Desultory?"

He shrugged. "The basilica did not open until 1951. I thought it might please you to see our old station, which is something of an attraction for tourists. I hope I have done right; if you wish I can order a cab to carry us to the basilica at once."

He started to fish under his jersey, presumably for a cell phone. Annja stopped him.

"That's okay. I love ancient cathedrals, or I wouldn't have my specialty. But 1951 isn't ancient to anyone. And what I really wanted was to get as much of a feel for the origins of the story as I could."

"Regrettably," the little man with the big, bald head said, "very little indeed remains of the thirteenth-century village of Atocha within twenty-first-century Madrid."

She smiled at him. "Perhaps you'd at least fill me in on the story of the Holy Child."

"It would be my pleasure. You must first understand that the Santo Niño enjoys no great popularity in Spain today. His worship is far more prevalent in the colonies, Cebu, Mexico, Chimayó. Indeed, it appears to be the case that the earliest known image of the Holy Child as we know him today was the one sent as a present to the Mexican town of Plateros in the sixteenth century. In the thirteenth century the Moors, it is said, held the little village of Atocha, then well outside the walls of Madrid. Prisoners captured in the continuing war for freedom from the occupiers were kept in most deplorable conditions in a building in the town. The Moors refused to feed them, insisting that the local townsfolk should provide, which was not an uncommon arrangement for the time, however harsh. In time, suspecting the Christian villagers were all sympathizers with the insurgency—as no doubt they were—the local ruler forbade anyone to visit the prisoners except children under the age of twelve.

"Then lo! A child appeared, dressed as a pilgrim of the day, in robe and cape, sandals and hat with plume. He carried a staff with a water gourd suspended from it, and a basket of bread. The guards permitted him to enter. One story has it that no matter how much bread and water he distributed to the captives, neither his bread basket nor water gourd ever ran out—a clear linkage to the biblical miracle of loaves and fishes."

He raised his right leg behind him, grasped his instep, pulled. "Please forgive me. I have a tendency to cramp. A consequence of adult-onset diabetes, I fear. Another, even more miraculous version of the story has important resonances for these apparitions of the Holy Child you're having in the New World.

"In this rendition the jailers did not permit the

Holy Child to visit the prisoners. But they could not keep him out. They would hear talking from within the cells, rush in, find the captives just swallowing the last of their bread and water. But never a sign of the Holy Child."

"He vanished," Annja said, "just the way he supposedly vanishes from the backs of people's cars in New Mexico."

"Precisely! Moreover, when the women of Atocha went to give thanks to the image of the Santo Niño—in this account, Christ as a child in pilgrim's garb rather than the miraculous figure who brought succor to the Christian prisoners of Atocha—they found his shoes soiled and worn out. Leading to the charming custom in Chimayó of taking baby shoes to the image of the Santo Niño in the chapel there, I understand."

"So in that story we have the origins of the vanishing-hitchhiker elements of the Santo Niño," Annja said.

Bobadilla laughed. "I had not heard that connection drawn before. But yes, it is apt. Especially in view of these American sightings. And also of the tradition of the Holy Child succoring travelers in need or peril, which I also understand plays a role in these modern encounters."

"Yes." She hesitated. "What truth, if any, do you assign to the story?"

"I am not a particularly observant Catholic. I consider myself a man of reason. So naturally I will tend, at least intellectually, to discount the miraculous elements of the story. As for an unknown child appearing, dressed as a pilgrim, and bringing food to the suffering captives, I personally believe it almost certainly happened."

"Really?"

"Quite so. It makes sense. It did, after all, cleverly skirt the prohibition on adult visitors. And the pilgrim garb may be explained by the fact that Muslims then as now hold pilgrims in particular regard, even infidels. After all, while the Christians were undoubtedly subject to varying degrees of oppression, their religion was not forbidden.

"Moreover even the apparently inexhaustible supply of bread and water might have a factual basis—in extra baskets and gourds concealed beneath the flowing robe and cape, yes?"

Annja laughed. "That sounds quite plausible actually."

"I would not be surprised if the Moorish guards were wise to the ruse and went along with it. For all the real hostility existing between Muslims and Christians during the occupation, these people were neighbors. They lived far more of their lives peacefully together than they did in fighting one another."

"People depended on each other to survive," Annja said.

"Precisely! The lines were not drawn nearly so starkly at the time as they are now, in our pictures. Also there is a respect of cleverness and resourcefulness in many Islamic cultures. The guards may have thought the whole thing a capital joke, regardless of how seriously their commander took his edicts. And I think to see echoes in the tale, even at this essentially plausible level, from Sufi parables, which often involve degrees of deception. That strain of Muslim mysticism, as you well know, played an integral if often forgotten role in shaping our own Spanish intellectual and mystic traditions, after all."

"Yes," said Annja, who had studied Spanish history. "But what of the more…esoteric elements to the story?" she asked.

"I see two possibilities, which are far from exclusive. First, simple folk rumor, and the universal and long recognized tendency of any story to grow in the telling. The identification of the child bringing succor with the Christ child would be quite natural for people raised to believe unquestioningly in Christ's reality and dual nature, human and divine. The more so if in fact an image of the Christ child dressed in the pilgrim's characteristic garb preexisted the events that gave rise to the story, rather than came about as a result of them.

"The other possibilities? That Christian Spanish leaders, secular and of the church, deliberately created the tale, whether tailoring facts to fit or making it all of whole cloth, as a propaganda ploy. If you can credit the church fathers with such cynicism."

"You'd be surprised what I wouldn't put past the church. Please forgive me if I offend," Annja said.

Bobadilla laughed. "Not at all. In turn, forgive me if I presume, but something in your tone of voice— are you a lapsed Catholic?"

Annja nodded. "Raised by nuns," she said. "At a Catholic orphanage in New Orleans."

"*Pobrecita*," the professor said, clucking sympathetically. "We at least got to escape from our nuns by going home at the end of the school day!"

THE MONSOON HAD COME to Cebu Island, tucked into the Philippine archipelago between Luzon in the north and Mindanao to the south. Riding the taxi back from Cebu City to the international airport, across the Opon Channel on Mactan Island, Annja found the torrent falling from the sky perfectly appropriate. First, as a metaphor for her Philippine expedition, which was a total wash. And as portrayal of her mood.

The driver chattered cheerfully in Spanish, so incessantly and inconsequentially she wished she'd never let him know she understood the language.

It wasn't that difficult to tune him out, since not only did he not seem to require any response from his passenger, but he also seemed not to have to breathe. He rattled ceaselessly about local politics, corrupt and rife with coups and rumors of coups and the weather, which she could see for herself was lousy.

She had paid her visit that morning to the Basilica Minor del Santo Niño. The Cebu church was a typical colonial structure with two bell towers, built of coral blocks that gave it an unfortunate corroded appearance, as if it suffered severe acne. A pleasant young sacristan in a white gown over black trousers, who spoke excellent English, showed her the sights.

These included the Santo Niño himself, or rather a replica of the miraculous image, which had been given to the queen of the Cebuanos by Magellan. Forty-odd years later the Spanish returned and found the natives hostile. They set the village on fire and when it was subsequently found in a burned-out house, the image of the Santo Niño was either charred beyond recognition or miraculously unscathed. Her guide smilingly refused to say which. And since the original was kept under lock and key in the associated convent, she was not likely to find out.

It hardly mattered to her current quest.

As for local legends about the Holy Child, especially nocturnal perambulations and aid to the needy, the sacristan hadn't heard of any. The Santo Niño was mostly a pretext for a big annual party, it appeared.

Annja gazed out the window. In all the brochures in Annja's hotel, Cebu City portrayed itself as the real economic miracle city of Southeast Asia. For all Annja knew, it could be. It certainly had its share of gleaming new skyscrapers. But that didn't mean it lacked slums.

They drove through one. At this point of the mid-afternoon there was miraculously little traffic. The cab was like a blocky little sampan making its way down a vast, empty river between steep green slopes. Miserable shanties of rain-warped planks and rusted sheet metal stuck up out of the vegetation on stilts like exotic weeds. This, she knew too well, wasn't the worst of it. The real poverty was to be found in the city dumps, which were inhabited by tens if not thousands of truly desperate people.

But this slum smelled more than bad enough. The air carried the scents of petroleum fractions, rotting vegetation, untreated sewage, rancid peanut oil and general misery.

For this, she thought, I did such damage to my tailbone, my spine and my budget, with all this globe hopping? She was retrograding Magellan, circumnavigating the globe ass backward. She wasn't even sure why.

Her eyelids drooped. Her head dropped toward the glass of the door where she sat directly behind the driver, mainly so she couldn't hear him quite as well. Its impact against her forehead woke her.

The cab was slowing. A truck was stalled out in the lane right ahead of them with its hood up and engine steaming into the rain. Away up on a hillside across the highway a dirty white flower bloomed. She saw an intense blue-white light spiraling toward her, drawing a twisty white trail behind it.

She recognized it only because she had seen the movie *Black Hawk Down* five times when she had been going through an Orlando Bloom phase.

As the soldiers did in that movie, she shouted, "RPG! Get out *now!*"

The driver turned an almost comical gape of surprise and incomprehension toward her as she yanked her door open. He was not reacting. She grabbed the collar of his shirt and with her feet to the back of his seat kicked for all she was worth, hoping vaguely to yank him out the back door with her.

The shirt collar tore away in her hand. She flew backward out of the cab as white light dazzled her eyes and the most terrible crack of thunder she had ever heard drove sound from her ears. She rolled over and over backward at least three times before coming back to something like self-awareness. She was sitting on the wet asphalt with her back to a concrete lane barrier, her hair hanging like fresh-dredged kelp in her face, clutching a sorry half circle of sodden, once-white cloth in her hand.

She smelled gasoline. The little Toyota cab blazed quite merrily in the downpour. Tendrils of black, black smoke undulated out of the windows and grew together into an imposing black stalk that kept growing to meet the low-hanging, lead-colored clouds.

Annja steeled herself to charge the wreck. She could not permit the innocent driver to burn to death if she could help it.

Then she noticed the flame-wrapped silhouette behind the wheel lacked a head. The rocket grenade had apparently struck the post of the driver's door, right beside the windshield. The jet of incandescent copper it spewed, meant to cut deep into the entrails of a tank, had decapitated the man far more efficiently than a guillotine.

THE POLICE CALLED IT a random terrorist attack by Moro separatists. Since she had seen nothing beyond the flash and smoke of the RPG launch, they were even more eager to see her leave the country than the

Mexican cops had been. No doubt they feared she might sue them for psychological damage.

She cried halfway across the Pacific. When she did manage to drop off to sleep, she kept waking up sweating and shouting from visions of the little cheerful man, his word flow unkindly cut off, burning to death.

Another victim of her quest, her curse. Another innocent she could not save.

ANNJA WAS SO DRAGGED OUT that after disembarking at LAX, to the unspoken but unmistakable relief of the flight crew, she didn't think to turn her cell phone on until she had cleared customs.

The phone rang moments after she turned it on.

"Annja? This is Doug. Where the hell have you been?"

"About there. What do you want, Doug? I've had a long day."

"Long day? It's what, not even noon there?"

"Whatever. You wanted something?"

"Where is it?"

"Where's what?"

"Your proposal for a show on the stuff going down in Mexico, of course."

"Mexico?" She blinked. Was *Chasing History's Monsters* branching into true-crime or terrorism stories?

"Mexico. New Mexico. Old Mexico. Wherever. Where Santa Fe is."

"That'd be New Mexico, Doug. It's in a little country called the United States. Have you heard of it?" She was grateful for the enveloping blanket of sheer numbness that insulated her.

"Well, where's my show?"

"I don't know how to break this to you, Doug, but I don't think your audience is going to go for a nine-year-old kid dressed up like the baby Jesus as a *monster*."

"What? What are you on about? Hello." She heard the sound of nail clicking against the phone.

"Stop that, Doug. I hate when you do that," she said.

"I'm only talking about the biggest monster flap to hit the States in forever. I'm talking about this snowboarder who got mauled to death in the mountains out there by, lemme check my notes—what his terrified friends described as 'a giant black apelike being with glowing red eyes.' A freakin' ape, Annja. With glowing red eyes! This is television gold."

"Shit," she said.

"Annja? Are you okay? You never cuss."

"No," she said with a shudder.

"Well, jump right on that bad boy. I expect to see my e-mail inbox filling up with killer red-eyed ape data ten minutes ago."

"I'll do what I can for you, Doug," she said, "*after* I get some sleep.*"

"But—"

"No, Doug. Sleep, then ape. Or no ape." And if you throw that bimbo Kristie in my ear I'll reach through the phone and rip your tongue out.

"Whoa, whoa, calm down. Annja, sweetie, would I do that to you?" Doug said.

Did I actually say that out loud? she wondered. She almost cared.

"We're all good. Go get some sleep, Annja, honey. Then the ape. Deal?"

"Deal."

"Still friends?"

"Still friends, Doug. If you hang up now," Annja said.

The phone line went dead.

16

Albuquerque

"Please don't take this the wrong way, Annja," Byron Mondragón said, squeezing a teabag into his cup by holding it in his spoon and wrapping its string around it. "But you look as if the world is weighing you down."

She showed him a wan smile. "That's the nicest way anybody's ever told me I look like hell, Byron. Thank you."

She took a tentative bite of her *chile relleno*. It was a whole roasted green chili pod, stuffed with cheese and batter-fried. It was very good.

"So tell me something, Byron," she said when she finished a mouthful. "How is it possible for the infant Jesus to be wandering the Southwest helping out

Japanese tourists? Even if it is his ghost, he was a full-grown man when he died."

"You have to consider the notion of *timelessness*. It holds that spiritual elements, just like God Himself, are timeless. So Jesus is at one and the same time everything he was—an infant, a child, a man crucified, a man-god resurrected. He's just as much an eight-year-old Jewish kid as he is sitting at the side of God the Father. I admit, I do have to wonder about Jesus appearing in costume from twelve hundred years after he died," he said.

"Still—" He gave a little laugh. "You really have to figure that if Jesus is what they say he is, he can appear any way he likes."

"True." She stirred her refried beans meditatively with her fork. There was something in the notion of refried beans that struck her as somehow just wrong. It didn't mean they didn't taste good, though.

"Of course," he added, "that doesn't mean the Santo Niño everybody's seeing is actually Jesus. I'm just pointing out that in Catholic belief Jesus exists outside of time. So it could be him, sure. I'm not saying that it is."

"Who or what do you think the Holy Child is, then?"

He only smiled.

"Are you a Catholic?" she asked, to mask her frustration.

"I was raised that way. It doesn't mean I'm one now. Or that I'm not." He grinned mischievously. It struck her that if she was going to paint a faun, he'd be her model.

"But your paintings are mostly on religious themes," she said.

"That's an idiom I know. If anything, it's a sign of laziness, not anything profound."

"Why the Santo Niño in particular?"

"He seems handy for me to use to say some things about mankind, his relationship to the universe, the infinite. That kind of thing," he said. "Not that what I'm doing has any direct connection to what's going on in the state right now. Or anybody else's concept of the Holy Child, really. He's my current favorite subject, not necessarily what the paintings are *about*."

"What are they about?" Annja asked.

He shrugged. "Sorry. I don't feel comfortable talking about it any more than that. I feel like, if my paintings don't speak for themselves, I'm not doing my job. I'm not that good with words, anyway."

He's so innocent, she thought.

Outside the window a guy in a worn olive-drab army jacket, with a brown weed-patch of hair, stood with his back to one of the big windows and slowly raised hands in fingerless gloves out to his sides. He looked as if he were either supplicating Heaven or mimicking crucifixion. Neither the cars zooming past on Central nor the students eating at the tables on the other side of the big window paid him any heed. For some reason it gave Annja an eerie feeling.

Things just have me susceptible, she thought. She still had no idea who was after her. Besides Father Godin, she thought. And maybe Garin Braden. And perhaps even Roux. She shook her head. She had other mysteries to solve at the moment.

"How about these other sightings?" she asked him. "All these bizarre creatures. Do you have any insight on them?"

He turned sideways in the booth seat and crossed his legs. The question seemed to agitate him. "Why would you think I would?" he asked.

She shrugged. "I don't necessarily think you do," she said. "I'm just grasping at straws here. I wanted to get your, you know, your unique perception."

"I don't really know much about it. I don't really pay much attention to the news. I know from listening to my friends that people are seeing some scary things. And that poor kid got killed in the mountains north of Santa Fe, and now there seems to be some kind of media blackout about it."

That was, Annja thought, perhaps putting it mildly.

After getting back to her motel room not too long before midnight the previous night, she had collapsed straightaway into bed and slept almost around the clock. When she woke she couldn't tell from the media that anything resembling Doug's phone account to her of the evening before had ever happened at all. The local TV news program Annja put on talked about the death of the snowboarder as an accident.

When she logged on to her computer, after a shower and a restorative cup of coffee brewed in the little machine by the sink in the bathroom, she found a site linked to by Google News that spoke in terms of the state police investigating what they called "possible foul play." Yet when she clicked back to it several minutes later to recheck some details she found a new story claiming an accident.

Interesting.

Only by turning to alternative new sources was she able to find any mention at all of the killer-ape theory. It seemed a party of four—three young men and a woman—had been about to call an end to a day's snowboarding in the vicinity of an eleven-thousand-foot Sangre de Cristo peak called the Dome when something set upon them and killed one of them. Though none of the others was within a hundred yards of the victim when the attack occurred, at sunset with windblown snow screening the scene, all apparently agreed the attacker was an eight-foot-tall being, black, shaggy and vaguely humanoid. Despite the distance all three of the survivors spoke of seeing its horrible red eyes as it looked at them. Two of them recounted hearing its cry, which one described as sounding like screams and another like a baby crying.

The three survivors apparently fled several miles on foot before finding a signal to call 911 on their cell phones. Santa Fe County sheriff's officers who responded said the snowboarders were pale, hyperventilating and almost unable to speak from terror. The initial investigation was complicated by the fact that the attack seemed to have taken place just across the county line. After some back and forth between the neighboring sheriff's departments, the New Mexico State Police were called in.

THE AFTERNOON WAS actually warm as Annja walked back to her car. The only free parking space when she'd arrived to meet the artist had been a block and a half south of Central on Cornell Drive. The street was lined with little shops and apartments in somewhat shabby Southwestern stucco. And parked cars.

She found the image of Father Godin's grinning face coming back to mind. *Why?* she demanded of herself. She just kept thinking about him—his easy charm. His equally easy competence. The fact that he'd treated her with respect, not as if she were a little girl in a man's world, despite being totally an old-school European.

He knows my secret, she reminded herself forcibly. *Not to mention the fact that he tried to kill me.*

She had done some Internet research on him. It turned out he was quite notorious. He had a fascinating history. None of it was exactly confidence inspiring. Some was actively scary.

Still, Godin's smiling, homely yet charismatic face was far preferable to the image that hovered around the edge of her awareness, always looking to push inside, like a horrific specter at a banquet in a yarn by Poe or Lovecraft. The sight of that poor man burning in his own taxicab. Even if he was already dead.

Her phone rang. With a sigh of relief she flipped it open to her ear. "Annja."

"Ms. Creed? This is your doctor friend."

"Doctor?" she echoed, momentarily blank. Her first response was that this was a call from some fan of the show who had cadged her number somewhere. Maybe he offered Doug twenty bucks, she thought unkindly. She almost broke the connection then.

Almost. But the voice sounded familiar. Where earlier it had been jovial, now it was gruff.

She stopped walking. "Dr. Co—"

"Yes. Please. No more names. No questions. It is imperative that you listen. Will you?" Cogswell's voice sounded strained.

"Yes, of course."

"I have not been altogether open with you, I'm afraid. There is no more time for subterfuge. There may be no more time at all. Forces beyond your expectation are on the move. They may pose a danger to all humanity. They pose a highly specific danger to you. Do you understand?"

Her first response was to laugh. Cogswell was probably just a sad old monster crank, lonely and looking for a little drama to liven the aimless winding down of his life. Except—she clearly *was* the object of a conspiracy, of entirely deadly intent.

"Yes," she said.

"The sightings—you must study the sightings. Carefully, Annja. You have a scholar's mind. Treat them as puzzle pieces. Find how they fit—wait. Damn."

From the rush of wind into the phone it sounded as if he had turned his head momentarily away. He must be calling from a pay phone, she realized.

"Time's up," he said. "Seek the center, Annja Creed. Seek the—no! Damn your eyes, take your hands off—"

The connection died.

She stood there staring at the razor-thin flip phone in her hand. "A hoax," she said aloud. "Just theater."

But however much her mind wanted to believe that, her heart knew it lied.

17

What Annja gathered was a premature heavy snow-fall had laid a thick blanket of white over the low mountains surrounding Chimayó. Through breaks in thick cloud, the stars shone brightly enough to make the snow seem to glow.

She was still a good mile from the sanctuary when she started to see cars parked along the sides of the road. She had already come well off the beaten path here. Chimayó was solidly up into the lower reaches of the Sangre de Christos and not, from all indications, anybody's idea of a metropolis.

She parked the rented Honda on a shoulder of the road that was relatively flat and seemed to have a fair amount of bunch grass beneath the snow. The temperature was well above freezing and not likely to drop much, given the low ceiling of cloud. She had no desire to have her car bog down in mud—especially if she had to make a speedy getaway. She'd found herself having to do that with distressing frequency these days. The roots of the tough grass would tend to bind the soil and keep it from swallowing the car whole if the snow started to melt.

She got out. The air was surprisingly cold, especially after the mellow autumn afternoon she had left behind in Albuquerque. Her breath puffed out in clouds.

She made a face at the pine trees standing around with snow gleaming on their boughs. She had not brought a proper winter coat to New Mexico with her. Just days before the dig ended she had been working in shorts and halter top, and it was still flat-out hot. Even with a T-shirt and a long-sleeved flannel shirt on over it, her jacket was not likely to be terrifically warm. I'd better get moving, she thought.

Cars were rolling past her steadily if not very fast. A fair number were coming back the other way, cruising slowly, evidently in search of places to park. She chose to walk on the pavement, preferring to check behind herself frequently and moving off the road when vehicles approached rather than trying to slog along the snow-covered shoulder. Especially since that picture-postcard snow could hide all kinds of nasty pitfalls and snags to trip her or twist her ankle.

Striding briskly, she came around a forested ridge to see a double line of red taillights in front of her, with some flashlights waving a few hundred yards down the nearly static line. State police or sheriff's deputies were turning cars back. Apparently the sanctuary grounds were full enough already.

Other people made their way on foot around her.

Byron had filled her in on some curious details about the sanctuary. Aside from the chapel devoted to the Holy Child, where the faithful came to offer baby shoes and slippers, there was a pit dug behind the church. The blessed dirt was alleged to have healing properties. It had the miraculous character of never running low no matter how much was dug out. Annja suspected that was the sort of thing Dr. Lauren Perovich had been talking about when she enumerated reasons she loved living in New Mexico.

Byron had also told her of friends of his who came from the hills up here, who had served as altar boys. They'd been told to go and fill the hole with fresh sand when nobody was around. It appeared to be a semiopen secret. Yet each Easter attracted thousands of pilgrims to the sanctuary. Some walked from Albuquerque or farther away, others from Santa Fe— on their knees.

Approaching the police checkpoint, she felt a shiver run through her body that didn't have anything to do with the cold. Byron had told her that pilgrims were gathering for a memorial for the unfortunate snowboarder. They were also gathering out of fear from all the strange sightings.

As Annja got closer she could see the church was a conventional enough looking building in the Spanish Colonial style. It had a pitched roof flanked by two little square towers with belfries. A four-foot adobe wall surrounded it. An adobe-arched gate led into the courtyard. Its simplicity reflected the relative poverty and isolation of the area during the church's construction in the early 1800s. Yet, made of the local soil itself, with timber from local trees for its bones, it gave the appearance of strength, of enduring as the tiny community it served itself endured in the face of time and neglect and endemic poverty. As well as the encroachments of the modern world.

The light of candles danced above and among the gathered throng like fireflies. The effect would, under most circumstances, have put Annja in mind of a rock concert. But something about the mood of the crowd, the way everyone spoke in low, hushed tones as if in a church instead of outside it, gave it a far different feel.

No cars had been permitted to park within several hundred feet of the church. No new ones arrived, and no headlights shone. A few news crews stood off to the sides in isolated pools of glare, but otherwise very little artificial illumination was visible except a few lights from the village nearby. Annja saw a number of law-enforcement officers bundled in black fake-fur hats and dark bulky jackets with big reflective initials on the back.

The occasion itself enforced the mood. Even a group of mildly punked-out Anglo kids who had walked near Annja for the past few hundred yards, scoffing among themselves, paused to buy candles from a little card-table vendor set discreetly on the outskirts of the church grounds. Now they walked softly without speaking, their young faces showing mostly a sort of awed expectation in the lights of the fat little yellow or white votive candles they carried in gloved and mittened hands.

Annja approached the church through a grove of cruelly topped cottonwood trees, with thin shoots rising unnaturally vertically from the lopped-off stumps of once mighty limbs. Many leaves still clung to shoots and limbs, probably still colorful to judge by what she had seen of the rest of the river valley and its flanking mountains, where great stands of aspen had caught flame in autumn yellows and reds. The snow muted any color the dry leaves held, made them sodden and dull. On the outskirts of the little grove several ambulances and emergency vehicles were parked. The EMTs stood around or sat in open doors, chatting and smoking.

Annja's boots crunched in the new snow. Despite the solemnity of the setting and affair, and the overhanging sense of dread, Annja felt a certain schoolgirl's delight at walking through snow. It was still a relative novelty for her. Growing up in New Orleans she could remember seeing snow only twice, once during a freak dusting of the city, a second time during a field trip some of the girls unaccountably were taken on to Cleveland, Ohio around Thanksgiving.

"And how is our warrior maid this evening?" a voice called softly in French.

Annja turned quickly around to see the trim, erect form of Father Robert Godin standing beneath a tree with utterly bare limbs, his hands in the pockets of his scuffed leather jacket. She felt an urge to move away quickly, and another urge to walk right up and slap him.

What she did was sigh and walk toward him. She kept a hand discreetly ready to move for the butt of the compact .40-caliber Glock 23 she carried in a holster clipped at the small of her back. She was not going to be caught off guard again. It gave her range the sword lacked. Also, if she did have to defend herself its effects would be a lot easier to explain.

"I'm cold," she said. "I didn't pack for this weather. I wasn't really thinking of this as a skiing trip."

He laughed softly with that seamed hound's face of his. "Let us hope you don't find things too warm soon."

She recoiled slightly. He frowned and shook his head. "Ah. Forgive me. A careless choice of words, was it not? I intended no reference to your illustrious predecessor. But rather to the possibility of vigorous action. Please forgive a young, gauche Antwerp wharf rat grown into an old, gauche Antwerp wharf rat, if you will."

She laughed and shook her head.

She came and stood by him, all the while wondering why. Just seeking the comfort of familiar companionship, on such a strange and fraught occasion, she thought. Although the more cynical part of her wondered why she might take comfort from the presence of someone who'd recently tried, determinedly and skillfully, to disable or kill her. She was beginning to understand the complex connection between Roux and Garin a little better.

"What are you doing here?" she asked, still speaking French. It seemed a useful security measure. Many of the people she had overheard spoke Spanish, and most of the rest spoke English.

"The same as you," he said. He didn't look at her, but instead scanned the scene ceaselessly from behind his round lenses. "Something will happen here tonight."

He glanced at her then, with a hint of a smile. "Or do you pretend to yourself not to sense it?"

She shook her head, frowning. "I don't even know what the hell I'm doing here talking to you. Aside from the fact you tried to *shoot* me—"

"A misunderstanding, shall we say?"

"I did a little online research on you. You have quite the résumé. Belgian paratrooper. Congo mercenary. French Foreign Legionnaire. Ph.D.s in history and psychology."

"Please don't leave out civil engineering," he said. "That was the hardest, by far."

"Globally renowned antiterrorism expert. And if I paid attention to conspiracy sites, what you've done the past twenty years has been a lot spookier than what you did in your mercenary days, and not a lot less bloody."

His smile was abstracted. He was scanning the scene again. His weight was rotated forward on the balls of his athletic shoes. He seemed tense as a hunting dog who's caught the first whiff of prey and is straining at the leash.

"You're well advised to ignore them. Their purported facts are absurdly mistaken. If not necessarily their take on the *nature* of what I am about."

She stared at him with mingled disbelief and horror. "You admit it? You're actually a hit man for the Vatican?"

Several Latino couples passing nearby, middle-aged and dressed in their Sunday best, looked sternly over at her outburst. Fortunately, they gave no sign of understanding what Annja had said.

"My niece apologizes," Godin told them in Spanish. "She finds herself somewhat overwrought by the occasion. She is an impressionable child."

The matronly scowls softened into smiles and nods. The men smiled, too, trying not to look too closely, much less too approvingly, at the leggy young *gringa*.

The youngest of the women noticed Godin's collar. "Your blessing, Father?" she asked shyly.

"To be sure," he said warmly. He blessed them. They crossed themselves and murmured thanks.

A shadow passed over Godin's face. He set his mouth, coughed behind his lips. To Annja's look of concern he gave a quick shake of his head.

"Sometimes I don't know whether to hug you or punch you," she continued in French.

"If you don't answer my question I'm walking away," she said. "Are you really a secret enforcer from the Vatican?"

He stuck a thumb inside his collar and fished out a round silver medallion hung from a fine silver chain. She squinted to look at it in the uncertain light. Then her eyes widened in shocked surprise. It looked like a crudely struck coin. It prominently showed a cross, not of squared timbers, but logs knobbly with the stubs of hacked-off limbs. To the left the cross was flanked by a small bush, possibly laurel. To the right was an upright straight-bladed sword, not so very different from the one that answered Annja's call. Around it were inscribed tiny words.

"*Exurge domine et judica causam tuam,*" she said, half-breathlessly.

He nodded. "'Arise, O Lord, and judge thy cause,'" he translated, though certain she knew it. "Your eyes are very fine."

"I don't have to read it. That's the insignia of the Inquisition!" she exclaimed.

"Quite."

"I didn't think the holy office existed anymore."

"They have gone through some changes. And my functions are not—how shall we say?—openly acknowledged."

She took a step away from him. He laughed.

"You need have no fear of me. I have not the slightest interest in burning heretics or witches. But even as my somewhat questionable predecessors thought they were doing, I am engaged in protecting the body and soul of the church. And of humanity itself, communicant or otherwise."

"How?" she asked.

"You are familiar with the concept of spiritual warfare?" Godin asked.

"You wage spiritual warfare for the Vatican?"

He smiled. "Not exactly, my dear. When it ceases to be a metaphor—and moves beyond the purely spiritual, as it were—that is when my real work begins."

"You fight *demons?*" Annja asked.

"Demonic influences. When they break into our world and begin to cause actual destruction and pain. It happens far more frequently than you would feel comfortable believing. You will come to know the unsettling truth soon enough."

"Are you serious?"

"Only when absolutely necessary. On that subject you might consider lightening up somewhat. You're still young. There's time to head off certain tendencies toward humorlessness before they become set in the stone of habit. That frown, for example. Do you want that lovely face stuck that way?"

She laughed. Then quickly stifled herself and looked around, feeling guilty. She didn't want to incur any more matronly wrath. Nor did she wish to show disrespect for the event or the participants.

But she had little call to worry about being overheard. They stood apart from the crowd. The doors to the church itself had opened. The pilgrims had begun to file inside. Some sang hymns.

"Truce?" Godin asked.

She glared at him. "Why should I trust you?"

"Because we may face a common enemy," he said, "quite soon."

"But what about your determination to repossess your precious relic?"

"Let us say that the jury is still out about your suitability to carry it."

"What's that supposed to mean?"

"The sword does seem to have chosen you. In spite of your almost defiant refusal to believe. Yet you acquit yourself as a true warrior ought."

"Are you trying to flatter me into letting down my guard?" Annja asked.

"I would if I thought it would do any good," he said artlessly. "What do you feel are my intentions? Think deeply, if expeditiously. If you are worthy of the relic must your judgment not be of the utmost reliability?"

She thought a moment, drawing in a deep breath. The sense of responsibility his words evoked washed over her like a wave that threatened momentarily to swamp her.

No, she thought. *I must not doubt myself now.*

"You're right," she said. "I believe you're sincere. So far as the words you just spoke. So yes, I agree to a truce. But if you play me false, may your God have mercy on your soul. Because I won't hesitate to send it to him!"

He laughed and offered a black-gloved hand. She shook it firmly.

"Do you note the disparity of persons?" he asked quietly, turning away to nod at the throng entering the church. The sea of folk outside seemed scarcely diminished.

She did. The seekers gathered, at least a thousand strong, she guessed, were your proverbial all-walks-of-life assortment.

"What do you feel," Godin asked as they walked toward the church, "from the people?"

"Fear," she said without hesitation. "These people are genuinely afraid. They've come here looking for—"

She broke off, shaking her head.

Godin was not merciful. "Spiritual shelter? A sense of solace and reassurance that ruthless materialism cannot offer them?"

"I don't see how giving in to—superstition—can be a meaningful response to the problems of the world," she said.

"Why do you dismiss anything spiritual as superstition? Is that not itself a superstition from the days of the Age of Enlightenment, when men and women were defensive because professing *reason* carried genuine risks? Perhaps it's time to realize that there is no necessary conflict between science and spirituality?"

She still furrowed her brow and shook her head.

"It's just hard for me to reconcile reason with faith, with either witch-hunting righteousness or New Age goofiness."

"Which do you sense here, Annja Creed?"

"Neither," she said after a reluctant interval.

A sound trilled through the night nearby, from among the pilgrims now all around, their bodies dark or illuminated in front with the flickering orange of candlelight. Annja's face compressed in bewilderment.

"Is that the theme from *The Simpsons?*" she asked.

"I believe so," Godin said, even as the jaunty little tune cut off. To her right Annja heard classical music peal out, then a rap tune she was unfamiliar with, bars of a current chart-topper from some English band she could never bear to listen to, the epic fanfare of the *Star Wars* theme, a Kanye West song, electronic chirps and warbles in half a dozen keys. Each was soon cut off by a muted voice saying, "Hello?"

A middle-aged woman spoke into a cell phone held to her ear not fifteen feet from where Annja and Godin stood. With a start Annja recognized her as the woman she had seen in the Shed restaurant what seemed a lifetime or two ago, complaining about the furtive but frightening black creature that haunted the backyard of her expensive home on Lamy ridge.

"Saw him?" she said. "You saw the Holy Child?"

She turned to her companion, presumably her husband. "Harry, Margaret says she and Louis just parked their car and who do you think they saw? The Holy Child! He appeared right in front of them!"

"He told you what?" a man said in hasty Spanish, passing from Annja's right. Everywhere around them people were holding their hands to their ears and talking into them. More and more ringtones sounded, like a chorus of dissimilar crickets, filling the night with tinny dissonance.

"He told you to stay away from the church?" a young woman with a pierced eyebrow and lower lip said.

"—stay away—"

"—from the sanctuary?"

"—there's danger here?"

Annja looked from side to side and then at Godin's face. But his air of confident, slightly humorous detachment was gone. He was frowning.

From the church door, screams echoed.

The crowd went stiff as one. It was as if the bodies around Annja and Godin instantly changed state, like some sudden shift in crystalline structure.

A figure staggered from the open doors that led into the sanctuary. It was a priest, a stocky, middle-aged Latino. His glasses were askew on his face. He clutched the front of his surplice as if carrying some heavy load. The pristine white was splashed with some dark taint, gleaming wetly in the candlelight and the glow from thickening clouds overhead.

He fell to his knees. More screams rang from behind him, shrill as bat cries and edged with hysteria.

His arms sagged. Dark loops of entrails moistly glistening slopped out over them upon the stoop of the church.

18

Terrified people rushed from the church door. The first shied back like startled horses at the sight of the disemboweled priest lying right at their feet. The pressure of others behind thrust them forward irresistibly. Some were forced to trample the body or were crushed in the entryway in front of the door as the fleeing mob drove them onward to the gate.

The outflow met the crowd condensing and flowing in through the arched gateway. It produced swirling turbulence that filled the courtyard and jammed the gate.

Annja ran for the gate. Cell phones still went off all around. The Holy Child was a busy little apparition tonight, it appeared. People were listening to distraught friends and relatives on the other end while looking around trying to figure out why everybody around them was so upset.

Outside the courtyard wall people began to scream, seeing what was going on inside. The pressure of pilgrims seeking entry to the sanctuary ceased. People fell back from the gates in apprehension or frank terror, depending on how much they had seen.

Annja reached the gate.

It was all she could do to hold her ground against the human flood.

She glanced back. She could see Godin likewise just managing to stand and let the stampede flow around him. He had his stubby revolver out, pointed safely skyward in both gloved hands.

She vaulted to the top of the wall to the right of the quaint adobe arch over the gateway. Her feet slipped slightly in the snow. She teetered dangerously, windmilling her arms. She found her balance.

Celebrants still poured out of the church, breaking around the sealed well with the crucifix and the millstone set in the pedestal. From inside the church came shrieks that soared above the panicked noise of the crowd like a terrified bird.

Annja ran forward, pushing urgently against the crowd. She reached the doorway. The screaming from within had also ended. Cautiously she advanced inside.

As she entered, her nostrils wrinkled to a terrible stench. The church's interior was darker than outside. The low, heavy roof beams seemed to waver in the unsteady glow of candles. The shadows seemed to live. As her eyes adjusted, Annja made out uncomfortable-looking old-fashioned pews to either side of a narrow aisle.

Then her stomach clenched in horror. At the end of the aisle, in front of the gaily painted altar screen, sprawled a body dressed in black. It was an elderly lady, with a bun of gray hair. Her black pillbox hat with crepe veil had fallen to the side. The gray hair was daubed with red as by the careless stroke of a brush.

Slowly a black shape appeared from the shadows before the altar, looming above the prostrate body. It looked immense. Or was that exaggeration, conjured by adrenaline singing in her veins? The slope of its back to high withers suggested a wild boar. As did the strange grunting, gobbling sounds that seemed to emanate from its direction.

Slowly, Annja advanced.

The beast raised its head.

Dark fluid dripped from its muzzle as black lips drew back in a low snarl. The eyes that rose to chill Annja's soul glowed red in the gloom.

She formed her right hand as if grasping, extended

her will. The reassuring cool metal of the heavy hilt suddenly filled her palm and fingers.

"Come on, then," she whispered hoarsely to the horror. "Come on, and I'll send you back to Hell where you belong!"

The red eyes stared at her. The skin on her face and ears and shoulders seemed to contract in an emotion that transcended terror to achieve revulsion. This creature was *wrong*. Everything about it was wrong. It no more belonged on this Earth than the bloody horror it wrought belonged in the two-century-old air of peace and serenity within the church.

It hunched its shoulders and charged. Not at her. Rather to her left. To her despair Annja saw something she had missed before. A child in a dark winter coat and white-trimmed hat huddled against a carved and painted wooden panel in the whitewashed wall that showed the stations of the cross. The child whimpered, clearly trying to make no noise, but unable to remain silent in the face of such overwhelming terror.

Annja sprang up onto the back of a pew. It rocked beneath her weight. She began to move forward as fast as she could from seat back to seat back. She knew that she would never be able to interpose herself between the nightmare creature and its helpless prey.

The chapel echoed to a shattering boom. A second

followed. The beast flinched. It screamed like an anguished woman. It stopped its blinding rush to snap at flanks that had started to bleed.

At the first shot Annja had halted. Teetering on the back of a pew halfway to the altar, she glanced back. Father Godin strode down the aisle holding his big short-barreled revolver out in front of him in a black-gloved hand.

"The child," he called. "Hurry!"

In two springing steps Annja reached the child. The girl looked up in fear as the last pew overbalanced and toppled backward with a crash. Her olive face had gone ashen.

Annja touched down before her, holding her sword out to her right, in case the creature should charge again. As she did Godin fired twice more. He was answered by a furious, guttural snarl.

"Run, girl," Annja shouted in English. She repeated it in Spanish. The little girl stared at her as if doubtful and gave no sign of understanding.

Annja heard the scrabbling of great claws on a wooden floor polished by generations of pious feet. With no more time Annja grabbed the girl by the shoulder and propelled her bodily down the space between pews and wall. The little girl bounced off a heavy wooden pew eight or ten feet back with a little cry of pain that wrenched Annja's heart. But it seemed to snap her back to herself. In a flash she recovered her balance and raced toward the exit with surprising speed.

Godin had stopped ten feet inside the entrance. Now he advanced again to cover the little girl's retreat. He fired the final two shots in his cylinder. Behind him the child scuttled out into the snow.

Annja smelled something like burning fuel oil and hair. The monster rocked back as a little gout of flame jetted from one shoulder. A gash along its muzzle bled smoke.

Seeming to sense its tormentor was out of cartridges, it charged. Again it voiced its horrifying cry. Godin stood square. Still holding his huge revolver with its barrel tipped toward the ceiling, he reached behind him for the handgun Annja knew he carried there.

The heavy .45 slugs had not come close to incapacitating the beast. The lighter if faster 9 mm bullets would never stop the creature from smashing the Jesuit to the floor and mauling the life from him.

As the monster raced past Annja she sprang. High over it she soared. She slashed downward with her sword.

She felt it bite. The beast's scream was like a steam whistle. It put down its haunches and spun, skidding on the slick floor. It slammed into a pew and shattered it. Then it completed its turn to charge at Annja.

She had already jumped up to run toward the altar, leaping again from pew back to pew back, just succeeding in managing her balance so she didn't tip one beneath her.

The beast followed, head down. As it plowed into the pews behind her it tossed them aside with its head like a Mexican fighting bull. The hump of its back was apparently largely muscle, like a bison's, and gave its neck extraordinary strength.

She touched down on the rail before the painted altar screen. The horror overtook her. The beast tossed the last pew aside and smashed right through the rail. Annja fell over sideways as it was knocked splintering from under her.

She had to let the sword slip back to oblivion to throw out her right hand to catch herself. She felt a moment's fear she might snap wrist or forearm, crippling herself in the face of the horrific creature. Its stench filled her lungs.

She caught herself with her hand. Her right knee struck the floor hard, sending a white lance of pain stabbing through her thigh and brain.

With the sound of further splintering of heavy old wood the monster turned on her. She dove forward up the aisle. Its teeth raked her thigh, ripping open jeans and skin. She landed on her elbows, slid.

The creature jumped at her. Its mouth was a gape

of reeking scarlet-and-white teeth like curved ivory nails. She brought up her feet. The monstrous breast-bone slammed into them. She grabbed the sides of the hideous head behind the jaws, somehow, seizing great handfuls of slippery flesh and spiky fur. The beast's weight was unimaginable. It might have weighed a thousand pounds.

She didn't try to hold the crushing weight. Instead she braced and pulled as she rolled over backward, and let its own terrific momentum carry it on over the top of her in a fair approximation of a judo throw.

Black talons raked her right cheek. The wounds stung like acid. The creature landed on its back with a heavy thud.

Instantly it was up again. Annja heard Godin's pistol go off, like a string of firecrackers in the enclosed space.

The creature screamed. It lunged at Godin. He dodged aside. It ran past him out the door.

Annja picked herself up. She felt as if the aid of a cane would not be unwelcome. She felt as old as the church and much less well preserved. Her right cheek and the back of her left upper thigh stung as if from fire-ant bites.

Out the door she ran. To find herself staring down the barrels of at least a dozen handguns and shotguns pointed by terrified-looking law enforcers.

Annja just had time to throw herself down behind the cover of the sealed well as the police and sheriff's officers opened fire in a thunderous fusillade.

Chips and dust blasted from the facade of the church showered down on Annja. Most of the shots fired came nowhere near the monster. She realized with a fresh jolt that there were still people trapped in the courtyard—right in the line of heedless fire.

She shifted to a crouch to be ready to move.

The policemen's magazines all ran dry almost simultaneously. Silence fell like a lead curtain.

Annja whipped around the side of the well. She took quick stock of the situation. At least half a dozen people lay scattered around the little courtyard just in her field of view. How many of them were sensibly hugging the ground during the panicked barrage, and how many had fallen victim to the beast—or police gunfire—she did not know.

The courtyard was in chaos as people continued to flee. The police were searching frantically for the killer beast.

"What was that?" Annja asked as Godin approached her.

He merely shook his head.

"The police are taking control," Godin finally said, looking around, "and are starting to return. We should most likely absent ourselves."

"Amen to that," Annja replied. But she hesitated.

"There are injured people here," she said, gesturing at shapes lying supine in the muddy, trampled turf, beginning to stir and moan. "Shouldn't we—?"

"There are already several ambulances parked on hand," the Jesuit pointed out correctly. "More emergency personnel are undoubtedly on their way. They can help these poor ones far more efficiently than we can."

She nodded briskly—and gratefully. She had no more desire to answer official questions about all this than he appeared to. They walked quickly out the gates, turned left toward the nearest woods and walked as purposefully as they could without seeming to hurry.

So frantically had the crowd, including police and news crews, fled when the monster appeared that Annja suspected nobody had actually seen the beast's final moments. She and Godin appeared to be but two survivors eager to escape the sanctuary.

From above came the heavy chop of big rotor blades, descending fast. Out of the low ceiling of cloud a black helicopter appeared. Men wearing full-head ninja masks dangled black Nomex-clad legs from doors open in its sides. They carried machine pistols across their laps.

Powerful spotlights stabbed out from the descending Black Hawk. Bystanders raised their hands to shield their eyes from the glare. Snow from the ground swirled up all around, blown up by the downblast. It quickly shrouded the scene.

With no one paying any attention to them, Annja and Father Godin slipped in among the snowshrouded pine trees and quickly disappeared from that place of sorrow.

19

Her companion led her across the flank of a small peak overlooking the sanctuary. Beside a narrow dirt road running down a narrow valley with steep tree-crowded slopes, his vehicle waited, gleaming dully in the eerie shine between snow and cloud.

"An Escalade?" she asked as he opened the passenger door courteously for her.

"You know my order," he said. "We like to go first class."

"But what it costs to keep this boat's tank filled—"

"Expense account," he said, and closed the door.

He drove with lights out down slick mud-surfaced roads that were barely more than tracks. Even away from the sanctuary a surprising amount of light emanated from the swollen bellies of the clouds.

Perhaps they reflected the glow of nearby settlements, the blindingly illuminated tribal casinos, even Santa Fe twenty or more miles away. Annja's eyes were struggling to see well enough to drive. She wondered if Godin might be overestimating himself.

But I haven't noticed him doing much of that so far, she thought. Not everything he'd tried had worked. Against the monster—or her. But that seemed to be because he was intent upon *trying* even if odds didn't favor him, not out of cockiness.

He may be the most competent man I've ever met, she thought. "Where are we going?"

"Elsewhere," he said, not taking his eyes from the road. "The obvious egress routes from the sanctuary and the vicinity of Chimayó will be carefully watched."

"By the police?"

He chuckled. "Perhaps them, too."

She took in a deep breath and let it shudder out. She realized she was quivering like an aspen leaf in a brisk breeze. Her muscles and joints ached and the wounds in her cheek and thigh throbbed as if inflamed. "We need to talk," she said.

"Yes. Or rather, you need to listen," Godin replied.

She started to bridle at that. Then she settled back sideways on the wide seat with her arms folded tightly beneath her breasts and her nostrils flared. It was all futile display to salve her ego. He was right. She knew it.

"There is something…unexpected going on here," he said. She wondered briefly if he was driving at random through the mountains and foothills or had some plan in mind. She decided she'd just as soon not know right now.

"That's an understatement," she said.

"I have uncovered evidence of a secret research project being carried out in this vicinity. One of many, of course. But my interest is attracted by rumors my contacts in the counterterror and mercenary communities whisper in my shell-like ear. The security contract is held by a man with whom I am professionally familiar, a certain Colonel Thompson. He is a former U.S. Army Ranger and Delta Force operator. He is known for being very expensive and very good at what he does.

"He is also known as Mad Jack. He is well named. He's got a taste for methamphetamines, to give an edge to himself and his men. He has also, let us be candid, a taste for atrocity. To such an extent he was fired as a private contractor by U.S. occupation forces in Iraq for mysterious incidents late in 2003. Rumor has it he ambushed a patrol of SAS men dressed as Arabs near Ramadi and killed two of them. The U.S. command, which as you know seldom admits culpability for any misdeed or accident, would take no official corrective action. But the SAS swore vengeance. He was removed for his own safety."

"Lovely," Annja said.

"Some people believe times of great peril call for such men. Myself—having known many such—I feel the peril they themselves pose outweighs any benefit they incidentally confer on mankind. But leave that.

"The point is, if he is employed by this facility, it is doing something big. And whoever is in charge will go to literally any lengths to keep it secret."

"You mean to the extent of breaking the law," Annja said.

His only answer was a laugh.

"And you think this mysterious research may have something to do with these monster sightings?"

He turned his head toward her far enough to show her a raised eyebrow. "Sightings?"

"All right. These monsters?"

"Yes."

She shook her head. "Sounds like your typical antigovernment conspiracy theory."

"True enough," he acknowledged. "You yourself have clearly been targeted by a particularly pernicious conspiracy these past few weeks."

"What on earth do you mean?" she asked. Although she knew too well already.

"You have suffered some highly coincidental attacks recently. And I don't mean just the re-markably determined onslaught by street gangsters near that most delightful art gallery. Indeed, you seem to have appeared on the periphery of a pair of very violent, if not intrinsically common, incidents at what we might call the far ends of the Earth. Or, indeed, the former Spanish empire."

She blinked at him. She felt as if her flesh had grown chill beneath her skin. "How do you know about that?"

"I am here with the knowledge of your Department of Homeland Security. They tend to take an interest when American citizens are involved in possible terrorist incidents abroad, even peripherally. Fortunately they seemed willing to accept that you were merely an extraordinarily unlucky young woman, to turn up twice in the wrong place at such wrong times, in Mexico City and Cebu. Or perhaps they have knowledge they didn't care to share. Who can know?"

She uttered a shaky sigh. "Those aren't the only attacks," she said in a small voice. As concisely—and steadily—as she could she described the near kidnapping on the UNM campus.

"Aha," he said. "That is the most revealing incident of all."

"What do you mean?"

"That syringe likely contained a substance known as succinylcholine," he said, "or something most closely analogous. Its object is to stop your heart of an apparent heart attack. It is quite undetectable unless looked for by a forensic procedure done only in Sweden."

He glanced at her again. "A highly professional hit. And one favored by certain…official agencies engaged in unofficial activities."

She shook her head. "I can't believe my government would do such things."

"If it is any consolation, they may not be members of your government," he said. "Not directly, although acting on what they believe is its behalf. But do not deceive yourself."

He nodded his chin in a direction she thought was west. She had a reasonably good sense of direction, but the seemingly random twists and turns among the nighttime hills, and the eerie dissociative effects of coming off a colossal adrenaline jag—not to mention the totally unreal nature of the night's events—had totally scrambled it.

"Not so many miles away across these mountains they design and build devices to take the lives of millions—to extinguish, quite possibly, all life on Earth. Do you think such men would hesitate to snuff

your life, if they believed—or could convince themselves—some national interest lay at stake?"

"You speak as a man with lots of experience at ra-
tionalizing acts of violence," Annja said.

His smile was sad. "Because I am, dear lady," he
said. "Because I am."

"WHAT DO YOU MEAN it wasn't a demon?" Annja
almost screamed.

"What I said, as is my custom," Godin said, "is it
wasn't even evil. Hold still, please."

"But I felt it," she said, gritting her teeth briefly at
the stinging as he poured the hydrogen peroxide
they'd bought at a Walgreen's along the gouges torn
in the back of Annja's thigh. She lay on her belly on
the bed of a no-name motel room dressed in a long
T-shirt to allow the Jesuit to minister to her wounds.
"I *felt* its evil. It was almost tangible."

"It felt *like* evil," he said. "I felt it, too. That was
mostly its wrongness. But it was no demon. Believe
me. It was just a frightened animal. Vicious but not
evil. But it did not belong here."

"You sound like you're defending it."

"No. It attacked people. It had to die. But what we
experienced was its own fear and anger at finding
itself surrounded by creatures strange and doubtless
horrific to it. It was clearly a predator. We may have

resembled prey. And it certainly felt as horrible a sense of wrongness from us as we did from it. That, I think, is what you perceived as evil. First, empathetically, the terrible intensity of its emotion. Second, your sense of things being horribly wrong, resonating with its own."

"What do you mean, wrong? Ow."

He had given the peroxide time to work. Now he dabbed the pink-tinged white froth up with cotton balls.

"It wasn't from around here. That was surely obvious, yes?"

"But not demonic?"

"Not in the customary understanding of *demonic*. Although there are entities that might properly be so characterized who likewise sometimes penetrate our dimensions from their own."

"What do you mean?"

"Look at it this way. This at least is less unsettling to your faith in skepticism. What we fought tonight was not what you would call a supernatural entity. Although I would argue there is no such thing as supernatural, since all that exists in this world must surely be natural. However unanticipated it may be. But this creature's presence in our world was thoroughly *unnatural*. This will sting."

He poured alcohol on the tooth marks. She winced and clutched the bedspread.

"I hope that stuff kills any extradimensional microbes that thing may've left behind," Annja said.

"I suspect you have little to fear from such things," he said, daubing up the alcohol with more cotton balls. "They would be as likely to die from biting you as to do you harm, *non?* It is more terrestrial pathogens which concern me. Especially since you were not the first person the creature bit."

"True enough." She knew the diseases she most had to fear were those that might be transmitted from her fellow humans.

He put his hands on her thigh, manipulated the wound. She bit her lip. It hurt.

She was also aware that his hands were very strong. And very high up on her thigh. She felt extremely awkward and a little too vulnerable at that moment.

He's an old man, she reminded herself.

She was relieved when, with utterly clinical detachment, he told her to sit up so he could tend the claw marks on her cheek.

"I've been meaning to ask you," she said, voice distorted by the way he held her face to examine it. She was mostly speaking to take her attention off what she knew was coming. "Why a revolver?"

"No ejected empties for authorities to recover and inconveniently track," he said, reaching for the peroxide bottle on the bedside table. "It's a modified Smith & Wesson 625 in .45 Automatic Colt Pistol caliber, with a three-inch barrel and grips cut with finger grooves. An excellent piece for close-in work. Authoritative."

"I thought the authorities knew you were here. Or did you neglect to mention you were packing heat?"

"Ah, no. They are quite aware. The circumstances of my mission did not justify the risks of trying to smuggle firearms into your country illegally. Or obtain them in any contraband manner, for that matter. I am a recognized security operative, as well as fully credentialed law-enforcement officer of a sovereign nation, after all."

He had paused in what he was doing and stood beside her holding the brown plastic bottle. She felt as if she were at the dentist's office with a toothache, but trying desperately to stave off as long as possible the moment the dentist actually began to ply his drill.

"But why the precautions, then, if you're here with the blessings of Homeland Security?" she asked, still stalling. She wondered what exactly he'd told DHS he was doing here. It struck her they were unlikely to be too impressed with a demon hunter. She also knew that since the attempted assassination of Pope John Paul II, the Vatican had become obsessive about security. And of course it could afford the best. It was no surprise that Godin, coming from such an organization—not to mention his own background—should be readily accepted by his U.S. counterparts.

"First of all, I imagine you are sufficiently imaginative to envision circumstances in which I might find myself compelled to shoot someone, and your authorities would find it no less in their interests than mine not to be compelled to take official cognizance of the act."

"Yes," she said.

"Also, there are levels and layers within your government, and some very intense rivalries. There are those who would be most eager to cause trouble precisely because of my connections to DHS. Including some of your very most prominent law-enforcement agencies."

"That's hard to believe," she said.

He shrugged. "Naiveté is a charming trait, to be sure. But don't indulge yourself in it to so great an extent. No more delays, my clever girl. Hold still."

He held a rough white motel washcloth tightly against the line of her jaw to prevent peroxide from dripping down and discoloring the bedspread.

She gritted her teeth.

"These are most nasty cuts," Godin said. "Are you certain you won't let me take you to a clinic?"

"No! You aren't the only one who doesn't want to answer questions. Anyway, I'm tough."

"Indeed you are, Annja Creed. But still, it would be a shame to allow scars to disfigure such a lovely face. Especially as you are a popular television personality."

"That's what makeup's for," she said. "And I'm not that popular."

"Do not sell yourself short, my dear," Godin said, swabbing again. "There are fan sites devoted to you on the Internet."

"You're kidding!" Annja laughed and cringed simultaneously.

"Not at all," he said, tossing the used cotton ball into the wastebasket and picking up the alcohol bottle again. "You are not the only one to use the Internet to seek what is to be learned about other players in our little game."

"Great," she said throatily. "*That'll* make it easy to keep a low profile."

20

The news that morning had been full of the disaster at the candlelight vigil in Chimayó. It even made the national shows.

Impeccably chivalrous, Godin left Annja to sleep in the bed while he stretched out on the floor—somewhat melodramatically, she thought—at her feet. Although in fact the little room was not set up to make it easy to do so anyplace else. She passed a fitful night drifting in and out of sleep. Partly, what disturbed her were the dreams. Part was the sense of his proximity, the sound of his breathing, the illusion that she could feel the warmth of him from down there.

I've been alone too long, she had told herself that morning, brushing her teeth in the bathroom, using brush and paste picked up along with the first-aid supplies. But then, she'd been alone her whole life, in any way that mattered.

She emerged to find Godin doing a yoga head-stand in front of the television, his feet pointed in the air, his black trouser legs pooling midcalf. Well, there had to be *some* reason he stayed so limber. His legs were very white.

"Authorities continue their search at this hour," the newscaster was saying, "for what they describe as either a rabid mountain lion or an illegally owned melanistic leopard—often incorrectly referred to as a black panther—possibly made psychotic by abuse and neglect."

"Do mountain lions get rabies?" Annja asked aloud.

Father Godin lowered his legs and rolled easily to his feet.

"Does it matter?" he asked. "All they need is an explanation other than the truth. A rabid mountain lion is a rational explanation. Who but an equally rabid conspiracy buff would question it?"

Annja made a noise deep in her throat. Her world-view was getting rearranged in ways she didn't much like. Also she suspected she resembled his last remark.

But not even she could believe it had been a natural animal she'd fought last night.

I guess that wasn't an eagle, either, she thought.

After a subdued breakfast Godin drove her back up in the hills to where her car was parked. Dozens still dotted the roads. She wasn't the only one who had left the vicinity without recovering her vehicle, it appeared. The news had spoken repeatedly of three dead and eleven injured. She hoped these vehicles hadn't all been left by people in no shape to reclaim them. She was a lot less complacent right now about trusting what she saw on the news these days.

The sun had come out with New Mexican vengeance. Although the air was chilly the roads were clear, and most of the snow had vanished. Up ahead they could see state police utility vehicles blocking the road to the sanctuary.

Obviously investigations were continuing. She doubted either the state or the county authorities had much to do with them. She did not doubt the Black Hawk she had seen, unmarked and painted midnight-black, had belonged to some federal agency.

Unless it belonged to the security forces of some sinister and quasiprivate secret contractor.

In parting she gave Father Godin a quick but fervent hug and a quick kiss on the cheek. It seemed the least she could do. Then she got in her car and drove back to Albuquerque.

After a shower and a change of clothing Annja rooted around in the litter of random documents and sundry pocket artifacts that always seemed to accumulate on her dresser. She finally came up with the business card given her by Randy West, the burly Kiowa-looking artist who had greeted her at Chiaroscuro. He was on lunch break when she got him on his cell. She had offered, mostly from a sense of guilt, to buy him lunch in exchange for his arranging for her to meet a close friend of Byron Mondragón's at his day job stacking books at a store called Title Wave. *After* everything got sorted out.

THE YOUNG MAN'S watery blue eyes darted quickly left and right. He and Annja were alone in the science-fiction-and-fantasy stacks off in the back corner of the cheerfully lit used-book store in Albuquerque's Northeast Heights district. With only four feet of bookshelves to either side of them, making it hard for anyone to join them without being noticed, his caution struck her as excessive.

"Okay," he said. "Listen, though. You're sure nothing bad's going to happen to Byron over this, right?"

Annja had always loved the smell of used-book stores. This one didn't quite have the must of accumulated ages of antique or rare-book dealers. But she found the smell of ink and paper very pleasant. The not altogether subtle scent of weed wafting from her informant did little to detract from the effect.

"I'm not a cop and I'm not looking to cause him any trouble," she said. "And if I'm a crazy stalker, do you really think he'll mind?"

That struck her as bold and egotistical—as well as actively ridiculous—the instant it was out of her mouth.

But it seemed to hit the right chord. The young chiaroscuro art guerilla bobbed his head. He had a stiff brush of what was probably dark blond hair to start with, judging by his pale bluish-pink complexion. But the roots were currently dyed black, and it appeared that yellow paint, more or less, had been daubed on the rest with a brush. He wore a Rage against the Machine T-shirt, jeans almost falling, and rotting, off his near emaciated frame and black tennis shoes that seemed to be held together by sheer force of habit.

"All right," he said. "You're right. And I don't see what harm it'll do to tell you what you want to know."

"I am right," she said, stifling the urge to grab him and shake him.

Annja tore her eyes away from his piercing. It was a silver hoop through the septum, culminating in a pair of balls right beneath his nose. To be sure, living in New York City, she was not unaccustomed to seeing piercings, some much more exotic than this.

But this particular type always exerted a certain sickening fascination for her.

"All right," he said. "All right, I saw him."

"Who? Byron?"

"No." Another eye slide. "The Holy Child. I guess."

"What?"

"Some little kid dressed like him, anyway." The young man named Quade seemed unhappy. "It was pretty late at night. Sometimes I go there to work on things. It's about the only time I get." From Randy she knew that Quade did metal sculpture. He was also taking classes in welding at the Central New Mexico Community College.

"Go on," she said when he bogged down.

"Well, like, I totally saw him. This kid. All dressed in these funny clothes, you know? Just like those paintings Byron does. Walking around the yard all by himself late at night."

"Didn't you say anything to anyone about it?"

He seemed to shake all over rather than just his head. "I don't really believe in all this religious stuff, you know? And anyway I may have been a little stoned the time I saw him."

"Really? Well, thank you, Quade. You've been a real help," Annja said.

"Please don't tell Byron about any of this. *Please.*"

She smiled broadly. "And you are who?"

SHE WONDERED, as she hopped down from the top of the elaborate ironwork arch over the narrow front gate to the Chiaroscuro Guerrilla Art Compound, if she was trespassing. Or breaking and entering.

Feeling a little gun-shy, literally, about the street north of the gallery, she had parked on a more industrial side street a block south, just up from a gas station that was closed for the night. A quick reconnaissance on foot had convinced her that any other means of getting into the compound would be too challenging. The compound was surrounded on three sides by a nine-foot cinder-block wall topped with gleaming rolls of razor tape. Perhaps it was a relic of its days as a warehouse and industrial lot. And possibly not. There was some valuable equipment on the grounds, as well as the artwork.

Getting in this way required Annja to do so in plain view on a wide, well-lit street. Fortunately there was little traffic going by at the late hour.

It was a pleasantly cool evening, tinted with the remnants of the day's chili roasting and some other, less distinctive and also pleasant burn smells that she rather hoped came from the ritual cremation of autumn leaves. A fingernail moon did little to illuminate the area.

Inside the front gate the narrow passage between buildings was dark. She dropped into a three-point landing, froze, listened. Nothing.

She wore her dark jacket zipped over a canary-yellow T-shirt and dark blue running pants. She had opted for a compromise between low visibility and going around dressed like, well, a burglar. She figured if she bumped into anyone official she could quickly unzip her jacket. The blazing hue of her shirt would bolster the desired presumption of her innocence. She hoped.

There were some floodlights shining sloshing bright light among the buildings and the courtyard. They were not many nor particularly well sited. They left big, irregular bands and blotches of shadow ideal for slipping through on sneaky business. Annja half stood and crept forward, quietly.

Quade said Byron has a studio apartment in the southwest corner of the courtyard, she thought. That's just ahead and to the right.

She reached the end of the dark-stuccoed building to her right, paused, listened. She sensed no sign of any other life within the compound. She slipped around the corner.

A man stood scarcely six feet in front of her. She gasped.

"I believe the line is, 'We've got to stop meeting like this,'" Father Godin said.

"What are you *doing* here?" She managed to

whisper even as she struggled to breathe again. He'd startled the air clean out of her.

"Steady, there," he said softly. He shook his head in exaggerated reproof. A black watch cap covered his silver plush hair. Other than that, he was dressed as usual. "I thought we were going to be working together."

"Really. Well, it occurred to me that might not be the brightest idea for me," Annja said.

"It's better than working at cross-purposes, is it not?"

"Am I going to keep stumbling over you everywhere I go?"

She saw his grin in the darkness. "I might ask the same."

A train began to rock and clatter along the tracks a couple of blocks to the west. By its sound it had not slowed for the station a little way north.

"All right. I should've known you'd be thinking along the same lines I am. And if we're going to be following parallel lines, I'd rather have you on my side," she said begrudgingly.

He held a finger to his lips. It momentarily infuriated her.

He had turned around and started walking along the back of the brown building toward the right edge of the little courtyard. The tree and the twisted-metal sculptures went beyond bizarre to outright menacing in the random mixing of glare and shadow.

She followed. The train sounds subsided. Godin reached the long, slumpy porch shared by the apartments and paused. She moved up beside him. He glanced at her, eyes invisible behind his circular lenses. Then he walked toward Byron's door. He stopped suddenly. Coming up behind, she sensed tension in him, like a hunting dog on point.

The door of the artist's studio apartment stood open just a handsbreadth behind the swayback, fraying screen. Inside it was dark.

From within came a tortured moan.

21

Godin's right hand came out of his jacket holding his revolver. He opened the screen slowly. Annja held it for him. From somewhere he produced a short, thick flashlight. Holding it reversed in his left hand, he crossed wrists, bracing his gun hand on top. Clicking the flashlight on, he kicked open the door, stepped inward and immediately out of sight to the right.

None too sure what was expected of her, Annja went through the door after him. She did not summon the sword. It was unwieldy in close quarters, and she didn't want to accidentally stick Godin. Or Byron, should the young artist still be on his feet.

With Godin a dimly sensed presence hard on her right, her attention was drawn by the intense beam of white light angled downward. It illuminated a shape sprawled with its head toward the door. The head had wild, wavy dark hair. Parts of it seemed matted to the big, round skull.

With a cry Annja dropped to her knees beside the youth. She helped him sit up gingerly as Godin moved through the small apartment, checking room by room with light and handgun ready. She remembered vaguely that such room-clearing was supposed to be done by more than one person. But he knew what he was doing and she didn't. She deemed it best to keep out of the way and tend to Byron.

He wore a gray sweatshirt, dark sweatpants. His feet were bare. The shirt was ripped and spattered with blood. He had drying blood trailing down over his mouth, and his skin looked very pale.

"The house is clear," Godin reported, coming out of the back. He clicked off his flashlight, put it away, then moved to right a lamp on its end table and turn it on. The shade, madly askew, cast dizzying shadows up the wall.

The place looked as if a struggle had taken place, but was not thoroughly trashed or ransacked. Whatever the intruders wanted they had got without much searching. She doubted the goal was merely to rough up Byron Mondragón.

She examined him as best she could. His face was puffed to a weird asymmetric caricature of its usual fine-boned beauty. It was mottled with the blue-black of a truly brutal bruising. Though he winced frequently to her unskilled probing, she found no broken bones. Godin came and squatted next to them, shone his flashlight briefly in Byron's eyes.

"No pupil dilation," he pronounced with grim satisfaction. "No concussion, and probably no subdural hematoma to kill you in a few hours. *Bon*. You would appear to have been subjected to a thoroughly professional beating, young man."

"They seemed to know what they were doing," Byron croaked, feeling the back of his head. They were the first words he had spoken. "That didn't make it fun."

Annja rose and went through the door into the back. She found a little kitchen, fairly clean but none too tidy, with cracked gray linoleum tiles on the floor and cabinets with peeling facades. A dish rack by the sink held a jumble of plastic cups and plates. She found a roll of paper towels, ripped off a big wad and soaked them in cool water. Filling a big red plastic cup with water, she went back into the living room.

Godin sat on the couch with his elbows braced inside splayed knees and his fists to either side of his chin, studying the young artist. Annja allowed herself to notice now that the walls were a riot of paintings in a multiplicity of styles. None of them suggested

Byron's own hand to her. Most favored broad strokes and big colors. Not his trademark near obsessive precision and attention to detail.

"You like to hang your friends' artwork?" she asked, kneeling beside him and giving him the water. His hand shook slightly. She helped guide the cup to his lips.

He drank deeply, choked, coughed, drank a little more. Then he nodded as Annja began to daub blood from his face.

"They're a very talented bunch," he said. "And it's cheap. They lend it to me, then they don't have to store it. A lot of it's Billie's. She's one of the best."

"Your studio in back is in disarray, too," Godin said. "Suppose you tell us what happened."

The young artist sighed. His eyes were infinitely sad. They were also well blackened—he'd look like a raccoon by morning.

"They took him," he said.

"Who's 'he'?" Godin asked.

"Who's 'they'?" Annja asked.

He drank some more. His hand still shook. Water ran down his chin, diluting the blood that had halfway dried there. Annja availed herself of the opportunity to wipe most of it away when he lowered the cup to his lap. He was sitting cross-legged on a rumpled dusty throw rug in the center of the hardwood floor.

"I've been painting mostly from a sitting model,"

he said. He showed Annja a shy smile. "I think you suspected it from the first."

"I did," she said. Not really, she thought. But maybe. Somehow.

"As for who 'they' were—" He shrugged, then grimaced at the pain the movement caused. "*They* are whoever comes in the night to capture beings like the Santo Niño. Men in black suits with masks. And guns. Machine guns."

Annja looked quickly to Godin, who shrugged. They might have been the same men last seen descending from the clouds to the slaughter scene at Chimayó. They might just as well have come from any number of federal, state or even local agencies. Or from some government contractor. Or even been conventional if well-equipped criminals, although that seemed unlikely.

"How do you capture a being who can walk through walls?" she asked.

"They used Tasers to stun him," Byron said mournfully. "They were holding me down by then. Then they put him in a sort of sack. That's when they started to beat me so I didn't see what happened other than that they carried him out. I—I thought I heard a helicopter. But it was hard to tell with them hitting me."

"An eight-year-old boy?" Annja said, aghast. "Who on earth would Taser an eight-year-old boy?"

"Any of a number of your local American police agencies, to judge by the wire services," Father Godin said. "That would certainly explain his inability to escape."

"I think he wanted to help me," Byron said. "He couldn't. He isn't violent. He doesn't have that capability. He tried to talk to them, reason with them. But they just shot him with those darts and shocked him."

"Jesus," Annja said.

"He spoke to you?" Godin said, leaning forward slightly. He was twining his fists together between his knees now.

"Often," Byron said as Annja finished cleaning his face, or at least smearing the blood and grime around to a more consistent film. There was no hope of effecting any better cleanup with the tools at hand, so she tossed the pink-stained paper towel aside and sat back to give the young man space to breathe. And talk.

"Of what?" the priest asked.

Byron smiled sadly and shook his head. "Many things. Some of the same things he said to the people he met on the roads. He seemed sad tonight. That was strange. Usually he's very cheerful. That makes his prognostications of doom a little more shocking. If effective. He would never specify what exactly was going to happen, though. Only that it was bad.

"Other things we talked about—those were just for me. Please."

"It could be vital—"

Annja held up a hand, cutting the Jesuit off. "What is he?"

Byron's smile was magical. It lit his face. It seemed to light the room, small, cramped and dingy though it was. "A marvelous child."

"Is he—?" She could not force herself to pick a next word, much less say it. *Jesus? An alien? A remarkably clever impostor?*

A siren cut the night like a razor. It was still thin, with distance. But unmistakable. Godin stood up. "Time to go," he said.

Annja rose. Byron waved off her attempt to help him up. "I think I'll be fine here. I'd better let them take me to the hospital."

"Good idea," Godin said. "Get X-rays, in case my field-expedient diagnosis was wrong."

"Byron, this is important," Annja said. "Is there anything else you can tell us?"

"Oh, yes," Byron said. "Just before the men burst in he said to give you a message."

"*What?*" Annja was gratified, if slightly, to hear Godin utter the incredulous monosyllable in unison with her.

He nodded carefully. "He said to tell what he

called 'those who come after' to seek for him 'within three leagues' of the spot he was first found."

Godin stood by the door, poised to exit. The slight frown furrowing his brow indicated he was very upset. Puzzled but knowing no time remained, Annja joined him.

As he held the door for her, Annja's conscience twinged. She looked back at Byron, who now sat holding his head in his hands. He's hurt. He's innocent. Isn't my duty to look after him?

Byron looked up at her and smiled. "Don't worry, Annja," he said beatifically. "I'm not the one you're meant to look out for."

"Leagues?" Annja said.

Godin lay on his back on her motel-room bed with his shoes off and the backs of his hands over his eyes. "You're a historian," he said with unaccustomed asperity. "Surely you know what a league is."

He had experienced a savage coughing fit shortly after they came into the room. He had gone into the bathroom for quite a while. Even now he seemed to be slow recovering. She tried not to let herself feel concern as she sat at a round table by the floor-length curtains covering the window, waiting for her notebook PC to connect with the motel's broadband network.

"It's just not a term I'm used to hearing in everyday speech."

"What about this affair suggests the everyday?" Godin said.

She made a sound from the base of her throat and shook her head. Her insides seemed to writhe with frustration and urgency. They have the child! What are they doing to the poor little thing?

"Forget leagues," she muttered, typing furiously. She was barraging Google with sets of search terms, trying to track down all known Holy Child reports. "How the hell are we supposed to know where he was first found? We have dozens of encounter reports. Some of them are certainly phony. And how do we know how many sightings happened without anyone even reporting them? What if there's no way to find out the first time he was picked up? And does that mean this time around? In New Mexico? Or every Holy Child sighting clear back to Spain?"

"What if he does not mean being found in person?" the Jesuit asked.

She looked hard at him. "What do you mean?"

"Think back on the history of the sanctuary of Chimayó. Was there not some story associated with the miraculous discovery of the image on display there?"

She blinked. "I think you're right."

She started yet another Google search. The truth

was, she had gotten so overloaded and jaded with tracking various images and origins of the Santo Niño, literally around the world, that she had simply glossed over the Chimayó legend.

"The quickest and easiest story to check first-hand," she said, "and the last I actually follow. I have a lot to learn about this hero business."

"Life is a process of on-the-job training," Godin said.

She was worried. His voice sounded weak. *Maybe he's just showing his age.* He was not a young man, not by any means, although that fact was hard to keep in mind if one spent any time in his company. His silver-gray hair, seamed face and air of worldly experience were more than counterbalanced by his vigor, physically and mentally, and a sprightly, youthful—or perhaps ageless—spirit.

And then again the events of the past few days had Annja worn to a nub, physically and emotionally. And she *was* a remarkably fit young woman even before the sword had brought her capabilities whose full extent she had yet to learn.

"Here we go," she said, attending to the screen. "I could kick myself for spacing this out. Legend has it that some time in the 1800s a man was out plowing the fields near the town of Chimayó. His daughter told him she heard church bells ringing from underground. When he dug down he found a wooden statue of the Holy Child. It's the one kept in the chapel next to the sanctuary. The hole the father dug is where the holy dirt supposedly comes from."

She clicked back and forth between several other citations. "Basically what I get are all on the same theme, with slight variations."

She looked over to Godin. "Want to hear some other versions?"

"As the accounts are likely to bear only passing resemblance to any kind of historical accuracy," he said, "I think I shall pass."

Her shoulders sagged and her back rounded. "You don't think this has any significance?"

"I didn't say that. Whatever or whoever the Holy Child—*our* Holy Child, as it were—may be, I doubt literal history holds much importance to him."

She rocked back in her chair and tapped her fingers on the tabletop beside her computer. "I know we're pressed for time," she said, "but would you care to elaborate on that? It seems like it ought to be significant, but I'm too fuzzed to figure out where you're going."

"Understandably, my dear." He sat up, coughed slightly into a fist, shook his head. Then, seeming to rally, he went on.

"I think we can take it for granted that our Holy

Child is not literally a thirteenth-century child roaming the Earth."

"Since I seem to be stuck accepting impossibilities a lot these days," she said, "why not? Couldn't he be a ghost of the real kid who smuggled bread and water to the prisoners?"

"The shell," Godin said.

He smiled at Annja's look of puzzlement. "The golden brooch the Santo Niño wears on his cape is called a St. James shell. It was not added to portrayals of the Santo Niño until two centuries after the supposed events in Atocha."

"All right. But couldn't a ghost appear wearing it? Whatever it wanted to?" She shook her head. "Forgive me for not being too up on the habits and abilities of ghosts, since I don't believe in them and all."

"You will learn," Father Godin said with a knowing smile. "In the meantime, I believe you make my point for me. Whatever this entity is, he—I prefer to call him *he,* rather than *it,* because I am a sentimental old fool—chooses to present the appearance we see."

"Okay. I'll give you that. And so—"

"He chooses, specifically, to present himself as a figure out of legend, fraught with spiritual significance. Why is that? I suspect the full truth is as unknowable as the true mind of God. But does it not suggest that our little friend is concerned more with symbology and myth than the world of the literal and material?"

"I guess," Annja said.

She turned back to her computer and brought up a Google map for Chimayó and its environs. "But what does that really do for us? A nine-mile radius around the sanctuary is a lot of terrain."

"True. And that particular region of the Rio Grande Valley north of Santa Fe happens to be full of restricted Los Alamos satellite sites, which complicates our search. My intuition tells me wherever the Santo Niño has been taken has something to do with one of those sites."

"You think this shadowy agency—or contractor— that hired your friend Mad Jack—"

"We're hardly friends," Godin said in tones of mild reproof. "Indeed, he and I have each tried to kill the other more than once. Although those were in the course of our professional lives, and so had nothing to do with friendship one way or another."

22

She couldn't tell whether or how much the grizzled Jesuit was kidding her. She decided not to ask. "You think they're the ones who roughed up poor Byron and snatched the Holy Child?"

"You were thinking perhaps al-Qaeda?" Godin asked.

"No," Annja replied.

But she was thinking of Dr. Cogswell and his portentous warnings. She had not told Godin about the retired professor turned monster hunter. She wasn't sure why. But even now she could not bring herself to mention what Cogswell had said to her. Or how their last exchange had ended.

Yet the words of that last, interrupted call returned to ring like alarms in her brain. "You must study the sightings," he had said. "Treat them as puzzle pieces. Find how they fit…"

"Seek the center, Annja Creed," she muttered to herself.

"I beg your pardon?" Godin said.

She shook her head. Damn! A sure sign I'm wearing down—I start thinking aloud without knowing it.

She opened her geographic-information-system software.

"Okay," she said, pushing her chair back and inviting Godin to come and look. "I've got something."

He swung off the bed and came to join her. She was pleased to see that he displayed his customary vigor, and the color had come back to his cheeks. The skin looked a little tauter and less porous, too, as he leaned in close.

"I've plotted all reports of Holy Child encounters from the latest flap," she said. The screen displayed a map of New Mexico covered with a surprising number of little red dots. A sort of vague pink paramecium shape enveloped them, defining the area where sightings had occurred.

"The distribution is nowhere near circular—that Murakami case skews it all to heck and gone to the West. But look what happens if I weight by total *number* of sightings," she said.

She pressed a key. A darker pink circle appeared, much smaller. A blinking red cross indicated its geometric center.

"That's the sanctuary of Chimayó," she said. "Cool. No?"

"Indeed. But your objection would still seem to apply. A diameter of nearly twenty miles gives us a great deal of ground to cover."

She slumped back in her chair. Deflated again. "Betrayed once more by technology's bright promise."

"Wait," he said.

She looked up at him.

"What about the monster sightings?" he asked.

"What about them?"

"Can you plot them, as well?"

She felt a weird falling-elevator sensation in her throat. "You must study the sightings." She recalled Cogswell's words. "Seek the center…"

What if he was talking about the creature reports? *They* were his main interest. Monsters. Not the Holy Child.

"You know," she said, typing furiously, "you're probably almost as clever as you think you are."

"My dear, I have inhabited this mortal shell long enough, and in alarming enough circumstances, that I believe I can honestly say I know *exactly* how clever

I actually am. But as a Jesuit, might I not choose to pose as *deeming* myself more or less clever than I am? Or perhaps—"

She held up a palm. "Okay, we've just reached my maximum recommended dose of Jesuitry for one day. Feel free to run that by me tomorrow if you want. But you'd better do it early," she said.

He laughed.

She turned back to the screen and pumped her fist. "Yes! I've got you now, you little—"

She felt Godin's deceptively bland gaze upon her, and decided not to finish the sentence.

"Behold. We have the anomalous-creature reports plotted in shades of blue. Courtesy of a cryptozoology Web site that kept a running of them all."

"A wondrous thing is the Internet," Godin said drily. The variegated colors of the screen reflected on the lenses of his glasses.

"A wondrous thing is nerds." That didn't sound quite grammatical, but she was tired and on a roll. "And *here*—"

She stabbed the screen with a triumphant forefinger. It flexed slightly to her touch, momentarily distorting the image in a polychrome swirl. "The statistical center of the monster reports. *Including* the ones I was involved in."

Godin's eyebrows rose from behind his spectacles. "Just within our three-league limit," he said, "and north-northwest of the sanctuary."

Annja sucked in a deep breath and made a fretful sound, half nasal, half hum. "But we still don't have any evidence. Just circles on a computer screen. And one thing going on digs has taught me—computer projections are one thing. What's really in the ground is another."

The Jesuit smiled. "I think I've got something to contribute here." With his first two fingers extended he made a rolling gesture at her notebook computer. "If I may?"

She pushed back from the table. "Knock yourself out."

He sat in the chair across from her and swung the computer around to face him. Frowning slightly, she got up to come around and look over his shoulder.

He held up a finger.

She stopped. "You have *got* to be kidding me!"

The finger wagged. "Please. Allow me a few secrets. Or at least a little professional mystification."

She jutted her chin and scowled. Ignoring her, he began to type.

"I've had enough run-ins with guys in black helicopters," she said finally. "Don't do anything that's going to get my motel room door kicked in, okay?"

"I assure you," he said, gazing intently at the screen, "I will do nothing that is illegal. For me."

She spun and walked huffily into the bathroom to splash water on her face. "Dämn him," she said to her image in the mirror, behind a safely closed door. "I do all this awesome sleuthing, and he dismisses me as if I'm a schoolgirl."

She scowled more fiercely and flared her nostrils at herself. Then she exhaled and relaxed, laughing softly. "He's right," she said. For all the mad exigency of her curiosity it occurred to her there might be some things she was best off not seeing. Especially if they did happen to draw official interest. "And I am acting like a schoolgirl. A little bit."

She felt better when she opened the door and went back into the main room.

He had thrust himself back from the table and was sitting with long legs stretched out before him, arms folded and chin on clavicle, gazing at the screen.

"No luck?" she asked, coming around to stand behind him.

"It depends, I suppose, upon one's definition of luck."

He swiveled the PC toward her. Its screen showed an overhead shot of what looked like a farmhouse with a pitched tin roof. It was hard to tell exactly. The picture was slightly blurry. She got an impression of general disuse and disrepair.

"There is indeed an underground facility in the vicinity of our epicenter," he said. "It was built late in WWII as a Los Alamos auxiliary. Nothing so unusual in that—the Manhattan Project was scattered all over the United States."

"And we know the labs still keep numerous facilities in the area," Annja said.

"Just so. This particular facility was greatly expanded during the fifties."

"The height of Cold War paranoia."

"It was decommissioned and abandoned in the sixties. Allegedly. While its location, even its existence, were not classified per se, they were, shall we say, never publicly announced," Godin said.

"Where would you find information like that?" she asked. "Who'd keep it online, I mean? Or would you have to kill me if you told me?"

He raised a brow at her. "You must be fatigued for your originality to slip so."

"Point taken."

"Various possibilities exist. For example, a former adversary, an erstwhile Warsaw Pact nation, say, seeking to tweak an old foe." He chuckled. "Or I could be mystifying again. Americans maintain databases of such facilities as well, mostly those concerned with monitoring either government profligacy or encroachment on civil liberties. But look here."

He leaned forward to click the forward button in her browser. The picture pulled back to a view of what looked like the same farmhouse, but from either higher up or at lower magnification. The building stood, she now saw, nestled by a creek between a forested ridge and a small, blotch-shaped hill. A semitrailer was visible on a dirt road on the far side of the ridge.

"Subtle," she said.

"It is hard, in this day, to avoid entirely the scrutiny of satellites."

He clicked through more pictures, all showing vehicles of various sizes near the apparently derelict structure. "These are simple archive images for our target location. If anyone attaches particular significance to them, it is not made evident by the service I purchased them from."

A new reason occurred to her for his caginess in doing his online work out of her sight. The satellite shots apparently came from some commercial site. He may not have wanted her witnessing the details of the transaction, even if entirely aboveboard. The account he used to pay, for example, could be something she had no need to know.

She straightened up, smoothing her hair back from her forehead. It was warm in the room—she always had trouble in motel rooms, finding a balance point between gooseflesh and sweat.

"So there's our target," she said with a sigh.

"It's a leading candidate," he said.

She moved up close and put a hand on his shoulder. "Where does that leave us?" she asked.

He looked up at her with a grin. "With a job excellently done."

"I know what happened last time I asked a question like this," she said, "but what now?"

"There are certain arrangements I must make," he told her. "Give me a day. Then we shall go together to reconnoiter this mysterious farmhouse."

"But what about the child? What might they be doing to him?"

"Nothing we shall be able to rescue him from if we rush in lacking adequate preparation."

"All right," she said.

23

Through the binoculars, the dilapidated abandoned farmhouse looked like exactly that.

The vagaries of the New Mexico autumn had swept the snow almost clean off the landscape. Though the late morning was not exactly what Annja would call warm, the sun was bright, and that did the trick. Of the heavy snow that had fallen on the area two nights before, all that remained were a few drifted deposits in shaded areas, such as among the pines on the ridge from where Annja surveilled her objective.

High up in the air a dark shape drifted, wheeling against a sky like an endless well filled with blue. Whether it was an eagle or a red-tailed hawk, or some other large bird of prey, she couldn't tell. She'd never been good at identifying birds, although she enjoyed looking at them.

She turned her attention back to the farmhouse. Nothing had happened in the hour she'd been there. She had made a wide, careful circuit to reconnoiter after she arrived from parking her rented car among some trees about two miles away. She had seen no sign of any activity, nor any signs that some vast underground facility slumbered beneath the hill.

With a sigh she slung the binoculars around her neck, stood up and began walking toward the farmhouse two hundred yards away.

I'm going to feel like a fool if I ditched Robert for nothing, she thought.

The sun was warm on her face. Some big clouds hung over the mountains to the south, behind her, and also away in the northeast. Overhead the sky was clear but for some drifty cotton-ball cumulus. Little birds called to each other. As she walked down into the small valley between the forested ridge and the hill where the house stood, she passed through little clouds of near invisible midges that swarmed around her face.

The night before in the motel room, when Annja had agreed to wait a day for Godin to put his affairs in order, she had literally had her fingers crossed behind her back. She knew that was childish.

But she had known, even then, exactly what she had to do. She could not risk having his charmingly anachronistic gallantry interfere.

He had left her just before sunrise, slipping away with a quiet promise to return quickly. She had risen as soon as she was sure he was well away. She ate breakfast at a nearby Denny's, then drove north on I-25 paralleling the Rio Grande, grateful that the balloon fiesta had finally ended. The early-morning traffic heading north to day jobs in Santa Fe and Los Alamos was maddeningly slow enough.

She saw no point in trying to sneak around now. If this was an entrance to a supersecret installation of some sort, she guessed various undetectable sensors or surveillance devices would certainly have picked her up long ago. The most she could hope for was that they would take her for a casual hiker whose curiosity got the better of her sense of propriety.

The house did not look so badly decayed up close. It seemed structurally sound enough. The elevated porch was not sagging at top or bottom. Cosmetically it looked rough, with paint faded to shades of gray and peeling and the tin roof looking battered as if by hailstones. The windows were covered from the inside with plywood. The front door looked solid. And it was closed.

She slowed, frowning. "What if this *isn't* an abandoned farmhouse?" she asked herself aloud. If she went traipsing into somebody's home she was going to feel bad about it, not to mention the fact that folks hereabouts tended to keep guns near to hand. Also there was the little matter of the law calling it "breaking and entering."

From somewhere behind her she heard the sound of a baby crying.

Every muscle wound itself taut. Her pulse began to boom like Japanese drums in her ears. She stopped just feet shy of the porch and looked around.

She saw nothing. Just the placid meadows swooping with deceptive gentleness between the rises, tall, tan tufts of grass nodding in the breeze, pools of tiny white-and-pale-lavender wildflowers nodding in the sun, defiant as the bugs of the early onset, and rapid retreat, of winter. A larger insect, a horsefly perhaps, buzzed by her cheek.

The crying sound came from the same direction as before. It raised the short hairs on her arm and at her nape. She looked that way. Nothing.

The sound rose in volume and came from several directions at once. The unseen source seemed to be getting closer.

In a leap Annja was on the porch. The doorknob was dull, as if stained from hand grease and weather. It turned beneath her hand. The door opened into dim coolness that smelled of dust and mold as the blood-freezing cries rose to a crescendo behind her.

She spun and slammed the door shut. Inside was a surprisingly bright yellow lock plate with a dead-bolt toggle, visible in light slanting in over the tops of the plywood plates in the windows. She locked the door with a convulsive twist.

She stood for a moment, panting, trying to force herself to breathe regularly through flared nostrils, not through her mouth. The horrid cries had stopped. She did not think the door or walls were enough to keep the sound out.

She turned then. She stood in a short foyer with doors opening to either side into small rooms filled so far as she could see only with darkness. Ahead was deeper darkness. To her left a stairway mounted, likewise into black.

She took a red steel flashlight from her light backpack and turned it on. Its beam was narrow but intense. It gave her absurdly disproportionate comfort.

Get ahold of yourself! she admonished herself fiercely. She was tempted but did not summon the sword. It would only get in the way exploring the darkened house.

Annja rummaged in her pack again and brought out her Glock. Holding the compact flashlight in her mouth, she pulled the handgun's black slide back

enough to see the confirming silver glint of a cartridge inside. The Triton high-velocity 135-grain hol-
lowpoint bullets had proved themselves among the
world's very most effective defensive rounds against
human attackers.

She hoped not to have to test them on monsters.

Her training had not included handling flashlight
and firearm together. Not feeling confident about
using the crossed-wrist brace Godin had employed,
she held the gun at arm's length before her. With her
left hand she held the light out away from her hips.
She knew the biggest consideration in using the two
in concert was to keep her flashlight hand from
straying into her own line of fire.

She moved forward, knees flexed, shuffling so as
not to cross her legs or compromise her balance. She
passed through the open doorway ahead of her. She
found herself in a large room, longer before her than
wide, with more black rectangles of doors on the
three sides. She guessed it might have been a dining
room.

She listened intently. She could hear nothing but
the random creaking and low booming of wind of any
old house in such a setting. She thought that she
smelled less dust than she should if the place were
truly derelict. She should be raising choking clouds
of it no matter how carefully she walked.

Advancing into the room's center she felt a strange sense of dislocation ripple through her. She swayed, put hands out to her sides to steady herself. Have I been missing that much sleep? she wondered.

Something big dropped right behind her. It thumped loudly on the hardwood floorboards.

She spun, pointing the Glock. A blow struck it from her hand. A blue-white beam of light lanced directly into her dark-adjusted eyes, dazzling her.

Boots thumped all around her. She saw black forms looming with round, distorted skulls and weird, protuberant eyes. More blinding light beams converged upon her as if pinning her like an insect to a board.

"On your belly! Down-down-down!" a harsh masculine voice barked. In the glare she saw that the forms surrounding her, distorted as they were, were men in helmets, and masks and armor, all the shade of midnight. Their lights were clamped beneath the fat barrels of their assault rifles.

The flashlight was torqued from her hand as she went to her knees to obey. She was allowed to lower herself under her own power before knees descended on her shoulders to clamp her to the floorboards. The floor smelled of old wood and ancient varnish. Her arms were twisted behind her, not cruelly but without concern for her comfort. She felt plastic ties being fastened about her wrists. Then she was frisked with impersonal efficiency.

Captured! The word tolled like a bell in her brain. With a sick stirring in her stomach she recalled the fate of the previous sword bearer.

ANNJA WAS FROG-MARCHED down fifty yards of glass-walled tunnel with the occasional closed steel door to either side. She was escorted into an elevator. That they went down was all she could tell. She was marched in to face the rear, and hands on her arms prevented her turning to see any level indicators. She had no clue as to how far underground they'd descended.

She felt a slight jar beneath her feet as the door hissed open. She was marched backward and lifted bodily when she experimentally let her feet falter. She was deposited in another corridor identical to the one somewhere above. As the elevator door slid shut she was urged along at a brisk if by no means uncomfortable clip. Though no one spoke—and their faces were turned into weird, insectile shapes by their goggles and masks—their body language suggested that if she did not keep up they'd be more than happy to drag her.

She wasn't in immediate fear for her life. She knew if they wanted her dead, she'd already be there.

That they took this much trouble with her meant that she was safe. For the moment.

The size of the men's backs, already wedge shaped from weight-room bulk if not steroids, were exaggerated by the flexible armor they obviously wore beneath their black uniforms. On every back was a panel that announced in big reflective white letters, Federal Agent. It was, she thought, indicative of arrogance. It announced to all mere civilians, including lesser law enforcers such as state and local cops, that these men could act as they wished, with impunity, and bulldoze through any resistance, while conveying no actual information about their identities or that of the entity they worked for.

She also knew enough to realize that the nicety of legalism meant the words *federal agent* did not imply they were direct employees of any agency of the United States government. The words could refer to private contractors, as well. Although being driven along by them somewhere through the bowels of the Earth she couldn't see what difference it might conceivably make. They had the whip hand over her. What else mattered?

They led her to another steel door indistinguishable from the rest. Without any action on their part that she could see the door slid open as they reached it. Most fell out in the corridor as the two immediately behind her shoulders once more grasped her upper arms and steered her firmly inside.

The room was congruously paneled in glossy brown wood. Two walls were plastered baseboard to ceiling with pictures of a man whose crisply tailored suits, even with padded shoulders, could not conceal the slightness of his frame, which was in turn emphasized by the relative largeness of his head. He had thinning, slicked-back, light-colored hair and narrow features dominated by large eyeglasses. He was meeting rich and powerful men and the odd woman. The current President, the past President, the likely next one, senators and congressmen and movie stars and powerful business people smiled all around.

The man himself was standing and moving around a huge mahogany desk. In his dark-blue suit he looked even weedier and frailer than in the pictures, and his blue eyes were surrounded by bruise-colored bags behind his eyeglasses, as if he hadn't slept in days. But his smile was as large and patently phony as in his photos.

"Ah, Ms. Creed," he said. His voice was a bit high-pitched, but beautifully modulated, as if a great tenor had taught him to sing his words. "Believe me when I say it is a pleasure to make your acquaintance. You prove yourself a most resourceful young woman."

He held out his hand.

"Stand down!" snapped the man who stood to the side of the landing-strip desk. He was a big, red-faced man in desert-camouflage battledress without decoration or rank markings she could see. He had a peculiar sort of Mohawk strip of somewhat unruly straw-colored hair on top of his head, an affectation meant, she supposed, to make him resemble a World War II paratrooper. In spite of the middle-aged paunch pushing the front of his mottled-brown-and-gray blouse out over a Ripstop belt, he showed an impressive rack of shoulder and chest. He was obviously fit and muscular even if not as trim as he could be.

Annja could not help wondering, If he's into speed, how does he maintain that much gut?

Her escorts released Annja's biceps. "Cut her loose," the big soldier-for-hire ordered. She heard a snap behind her, felt the plastic restraints drop from her wrists. Each began to tingle as long interrupted blood flow resumed.

She flexed her hands while resolutely looking into the eyes of the man in the dark suit and ignoring his proffered hand.

He smiled regretfully and withdrew it. "Ah. I suppose not. And who can blame you. Well. I am Dr. Oliver Hanratty, director of this facility. The large, authoritative gentleman in the uniform is our chief of security, Colonel Jack Thompson. And here—" he half turned to nod to an older man pushing his bulk up from a chair to Annja's right "—is our distinguished chief scientist, Dr. Nils Bergstrom."

Annja nodded curtly. She'd allowed herself to look at Bergstrom, as if accepting the introduction, then looked back at Hanratty as quickly as she could without being obvious.

She did not want to risk betraying herself by letting her eyes linger too long on Bergstrom.

She'd already spotted retired professor and current monster hunter Dr. Raywood Cogswell.

24

"It's all bullshit, Creed," Thompson said in a voice like a nail gun. She doubted he could bring himself to say anything that didn't sound like a command. "We're not glad to see you and we don't respect your resourcefulness and determination. A damned pain in the ass is all you are."

Hanratty's eyelids fluttered behind his lenses. His lips twisted in a weak, moist smile. "Now, now, Ms. Creed. Please don't take our Colonel Thompson too seriously. He seems to feel a certain bluster befits his position."

"Bluster, my ass. Why the hell didn't you back off after all the warnings you got?"

"Warnings?" she asked.

"That parking lot at UNM?" he said. "Mexico

City? The Philippines? That hippie art gallery in Albuquerque? Your little artist friend. Did those slip your alleged mind?"

"They seemed more like assassination attempts to me," she said coolly. She thought it important to show him his bluster could not intimidate her.

"Didn't it ever penetrate that thick head that if you were pissing people off that bad, it might be a good idea to jump back?" Thompson raged.

"Now, now," Hanratty said mildly, fluttering a pale, well-manicured hand at his security chief on his way back to the desk. "There's no call to take such a tone with our guest."

Glaring, his face even redder than it had been when she first walked in, Mad Jack subsided with the good grace of a junkyard dog who'd had his leash yanked hard. It did not escape Annja's notice that Hanratty had refrained from yanking the lead until after Thompson got to establish his bad cop credentials.

Hanratty smiled. "Would you care to sit down, Ms. Creed?" he asked, indicating a chair across from his desk.

"Do I have a choice?"

"Of course, of course." Hanratty bounced his head like a bobble-head doll.

"Then I'll sit." She slid into the chair and tried to

relax. It was not so much for the impression she gave her captors. She knew, especially from her study of meditation and martial arts, that allowing herself to remain in a state of tension would only drain her and tighten her up so neither mind nor body could respond with rapid flexibility should the opportunity arise.

"I'm sure you will understand, Ms. Creed," Hanratty said, "that we regret the necessity of constraining your person—as well as the unfortunate incidents to which my esteemed associate referred. You must understand our position, though. We are engaged in research of the utmost importance to our nation, especially engaged as we are in a generations-long war on terror."

"Cut to the chase," Annja said. "What's with the monsters? I'm presuming they're yours."

Cogswell shrugged his big shoulders. He was dressed in the same knobbly houndstooth coat he had worn when she met him, although his waistcoat and tie were of more subdued shades. "Our experiments have enjoyed varied levels of success."

He tipped his big, round, bristle-haired head briefly to the side. "There have been various levels of side effects. Ranging, primarily, from alarming to extremely alarming."

"Why are you running your damned mouth like

that, Bergstrom?" Thompson shouted. "She's a god-damned TV reporter. You want to give her the frigging story?"

Annja scowled at that characterization of her. She found it even more demeaning than unflattering comparisons with Kristie Chatham. She said nothing. There was no point in letting him know he'd scored off her.

"Now, Nils," Hanratty said, "I know you love your theatrics. But please don't exaggerate the situation quite so excessively." He clasped his hands on the old-fashioned green blotter before him and turned to Annja. "Of course everything is really going well with the project. Quite well. Indeed, we are ahead of schedule. It's just that there have been certain un-avoidable side effects—"

"Like three dead and eleven injured at the sanctuary?"

His brows came together like a large caterpillar. "Well, with the best of will, you surely cannot expect us to make omelets without breaking a few eggs. Can you?"

"I always hated that cliché," Annja said. "People aren't eggs. Multiple homicides aren't omelets. Maybe I just don't see the connection."

"You have an awfully smart damned mouth on you for a woman in your position," Thompson said, though at reduced volume from before.

"How unexpected of you to notice," she said, making him blink and then glare. "My intelligence, I mean. So you're somehow letting these horrors loose to terrorize the population, Dr. Hanratty. That doesn't sound to me as if you've got the situation all under control. What have you done to the child?" she asked.

Thompson barked a laugh.

"You must be dumber than you look, if you bought all that 'baby Jesus' shit," he said.

"We don't really have words to describe our experiments," Cogswell said. "What we see, quite candidly, are results far in excess of our ability to comprehend their causes."

"So what you're telling me, Doctor," she said, looking directly at Bergstrom, "is that you are messing with forces you don't understand."

His black eyes looked right back into her amber-green ones. "Precisely."

"Wonks," Thompson said in disgust. "What the hell good are you?"

"Fortunately that determination lies in the provenance of people with larger and more powerful heads," Bergstrom said, "if only marginally."

Thompson's red face purpled. "Listen, you overstuffed sack of ivory-tower shit—"

"Gentlemen, please," Hanratty said with a briskness that surprised Annja.

"We do not wish to give our guest the impression of discord among our ranks, do we?" Hanratty said.

"In any event," Bergstrom said to Annja, "we've run into some trouble with anomalous creatures that have appeared in various parts of the state."

She leaned back in her chair and folded her arms. "So why are you telling me this, anyway? Why is this happening? I'm not your guest. I'm a prisoner."

Mad Jack Thompson's laugh was harsh as a steel brush on her bare cheek. "We want you in the right frame of mind when we interrogate you," he said.

"It's important, Ms. Creed," Hanratty said apologetically, polishing his spectacles with a monogrammed silk handkerchief. "You must understand the vital importance of this project…"

"Oh, stuff it," Thompson said. "After Little Miss Muffet here gets a taste of our meds, she'll be only too eager to tell us everything she knows."

He turned to Annja. "I want to know how you found out about us, who you told. Everything. We're going to discover every secret you're keeping."

25

Carefully Annja paced the stark white cell. Four steps by four. Allowing for detours around the bed and the sink and the chrome-steel toilet, all seeming to sprout from the floor on gleaming metal pedestals.

The padding on the bed was just that, a pad, plush enough, with a pillow-like protrusion at the head end, but integral with the pedestal bed. It was covered with some soft, resilient material that resisted a tentative attempt to tear it with her fingernails. Certain that she was being constantly watched by hidden cameras, she tried nothing too extreme. The point was there was nothing, sheet or otherwise, that a captive might tear into strips to hang herself.

Not that much presented itself to hang oneself

from. The light, which she had not seen dim and suspected never did, was inset in the ceiling, no doubt shielded with polycarbonate or some other unbreakable synthetic. The air vents were high up, covered with heavy grilles well bolted, and too small in any event to pass any body larger than a house cat. There would be no escape by crawling through the HVAC ducts.

Another broken promise of action movies, she thought. She was beginning to wonder if it had been such a hot idea to let herself get caught.

She sat on the floor with her back to the metal base of the bed facing the door. The white floor tiles gave slightly beneath her.

She was in total confusion over Cogswell. Was this all some bizarre setup on his part? He had to know that his role in feeding her information about the secret facility and its bizarre research—which, however elliptical, had proved all too accurate— would come out sooner or later once they subjected her to questioning under drugs.

It was my decision to blunder in and get captured, intending to bust loose at the first opportunity, find the Santo Niño and spring us both. Was it possible Cogswell—when he was acting as Cogswell, anyway—had somehow intended to put that thought in her mind all along?

She shook her head. It didn't make much practical difference at this point.

She wasn't hopelessly trapped in the cell. But if she somehow hacked her way out, the facility was swarming with heavily armed men, no doubt too many for her to fight off. Especially if she roused the whole place, while betraying the existence of the sword to those hidden cameras. She had little sensible choice but to bide her time and wait for some opening.

She closed her eyes. It was cool in the cell, even with her jacket still on. But not cold enough to be a distraction. Drawing in a deep abdominal breath, she blanked herself in meditation.

"WAKEY-WAKEY."

Never asleep, Annja had returned to full awareness from her deep meditative state the instant the door of her cell hissed open. She opened her eyes.

The derisive voice, vaguely familiar, had sounded somehow wrong to Annja. Now she saw why.

Three men had entered her cell. They were young and lean and dressed in black security uniforms. They also looked as if they had wandered right out of the infirmary.

"Remember me, shweetie?" said the man who had spoken first. He had black hair and held himself so rigidly upright that Annja suspected he wore some kind of brace beneath his shirt. The distortion in his speech came from the obvious fact his jaw was wired shut.

He and his companions looked different from the last time she'd seen them. They were cleaned up considerably, if visibly the worse for wear.

"Yes," she said. "I do. I thought I broke your neck with that spin kick. Too bad I didn't."

"Yeah," the gangly blond guy on his right said. Like his leader's, his beard had been shaved clean. "Too bad for you." Aside from a certain puffiness to what would naturally have been somewhat craggy features, he looked the least damaged. Until he grinned. The whistle of excess air escaping when he spoke indicated that the gap in his top teeth was fully authentic this time.

"You should have made sure of us, sweet cheeks," the third member of the trio said. He was a wiry Latino with a flexible cast on his right wrist.

"I have a tendency to be merciful," she said. "I won't make the same mistake twice."

"Yeah, well, the shoe is on the other foot here," the gap-toothed blonde said.

"Won't Mad Jack have a thing or two to say if you damage the merchandise?" Annja said.

They passed a look around and laughed. "Shit,

girly, he sent us here," the Latino said. "He told us to make sure you spill your guts."

The dark-haired leader's grin bared his wired teeth. It was a terrible expression.

Annja decided the time had come to act.

As the leader moved in, Annja reached out and grabbed him by the broken lower jaw. She squeezed. His dark eyes flew wide and he squealed with pain. He tried to slash at her with his fingernails.

She pushed him away from her. Hard. The back of his head struck the side of the stainless-steel sink with a crunch. His lanky body spasmed. His eyes rolled up and locked there. He slid to the floor. There was a blood-smeared dent in the side of the sink.

The blond man launched an overhand right at her face. She leaned her upper body back. His knuckles lanced off her left cheekbone.

The sword appeared in her hand. She heard the Latino cry a shrill, wordless warning.

It was too late for the blond man. Before he could recover from throwing himself off balance with his mostly missed punch, the sword came whistling down.

Its tip raked a bloody furrow down his cheek as the blade sliced his shoulder at an angle. He reeled back, spraying blood from his arm. Annja spun to her right, lashing out horizontally. The sword slashed the

Latino across his screaming mouth. She stepped into him and cut him down. Then she turned back to the blond man. Clutching at his shoulder with blood spurting through his fingers, he had backed against the wall by the still open cell door. He sidled toward it, leaving a wide smear of blood, shockingly brilliant red. Then he went limp.

She looked around the cell at the fallen men.

"I told you," she said. "I wasn't going to make the mistake of sparing you twice."

26

She sprang into the corridor with the sword ready in both hands. Her peripheral vision showed no sign of anyone to the left or right. She looked both ways quickly, confirming that she was alone. She began to walk forward.

Her nerves were jangled and her blood sang with fury. She felt as if she were about to burst with anger. And the horror of the fate she had narrowly escaped. There was something about having that hostility—that foul, purely evil intent—directed at her that was like a strange and violent drug.

She knew she had to control the rage, to keep herself from turning into a soulless killing machine, or worse, a monster who presumed to judge and execute any and all unlucky enough to cross her path.

That was the burden she must bear as she carried the sword.

To her left was a small alcove. She stopped, frowning. For a moment she stood, breathing deeply. Then she plunged inside.

"You're a welcome sight," Dr. Nils Bergstrom said from the bed of his cell. It was identical to the one she had just escaped.

He had his coat off. He sat with his legs dangling over the side. His manner was mild.

He raised a dark brow at the sword she still held in her hand. "So our gangster friends were neither confabulating nor lying," he said. "You really do carry a medieval-style broadsword with you."

"Early Renaissance, actually," she said, wondering if it mattered.

He passed it off with an easy gesture. "Outside my area of expertise. Remarkable how you manage to carry it without discovery."

"Why are you in a cell?" she asked.

"Apparently I failed to cover my tracks as well as I thought," he said. "Or perhaps our friend Mad Jack was merely allowing me enough rope to well and truly hang myself before he yanked it tight. He's not as stupid as he acts. Which would beggar possibility, of course."

"Why did you pretend to be somebody named

Raywood Cogswell? Who is Raywood Cogswell? And why did you get in touch with me?"

"I did not pretend, my dear," he said. "Raywood Cogswell is me. Rather, a fictitious identity concocted for me."

"Why?" Annja asked.

"To position me to spread disinformation. Are you familiar with the phrase 'giggle spin'? Enthusiasts of the paranormal frequently stray uncomfortably near to truths we would just as soon no one learn. Occasionally they trip and fall right over them. We find it useful to have our people inside the movement, as it were. To spread silly stories, to plant superficially convincing evidence that can subsequently be proved to be false, in general to muddy the waters. Ridicule and sheer obfuscation are among the most potent weapons for protecting classified information."

She drew in a deep breath and let it hiss out between pursed lips. "We're getting off track here. Why did you get in touch with me?"

"I'd hoped you might use your television connections to shed light on what this facility is doing. Get the program canceled."

"Canceled? But isn't this a U.S. government black project?" Annja asked.

"Yes and no," Bergstrom said. "The program is

illegal. Or at least deniable. The black-budget money being spent here is earmarked for other researches. The Department of Defense would shut us down at once if they realized what we were up to."

He sighed. "Once I thought this research was important and worthwhile. Unfortunately, the situation is deteriorating so rapidly that time has simply run out on us."

"What do you mean by that?"

Another wave of strangeness like the one she had felt in the abandoned farmhouse passed through her. She winced, swayed.

Klaxon-style horns began to blare, a cacophony of rising-falling sounds that grated, as though across the exposed nerves of broken teeth. Annja jumped, looked frantically about. The sword seemed to quiver like a living thing in her hand, eager to strike.

"Don't worry, young lady," Bergstrom said, standing up and straightening his clothing. "That is not for us. Although it concerns us rather intimately."

"What is it?"

"Containment has been breached," he said. "The creatures are loose inside the facility now." His cell door opened, triggered by the alarms.

She stared at him. "We should go now."

"Yes."

BERGSTROM EXPLAINED as he led her through a trail of slick-walled passageways and narrow stairs. She had put the sword away and he didn't seem surprised. As he predicted, the scientists and technicians they encountered were far too preoccupied to pay them any mind, with the breach alarms still grinding away. His own detention was unlikely to be widely known. Customary practice within the facility was for those who became dissatisfied—or dissatisfactory—to disappear. Asking questions was not encouraged.

Any guards they encountered would, he predicted, have at least a fifty-fifty chance of ignoring them, as well. She was content to take him at his word. She didn't see she had much choice, especially since wandering the halls brandishing a four-foot broadsword could only lead to questions.

"Actually," Bergstrom said, in answer to a question Annja took a personal interest in, "you caught Thompson's eye first. We have—he has—a roomful of information-security nerds who constantly scan the Net for signs of security breaches. When our black flyer manifested near your dig site, and the report subsequently leaked out, one of them spotted it and made the connection between you and that television series. Our Mad Colonel leaped to the conclusion that you were onto us, and preparing to do a feature on the program. Which naturally could not be permitted. So in his inimitable style he shot from the hip, sent three of his removal specialists after you. I fear he's partial to certain chemical assistance that doesn't always lead to calm reflection."

"So I've heard," Annja said grimly.

"Hanratty was terribly distressed when he found out. Dear Oliver is always flustered when confronted with the…less agreeable aspects of our work. But once an attempt had been made, and Thompson's ace operators came back in dire need of repair, he felt he had no choice but to allow Mad Jack to try to finish what he had so impetuously started."

A gaggle of techs in pastel jumpsuits emerged from a door on their right. They chattered nervously as they walked quickly past in the other direction.

"I'm sure it's a drill," said the stocky black woman in lime-green coveralls with the plastic cap on her head. "It's always a drill."

"But what if it's not this time?" asked her similarly clad white male companion, flapping his hands.

"It's always a drill."

"As top scientist for the program, I naturally found out what was happening as soon as the director did. He isn't capable of making a decision without having others around him to tell him what to do. Unfortunately, Thompson can yell a good deal louder than I can. I decided to make my own attempts to contact you."

"You didn't warn me," she said.

"Would you have listened?"

"I suppose not. And that last phone call?"

"Matters were coming to a head here. I wanted to goad you to action."

"So you weren't interrupted by Thompson's goons?"

He smiled. "I performed quite convincingly, did I not? Of course, years of playing Cogswell gave me ample practice for my thespian skills."

"If you were the top scientist here," she said, "why did you want to shut it down?"

Before he could answer, a pair of black-clad guards turned from a side passage on the run, thirty yards ahead, and made straight for them.

27

The guards wore their bulky black uniforms and helmets, and carried weapons slung by straps they kept tense with thumbs hooked through them to prevent the steel-shod butts of their machine pistols from pounding their kidneys. They ran straight toward the unlikely pair, the rogue scientist and the tall young woman in hiking clothes.

Annja began to curl her hand. "Wait," Bergstrom said conversationally.

The two black-clad operators trotted by without a glance at them.

"Quickly, now," he said. "Our research led us out of our depth. Experimenting with DNA, we found it easier to breed hybrid animals than we'd dreamed. Controlling the breaches was the problem. Among other things, it has proved difficult to confine the beast to the facility."

He sighed. His exertion had him breathing heavily. He was also limping slightly, favoring his right leg. "In some cases there have been…controlled breaches. Or at least deliberate ones."

"Why?"

"In part to test our ability to control the creatures themselves. These experiments have not produced many positive results. Also, in order to test our ability to control the release of potentially damaging information, and manage public perceptions of it."

"You mean you were putting innocent people at risk to test how well you could *lie* to them?" Annja said.

"Yes. We are not the first. Nor the only. We will not be the last."

"That wasn't what made you decide to blow the whistle?"

"Alas, no."

"What could, if not something like that?"

"The fear that we are threatening the fabric of reality itself. Between Hanratty's bland ambition and that psychotic Thompson's growing influence over him, all my warnings were ignored. And I became increasingly desperate. If those creatures begin breeding in the wild…" He shuddered.

"It's one thing to joke about creating the means of destroying the world, and quite another to confront the immediate risk of actually doing so."

"What about the Holy Child sightings?" Annja asked.

"I don't know. That had nothing to do with us," he said.

She frowned and wanted to question that. But approaching a cross passage, he raised a hand to stop her.

"And now time and answers are alike at an end. What remains is action. There may yet be time."

"To prevent what?"

"The world being overrun with deadly monsters," he said.

She looked at him. The alarms continued their cacophony. The corridors were crowded with excited technicians. No one paid the least attention to them.

She wondered, briefly, what was really going on. What did "containment breach" actually mean? But she took Bergstrom at his word. She had little choice.

"All right," she said. "Action I can do. What now?"

"Around this corner is the entrance to a control station. It will likely be guarded inside and out. You must get me inside at all costs."

"And then?"

"You must get out of this facility," he said, "and as far away as you can, as fast as you can."

She drew the sword to her. Bergstrom took a step back.

"Marvelous," he breathed. "What a terrible shame I shall never get to study the means whereby you do that!"

She put the back of her shoulders to the wall. It felt cold and hard through the fabric of her shirt and jacket. She took a deep breath and spun into the cross corridor.

A score of people occupied the passage. They moved in both directions in clumps. She had no idea where they were going or what they were doing.

A pair of men in black stood thirty yards down from her. They had MP-5s in their gloved hands. Their body language suggested they were distrustful of the technicians leavened with lab-coated scientists.

The one farthest from Annja noticed her first. He stepped into the middle of the passage, shouldering his weapon. Startled technicians began to part, screaming, to either side.

They didn't move quickly enough. He opened fire. The sound suppressor kept the burst from being intolerably loud in the confines of the corridor. But it still sounded, like an unmuffled motorcycle engine.

Some of the screams went up in timbre—or stopped. The guard was spraying bullets toward Annja without caring who or what was in the way.

She was running but not fast enough to give her
any decent chance of closing with him before he put
a bullet into her, even though the panicked technicians made her a harder target. The guard's companion turned and began shooting from the hip, right into
the crowd, evoking more screams and causing two
technicians to fall right in front of her.

On impulse she jumped. She straightened her
body so that, just for an instant, she flew nearly horizontal. She lunged with the sword. She felt the blade
bite deep, heard a hoarse cry of pain.

She landed heavily, pulling the sword with her
as she fell.

The man had collapsed, his weapon stilled. She
wheeled to find the other shooter, hunched in pain,
the victim of a ricocheted bullet.

She swung her right foot and kicked away his
weapon. He didn't attempt to stop her.

Some of the fleeing personnel had dropped to the
floor. Now they were picking themselves up—those
that could. Several lay moaning. At least four lay
without moving or making any noise at all.

Through the wounded people Dr. Bergstrom made
his way. He was walking bent over, clutching the
right side of his substantial belly with his hand. The
shirt beneath was dyed bright pink.

"You're hit," Annja said.

"I'll live," he replied conversationally enough, although his hairline was beaded with sweat. "Long enough at least."

She found herself standing outside a sealed door. There was a keypad with a slot mounted next to it. It offered nothing she could use.

"What now?" she asked as Bergstrom limped up.

He raised a hand holding a plastic card toward the pad.

"No biometrics?" she asked as he swiped its magnetic strip down the slot.

"No money," he said. "Our budget was far from unlimited. Our security was assumed."

He punched a quick five-number combination. "Get ready," he said, through now gritted teeth.

The door slid open. A guard stood there with a Beretta in his hand.

Annja head-butted him in the face. He staggered back clutching his flattened nose. A second guard was fumbling the strap of an MP-5 off his shoulder. He never got the chance to finish.

A technician in powder blue rose from a swivel chair in front of a bank of monitors. He stared in horror at Annja, standing with the sword still in hand. Then his eyes slid past her.

"Dr. Bergstrom!" he exclaimed.

"Get out, Yee," Bergstrom said. His teeth were individually outlined in scarlet. The technician paled as he saw this, then darted past him and out into the corridor. As he did, a fresh spate of screams wafted in past him.

"It has begun," Bergstrom said, leaning with a hand on the table in front of the console and frowning at the monitors. Whether he referred to what he saw or the terrified cries from outside the small room Annja couldn't tell.

He looked at her. His features were rigidly held against the pain of his wound. She guessed the anesthetic effects of wound shock were already beginning to wear through.

"You must go now, as well," he said. "Turn right, down the corridor for forty yards. Left into the stairwell. Go up two flights. It will put you in a truck tunnel that leads to the outside. Remember what I told you—fast and far!"

28

A black thing flew level, straight for her eyes. Black wings seemed to span the corridor. All she could make out of the head were the two huge red eyes that shone upon her like malevolent lamps.

Annja screamed in response. She met it with a wild forehand slash. The blade caught the left eye, extinguishing its glare. She sheared clear through the beast, her blade exiting just behind the right wing. It fell thrashing and shrieking.

She ran, vaulting writhing black ruin. Before her a creature the size and shape of a natural wolf, but with a coat of that light-sucking black, looked up from the torn-out throat of the hapless Yee with red, glowing eyes. She raised her sword. But a second creature, longer and leaner and feline in outline and sinuous motion, attacked the wolf from behind. Squalling and snarling, they turned into a furious ball of fangs and claws. She ran past them.

Without looking back she sprinted to the door to the stairs, yanked it open and went rabbiting up.

The truck tunnel was all Bergstrom had suggested and more. It was another glass-walled circular bore big enough to accommodate a full semitrailer rig.

Annja began to realize how the huge facility was supplied. The tunnel was so wide that various crates and containers were stacked high to either side of the level floor, or roadway. Two hundred yards away she could see double concrete doors illuminated by the jittering light of fluorescents.

There was just one thing wrong with the tunnel that Annja could see. It was full of screaming red-eyed men fighting screaming red-eyed monsters.

The battle lines were anything but clear-cut. The black monsters seemed as ferociously—or desperately—eager to battle one another as the black-clad humans. The humans, meanwhile, seemed almost as inclined to turn their guns, knives and fists on one another as on the animal horrors.

Guns flashed and roared. Men howled as their flesh was torn by great taloned paws. Empty cartridge cases crashed on fused stone, adding a madly whimsical wind-chime effect to the aural horror show.

Annja climbed to the top of a stack of crates. On the far side a security operator stood firing down into the melee. As she moved toward him he was distracted. Two wolflike creatures seized him by an arm and a leg and commenced a snarling tug-of-war.

With a shrill scream something glided toward her from the ceiling. She ducked out of its way. It wheeled, buffeted her with its wings. She took a stunning blow across the face, reeled. She felt her right heel come down on nothing, just caught herself with the corrugated toe of her shoe.

A wing struck her again. She windmilled her arms briefly. Her balance training saved her; she caught herself, lashed out with the sword as she moved toward the middle of the flat upper surface. The blade slashed a leading edge of wing. The creature recoiled with a shriek. Annja ran the sword through its belly.

She twisted her blade and tore it free. The winged attacker fell brokenly to the floor.

Bullets smashed into crates below Annja. She dropped flat. More bullets cracked over her head to punch holes through the plastic walls.

She crawled across more containers. She could see a smaller door beside the outsize truck doors. She began to hope she might see the sun again.

As she reached the end of the row she jumped down. As she hit the ground she encountered an eight-foot apelike creature. She ran straight at the monster, which seemed momentarily stunned by her appearance out of nowhere. She cut it across the belly, left and right then darted past.

A man with his helmet askew confronted her with a mad eye glaring through the combat sights of his shouldered MP-5. "You bitch," he shouted. "I'll—"

She raced past him to his left. As she did she snatched his loose-hanging sling with her left hand. Her momentum as she passed tore the weapon right out of his gloved hands and cracked him sharply across the face. She pulled him over backward to slam him heavily on his back on the stone. The thin rubber mat on the walkway did nothing to cushion his landing.

The air was knocked out of him but his helmet protected his head. He wasn't even stunned. As he moved to rise, one of the wolflike creatures pounced and pinned the man's lower leg between black, slavering jaws.

Annja reached the door with a last grateful bound. Her lungs burned so fiercely she wondered if some toxic fumes had been released. She reached for the door handle.

There wasn't one. There was another alphanumeric keypad. She was trapped without the code at the mouth of a seething bottle of raging violence.

A low sobbing sound, deceptively soft, made Annja spin away from the door.

A trio of catlike monsters approached her, slinking with their bristling belly fur almost brushing the tunnel floor. Their fangs gleamed against their black faces. Great, she thought, they're smart enough to flank me.

Her best shot was to try to race past one and disable it with a sword-cut. But that would mean charging right back into the midst of the frenzied man-and-monster scrum. She steeled herself to do it anyway.

Just then the smaller door blew off its hinges behind her with an end-of-the-world crash.

29

Dr. Nils Bergstrom looked away from his monitor at last. Mad Jack Thompson crawled, broken and bloodied, toward him. With arms outstretched, desperately clinging to the sides of the door, he screamed in terror. A black immensity filled the doorway behind him, trying to drag him out into the corridor.

Thompson's mad eyes met Bergstrom. "Help me," the security chief groaned. "Please."

Bergstrom's smile was ghastly red. "As you wish."

Turning back to his keyboard, he pressed Enter.

ANNJA STAGGERED from the force of the explosion. The door flew off to one side, smashing to the floor ten feet away.

Annja turned and was through the door like a shot.

Outside, the sun had already dropped behind the high peaks to the west, filling the valley with purple-gray shadow. She ran as fast as she could, down a road graveled with crushed white pumice toward a tree-lined ridge a quarter mile away. Midway between the door and the ridge a familiar figure stood and cast away an antitank missile launcher. Annja ran toward him with great bounds.

"How did you know I'd come out this way?" she asked Father Godin, slowing as she came up to him.

"I had help," he said. Though he smiled his voice was ragged. He bent forward to unlimber a heavy rifle from his back. "Mad Jack called about the security breach. He thought I might come and help out my old comrade. I did, but not the comrade he'd hoped."

She stopped to breathe hard and glance back at the exit. The great gray doors seemed to have been carved in a hillside, out of sight beneath a jutting slab of what looked like and might have been natural rock. Black shapes poured out through the lesser opening beside them.

"Run," Godin suggested. He pulled a long, heavy-looking weapon to his shoulder. It roared like a cannon and rocked the well-braced Jesuit back on his heels when he fired it.

An impressive tongue of orange flame licked

toward the animals in the twilight. Several fell howling and snapping at themselves.

Annja fled to the top of the slope, stopped, turned back. Godin was laboring behind her, face ashen. "They're gaining," he said.

A wolf shape bounded up the hill almost on his heels. He turned, dropped to one knee, bringing the rifle to his shoulder again. When he fired, the rifle's muzzle was barely a yard from its target.

The black canine shape fell thrashing and voicing its horribly human cries. Annja stared wide-eyed.

The sword sprang into Annja's hand. She moved past Godin and struck down another monster. The flat skull split.

Annja braced herself and prepared to face whatever might come next.

Suddenly she saw a shaft of intolerably white light thrust upward into a sky of deepening blue from a ridge a thousand feet beyond the entrance to the hidden complex.

She grabbed Godin and flung him to the ground. She landed hard on top of him. She hoped it didn't hurt him half as much as it did her. He wasn't looking good.

An immense white glare washed everything out as Annja buried her face in Godin's clerical collar and squeezed her eyes tight. The earth shook as the underground facility imploded.

As quickly as it started, it was over. The valley seemed plunged into stygian darkness as Annja opened eyes that swam with afterimage.

"What's that smell?" she asked.

The priest's hands beat at the back of her jacket. "You. You're on fire."

She rolled off him and squirmed around on her back like a dog, hoping the autumn grass retained enough moisture from the recent snowfall that she could smother the fire before it really caught.

Godin had hauled himself to his feet. He reached down and helped pull her upright. Her heart jumped to see his old familiar grin.

But her joy was short-lived. The skin of his face was gray, grayer than the light could account for, and seemed to sag.

Old soldier that he was, he conscientiously reslung his rifle. "I'm surprised your lovely hair did not catch fire," he said.

"Me, too. The backs of my hands and my neck sure feel sunburned, though. I hope we didn't just take a lethal dose of radiation, after all that."

"The good Lord willing," Godin said.

She frowned over his shoulder. "Why are we casting a shadow," she said, "on a south-facing hill?"

He lifted his chin. "Look behind you."

She did.

A thousand yards away a great circular hole gaped in the top of what had been a ridge. A beam of white shot up into the sky like a colossal spotlight.

"The earth has fused to glass," Godin said. "It still glows white from the heat."

She shook her head. She could hardly believe what had happened. Much less that it was, at last, over.

"The creatures?" she asked.

"Dead," he said. "Along with any people who were in there."

A sudden coughing fit doubled him over. She held him as his body shook.

"We have to get you to a doctor," she said. "Where's your SUV?"

"It is parked just over this hill." Bracing himself with a hand on his knee, he handed her the keys. "You will please drive. But not to a doctor. It is much too late for that, you see."

THE STORY CAME out as she raced east.

As she drove higher and higher into the Sangre de Cristos on the east side of the river, she crossed the line of darkness and then stayed just above it. Down below where the exit from the underground lab had been, with mountains rising hard to the west, evening came early. On the western face of the peak day lingered far longer.

The snow still lay thick on the ground and clotted in the branches of the trees. Annja drove as carefully as she could, mindful of the risk of black ice, for all that Godin kept gently urging her to hurry.

He had cancer. It was terminal. It had riddled his body. Although he was a lifelong smoker, ironically his lungs were the most recent part of him to be invaded. He had kept himself going from sheer force of will.

Annja could not conceive of the agonies he must have undergone. He assured her it wasn't bad—most of the time.

On a wide pullout overlooking a sheer drop to the west he asked her to pull over. He got out of the car.

"What are we doing here?" she asked.

"I have come to the end of the road, my dear," he said.

"I won't give up the sword! No matter what you say, I can't."

His smile was strangely sweet for a man so hard, who looked so haggard. "No, you must not," he said. "Not ever. It is where it belongs."

"What makes you say that?"

"You have proved it, have you not? Now help me walk, if you will, please."

The sun had become a blinding ball of brilliance, almost level with them. At the same time snow began to fall, fierce and hard. A wind rose, whistling, driving flakes with stinging force into Annja's eyes.

He guided her toward the edge of the cliff. Uncertain of what he intended, she went reluctantly along.

A few feet from the brink he pulled away from her. "The sword is where it belongs," he said. "And a very great threat to the world is ended."

He dug a thumb in his collar and pulled out his silver medallion. "And now the time has come for me to pass along my own burden," he said, lifting it over his head. "I'd say I deserve a vacation."

Despite herself she recoiled from it. "Take it," he said. "Whatever it once stood for, this medallion now stands for what I have stood for. And what you now stand for, whether you wish to believe it or not."

Numbly she reached out her hand and took it.

He turned his face to the sun. Its light shone beneath the clouds and struck him full in the face, lighting his tired features despite the swirling snow, his own personal floodlight. He smiled.

"I have done many terrible things in my life," he told her. "All of them for what I believed to be the greater good. And all scarred my soul. But there is a child within me, still pure after all. I hope today I have redeemed myself."

And it seemed that as he spoke the last words his

voice was the voice of a child—of the innocent he had once been.

He turned a smile toward her. "Goodbye, Annja," he said. "Go with God."

He turned and walked away from her.

"No!" she shouted. Yet she made no move to restrain him. She knew she lacked the right.

The snow was alive with glare that seemed to enfold him. It blew against her face with redoubled fury.

Yet it seemed to her that she saw him walking on, impossibly, beyond the point where earth gave way to air.

Annja fell to her knees on the gravel and cried.

epilogue

Albuquerque

"Let me guess," the beautiful young man with the unruly black hair said. "What happened up in Rio Arriba didn't have anything to do with any long-forgotten WWII stockpile of bombs going up. And you were right in the middle of it."

Byron Mondragón traded glances with the young woman who sat beside him. She was a plump, pretty, pale girl with dark brown hair. He had introduced her to Annja as Dorothy Enright, his fiancée. Dorothy giggled and sipped her limeade through a straw from her old-fashioned flare-topped fountain glass.

Sitting sprawled into the corner of booth and wall

in the Frontier restaurant, Annja turned away from the window to look at her companions.

"You've got that about right," she said. "Except for the me being in the middle of it part. I wasn't. Or I wouldn't be here talking to you."

Annja told them the story. More than perhaps she should have, but far from all. She reckoned that after what he'd been through Byron was entitled to at least a major helping of truth. And if he chose to confide in his fiancée, she didn't feel like second-guessing him.

"I think I've figured out the creatures," she told the young couple. "The researchers used animals in their experiments. Maybe they even genetically-engineered some. They might have been intending to use them as living weapons. They were designed and probably tortured to be vicious."

She didn't mention the Holy Child. She knew Byron truly believed he'd seen him and tourists were still reporting sightings. Were all the sightings the product of overeager imaginations or the power of suggestion? She had no answers and knew she might never get any.

At the last, she left out what had become of Father Godin, as she left out certain details of what had passed between them. She gave the impression they had shaken hands and parted ways after the covert lab blew up, their work done.

Annja had called in an anonymous tip to 911 from

a payphone in the valley. She'd claimed she had seen a man fall from a scenic overlook up on the mountain. There had been no reports of a body being found.

When she was done Dorothy said, "Wow." Annja couldn't tell whether the girl believed her or was merely being polite.

Byron just nodded, smiling. "I knew you could do it," he said.

A vibration at her hip made her jump. Then she remembered she had set her cell phone to buzz her instead of ring.

"Hello?"

"Annja, baby," a voice said. "Remember me? Doug? Doug Morrell?"

"Of course I remember you, Doug," Annja said with a sigh.

"Doug, *please* don't tap on the damned mic."

"Where's the feature on that epic monster rally down in Nuevo México? See? I even learned the real name of the country. That's how much this story means to me. Now where's my show? I need it yesterday…"